PLANETS ABOVE & BELOW

GRUES & KIRNS

WILL SCHMITZ

ISBN-10: 0996414738
ISBN-13: 978-0-9964147-3-9

For Louis, Krells, & Indigenous Peoples

CHAPTER I

Albungo, the trepanner, who was to go to the Venerid's court in the morning to perform surgery on the master's fifth favorite mate. He was nervous, sleepless and kept on planning and replanning what his behavior should and would be (A sweep of the hand as his assistant brought him his instruments? No! No theatrics.) the next midday. After practicing his walk, form of address and trying on of his professional garment eight times, there were still six to pass before the light came.

Albungo's mate would normally be scolding him to come to bed but, this time, if the dodderer mismanaged his work, they'd all be executed. Let him be his overconfident self. She had the necessary possessions packed and Wambles hired along the route from the palace to warn her if anything went wrong.

As Albungo walked out of his house to check on his siksaks and also relieve himself beside the bleating creatures' pen, he looked up to see a fireball arcing over the mountain. While fixing his mind in admiration on all that was unknown, an insect stung him badly on the inside of his thigh. Albungo slapped at it much too late to avoid the poisonous discomfort it was sure to bring.

In the palace, the Venerid, Kabaya was trying to calm the fears of his mate, Demodex, who was of the Jow tribe. Jows were superstitious and nervous in the extreme.

Kabaya, after almost three ensiles of coaxing, had her almost calmed when Cilicrat, the heaven watcher, interrupted through an intermediary to report on an event that tonight augured the aged monarch's ultimate future. Cilicrat was denied permission to enter the Venerid's presence. The heaven watcher would utter his nonsense and further upset the Jow female before the potion in her drink could lift her spirits into willingness.

Kabaya wanted this one again. The operation would deform her and the Venerid, who couldn't tolerate the sight of physical deformity, would send her back to her originating village.

CHAPTER II

Bombylious was escorting four Grue ambassadors into the unconquered land. After helping to settle the camp and participating as the ambassadors joined the priest around the phallenphoric standard set up in front of the priest's tent, Bombylious, who hated this collection of hysterical cranks, ambled off to find a high place to rest away from the others. The being flesh-eaters still made frequent raids into this area and Bombylious thought the Grues ridiculously overestimated their immunity to an attack. The being flesh-eaters didn't care if it was Kirn or Grue they had for dinner. All the same to them. The haughty Grues never listened. The entire cursed empire was divided between ass-lovers and ass-lickers in Bombylious' mind. He found a lant tree and shimmed up. They had the most comfortable tops you could find. Smelly Grues controlled everything. Language even. "Couldn't even call a lant a lant, had to call it a flue."

Grues didn't have lant trees in their own home territory. "You tell them what it's properly called and they rename it for you in their 'oaf-ishal' tongue," Bombylious grumbled to himself as he curled up in the lush crown of the tree.

From the lant, Bombylious would also have seen the fireball falling over the Grue/Kirn territories and into the flesh-eaters' jungle had it not been for the attack launched against his charges below. Looking sleepily down when he should have been watching the galaxy's staggering star display, on his back, all above him. Ah, Bombylious.

The Grue officials were rousted from their tents and rounded up. Their servants and porters were tied and immediately throat-slit. Kirns making an attempt to credit an atrocity to flesh-eaters!

Although the Venerid could—and did—take his own sister as his first wife and queen, the Grues had death penalty laws against putting it up anyone's rear. The Kirns found this to be silly prudery so before the horror of watching their servants bleed to death could abate, the Grue officials were bent over and buggered by the largest of the Kirn tribal brothers. Screams, louder than those bemoaning the fates of their devoted attendants, issued from the Grue throats. The priest was disembowel, quartered and cut up into tear-sized pieces for the Kirns' always voracious and bellowing yates'.

Bombylious had to hold both hands over his mouth to keep from laughing. Lose your balance, attract unwanted attention— maybe lose your life.

The Kirns did their best to make the attack look like a flesh-eater affair. A second line of Kirns was banging away at the whimpering Grues while artifacts of attack such as feathers, poison darts, arrows, and stone deboning tools were planted around the burning tents of the camp.

Instead of killing the Grues, as expected, they were tied and led away. A flesh-eater prisoner was dragged into the camp and pillowed with a Grue club for final effect.

It was often fatal to bring the Venerid bad news. Kabaya associated the message inextricably with the messenger. He had once even executed an overable general who returned to Gregal, the Venerid's present capital, after subjugating a province he had not been instructed to take.

The general, an ambitious younger brother of Kabaya, was publicly flayed alive in the citadel's central square. Bombylious' best chance was to become a Kirn for awhile. He was uncertainly sure that the Kirns would accept his services, although Bomby thought he already foresaw himself performing menial, backbreaking labor and slaving like a Wamble for meals as he, ugh, descended his trees.

The Grues were destined, through their insatiable appetite for work and ability to smoothly plan and organize vast patterning networks, for masterhood over all they eventually chose to possess. The Kirns were one of the last tribes retarding Grue expansion. The only others were the flesh-eaters and they could keep their jungle.

The Grues had followed a solemn policy of divide and conquer for several generations. (Kabaya has just had a heart seizure while trying to fulfill himself on the luscious Demodex.) The successions to the monarchy had always been made smoothly, without severe internal rupture. (Demodex is trying to roll the Great Venerid's corpse off of her. She is crying for help, but the guards outside regard such pleas as a sure sign of normal —the Venerid having his fun.)

It's customary to be buried alive with the body of the Venerid if you happened to be part of his immediate household or staff. Madpash, the last Venerid before poor Kabaya, had sixty sent off to the other world with him.

The Jow is screaming, She doesn't quite remember the secret way out of the palace that was once shown her in a confiding moment. Now she won't be able to have her operation and the pains in her head get worse and worse! Tiny swords feel through her brain.

Bombylious has clambered back up into his lant tree and is afraid to leave it. A librar has wandered into the camp and is chewing on the Grue Ptilicoses' former headband tier and foot washer. The librar is joined by a pack of waltrots.

Bombylious is going to be baked senseless by the strong light of midday before he ever gets out of the 'who cares how it's named now!' tree.

The waltrots, scavenging and cowardly, dispersed when a group of spies (on their way to infiltrate Kirn territory before the conquest began) entered the clearing. The librar had abandoned his lunch upon first smelling the company, but waltrots are less than particular about the crowd they run with and had to be driven off.

News of the Venrid's demise was the topic of debate. Should they go ahead as ordered? The ambassadors are certainly dead. A smarter and obviously slyer spy named Volage, as Bombylious heard it, took the ground from the more frustrated and irritated of his fellows by saying, "The ambassadors are probably prisoners of the Kirns and are being tortured to answer questions they don't know the answers to."

"What!?" squawked Daw, a fat and black greasily feathered bird. "This is a being flesh-eater raid. Look at the evidence."

"Evidence, evidence," Volage contemptuously murmured.

The three other spies agreed with Daw—they should go ahead and do their work. "The ambassadors are feasted upon somewhere in the jungle," Copes, a squat and overeager servant declared.

"Of course, I'm going in with the rest of you," announced Volage.

"Why don't you believe being flesh-eaters did this?" demanded Daw.

"Oh, I do believe it now," answered Volage.

"Hmmm. I don't see how you ever saw it any other way," said Copes,

"Neither do I," admitted Volage. "Pardon me. Let's go ahead," he said sweeping a hand toward the Kirn territory.

Bombylious stayed in his lant for some time trying to decide what best way to turn. "Who the next Venerid is going to be, that s the determinate factor," he told himself, Bomby was about to climb down again when he saw Volage sneaking back across the clearing.

Instead of taking the direction to the capital, Volage headed in the opposite direction to the lake district.

Bombylious elected to become the one who went to the Kirns to tell them that the Venerid was dead. It was a fantastic opportunity to attack the temporarily unbalanced Grues. Bombylious was having trouble with his hand hold when Daw and Copes re-entered arguing and debating. He groped for the branch he had just let go and shoved himself back into the crown.

"Where are you going to go?" asked Copes.

"To my father's village in the highlands."

"What should we be?"

"Herders, gatherers. The things that are open to us to be when we're in such a place," Daw advised.

"I detest that kind of work," Copes fussed.

"So life becomes as uninteresting and difficult for you as it is for most others," Daw chided. "Take a young and pretty wife."

"The Grues take our young and pretty ones, put them in the Venerid's custody to take as he likes, give to the priesthood for temple maidens, or to reward soldiers. The ugliest are left," Copos soughed.

Daw saw that reasoning with Copes was like drinking peasant

alcohol—both ended up leaving you feeling ill and mean.

"Make the best you can of it and. remember to survive," Daw said giving Copes a salute and marching away before his friend dickered any further.

Copos was not as sure of himself. Was this how things were? After seating himself, stirring the ashes of the fire, and fooling with one of the dead men's hands, Copes resigned himself to his indecision and reached into a small sack tied around his neck and drew out a set of dice that he hoped would make a choice hop forth.

The librar could be heard returning for more and Copes scooped up his dice and began to scurry up a tree—Bombylious' tree. Reaching to hoist himself into the crown, Copes received an unexpected push down.

The fall seemed to have broken the superstitious spy's left leg and the librar had no trouble leaping to its preference for personally killed meat. Copes was dragged off into the scrub still managing to moan or yell, "Daw! Oh, Daw! Daw, dawda, aw."

Bombylious could hear him being loudly munched upon, so, before the waltrots came meandering back … Bombylious clambered out of his tree and ran at a lope to the nearest Kirn village to stick the note about the Grue's leaderless state into some ears.

Bombylious went to a village where he was friends with the chief. Going to the main village would have put him in a position too difficult to extricate himself from. Entering the Kirn village told you why the Grues were on the ascendancy. The Kirns were crafty and the men liked to stage an occasional raid when they felt they had to. They gave and took, gave and took. The Grues only took. No tribe could put an army into the field that was either well led, well equipped, or could be supplied. A war between tribes lasted as long as the stomach could hold out.

Kirn women cultivate plump thighs and calves by tying bands below their knees and on top of their legs. "Ouf!" Bomby thought as a cackling group of them led him into the center of chief Moco's town.

News of the captured and humiliated ambassadors was already joyously common and Moco, who had supplied three of his warriors for the raid, insisted that Bombylious drink Nuche with him and the subchiefs to celebrate the success.

Bombylious was escorted to the war hut where he was greeted with a mock round of cheers and then, sniggering laughter. The slobbery waltrots were all foul drunk! "This is how it's always going to be," observed Bomby as he took the first bitter taste of the stuff. "Satisfied with degrading a few unimportant oafs while the big threat continues to build unmolested."

Madoqua, a very self flattering sub who thought he could be funny, asked Bomby if he knew where his former charges were right then. Bomby looked down into the bright orange of the clay cup and responded, "After hanging by their hair in front of the populace for a respectably painful time, I suppose they've been retired to the librar pit where they've screamed their last."

"Yes. Correct," said Moco. "And here's to the next four!" he said, raising a toast to the hall. "May they die begging entrance into the next world!"

"Begging!" the chiefs shouted back in unison.

"You're drinking away the only chance you'll ever have to remain free!" Bombylious shouted above the swaying loudness of the crowd.

"What are you saying?" demanded Moco. He'd like to slit Bomby's impudent throat to elicit some loud approval from his Nuche swilling friends. Certainly. Yes. Loud!

Standing before the gathered chiefs, Bomby declared that,

"The Grues have lost their Venerid. Kabaya died last night!"

"The flaming ball!" someone hissed.

"I didn't see and don't know about any omens," Bombylious replied spreading his arms out for attention. "The Grue State is organized completely around their Venerid, the representative of the sun god in this life. The Grues are voiceless and actionless until another Venerid is crowned."

Bombylious' speech had started several small and arguments. The Venerid was old enough to be dead so the news of it as fact was not disputed. The Kirns were a little thick about how to interpret facts except through group dispute. Runners were dispatched to the other villages belonging to the Kirn federation to bring the chiefs together for council.

Moco knew Bombylious better than Bomby would like to have been known. The chief had him seized despite Bombylious' denials that he would try to slip away. And Bombylious possessed more information about the Grues that no Kirn had privy to.

Bomby displayed his displeasure by trying to bite his 'friend' Moco on the hand, but the guards cuffed him as he attempted the courtesy and they dragged him scornfully off and threw him, face down, in an abandoned hut. He did not regain consciousness for several hours.

In the middle of the night, Kirns with torches appeared and staked Bombylious, spread eagle, to the ground. The prisoner couldn't be tortured to a point past cooperation, so a more subtle revenge and test of strength had to be devised wherethrough Moco could recoup his offended honor. Bombylious was doused with urine to insure that he was ready to be stung by what was to follow. After being washed off, Bombylious stared up and found himself being glared back at by five of the village's oldest, fattest, smelliest toothless females.

They began to massage him skillfully over the entire exposed surface of his body. Then, after soothingly arousing him, they ceased the adulation and beat him—lightly, furiously, unrelentingly—with dried fronds. Pleasure, pain pleasure, pain, pleasure—until the two extremes devolved into one. One female uncovered Bombylious' groin and performed a most delicate fellatio while another clawed at the bottoms of his feet with jaggedly cut fingernails until they bled.

After ejaculating once, the areas of pleasure/pain reversed. The female massaged his organ until it again submitted to erection then began working on it, more vigorously and violently this second time, while his lacerated feet were bathed in a salve.

Bombylious thought that he could vaguely remember Moco having entered the hut at some point drunk, happy and laughing at Bombylious through the darkened hut's happy mask. With the coming of the light, the women stopped their work. Their victim had fallen unconscious upon realizing that his flag was going to be razed a third, and if possible, even a forth time. And they had continued to labor in some frustration. Their victim was untied, washed and freshly dressed. Upon stirring, Bomby was offered a drink that he thankfully accepted. It contained a heavy narcotic and he discovered himself spun into a dimension of unencouraging dreams.

Upon waking, Bomby looked into the face of Moco's ugliest and least marriageable daughter. She was riding him like she rode all the reluctant post adolescent males in the village, who she had size over and could bully. As soon as Bomb recognized where he was and (*ugh*) what was happening, he shouted at her to get her fat rear off of him. Moco rushed into the room, pretending that he did not know what had been happening and started to wail over the shameful seduction of his innocent daughter. The wedding was set for the next day. Bombylious spat in his future

11

wife's face as she was climbing off. For this he received a smash to his groin from his redescending beloved.

"She's the best cook in the village, you lucky chank," said Moco patting the bent-double Bombylious on the back. "Now behave like a groom should or make yourself ready for a slow crawl out of this world."

Moco continued. "You should know better than to think you can go stealing around a Kirn camp making love to the chief's favorite daughter without regard to the consequences. By the gods! She may already be fertilized!"

"You've got me trapped," Bombylious groaned.

"As tightly as the prey in a librar's jaws," Moco exclaimed with his daughter beaming at her prize from around the corner of the hut's opening.

After stepping outside, Bombylious could hear her thanking her father for "The wonderful present."

"See that he stays healthy or our librar pit gets you," Moco told his girl as he walked past her, late for the meeting with the assembled chiefs.

CHAPTER III

Kabaya had three principal heirs. The ablest of them was fighting a campaign to push the being flesh-eaters further into the jungle so that the Grues might obtain access to the ample food sources of the region. But he succumbed, on the morning of the arrival of the news of the Venerid's death, to a poison dart.

The other two half-brothers, one of whom had paid for the delivery of the dart (it remained a mystery and a controversy as to how one of the enemy had gotten so far inside the boundaries of the camp, but there was the prince, dead in his tent, sprawled over plans for a new city he was going to build in the recently conquered north lands), were Egerne and Emerod. They both held equal semi-legitimate claims to the Veneridship. Egerne was the cleverer, though Emerod was, by far, wealthier and kept the most experienced generals by him in his sumptuous court.

Egerne was fond of keeping to himself and working on what Emerod's spies reported back as "toys." When Emerod learned about what his brother did with his time, he began mocking him at parties and to anyone who might be a useful listen.

What Egerne did was to make models in his study out of

wood. In addition to model making, Egerne was discovering some of the basic chemical and physical laws of metallurgy.

The Grues were a stone culture as far as building goes. They were incomparable masons. The frequent earthquakes that were indigenous to the mountain empire's nucleus never shook loose a stone. The weapon that Egerne was developing was three times as strong as conventional. The Grues fought as a well disciplined organization while the tribes fought without foreplan and this was the reason for the Grues imperial progress as much as superior weaponry. Egerne was constructing a paradigm for a small army that would equal the capacity of one of the hordes that the Grues popularly believed had to be put into the field to guarantee victory.

Emerod followed custom (he was very strong on supporting the Grue 'traditions' that had made them the power they were) and consulted a priest. The priest sacrificed a pure white siksak and examined its entrails. The priest told Emerod what he had paid to hear and, turning to the assembled nobles, announced that Emerod was "truly among our chosen", although the entrails have been strangely decayed in such a young beast and reading the signs right would have meant telling the crowd that the prince was "among the chosen to soon perish."

The prophesy so delighted Emerod that he sent emissaries with offerings of 'peace' to Egerne who was presently governing the Southernmost province, Egerne had also summoned a priest who sacrificed a siksak, and although this siksak was not as pure and white as the one that Emerod had had sacrificed to tell his future, its guts weren't rotten either. The priest told Egerne that, though his brother was quite strong in the capital and elsewhere, the gods had definitely made Emerod a loser and to go ahead with any plan that Egerne had in mind.

Egerne responded to Emerod s emissaries by having them

decapitated. Their heads were thrown over Emerod's courtyard wall one night as he walked there among his gold and silver crafted artificial plants, animals, insects and flowers. The female he was seducing shrieked as her hand reached back and touched one of the heads whose eyes stared back at her in quiet puzzlement—and, sigh, just after the prince had coaxed her spine into his favorite position.

Emerod was furious and assembled his generals. The informants that Egerne had in Emerod's court soon delighted him with the news that Emerod had mustered his army and was on the march against Egerne. Egerne had his own tiny force ready, nicely equipped with metal weapons that were effortlessly wielded compared to the stone axes, clubs, spears and maces of his half-brother's army, The metal also sliced easily through standard Grue quilted armor. Was there going to be a real battle or only a slaughter? Egerne's fears mostly centered around the confidence of his troops. They were sure that they would either all die, overwhelmed by the eleven to one odds against them, or that *most* of them would die. It was hoped among them that they would be offered the opportunity to surrender if the contest became an apparent and open farce.

CHAPTER IV

The Grues, having become conquerors originally to escape starvation, improved agriculture in the lands they mastered. Grains and roots and berries made up the diet until fruits, fish and vegetables were 'discovered' in the new parts of the kingdom. Fish were brought to the Grue court via runners. Fresh game and fruit remained unobtainable while the jungle was still dominated by the flesh-eaters. The Grues built storage chambers for the grain and used it to supply armies in the field or the general populace in times of famine. Every Grue subject paid tribute in the form of whatever he could produce by hand or from herds and land to the state. The craftless, herdless, or landless were conscripted to either work on public projects or serve in the army.

Bone ear ornaments, finger rings, bracelets, wristlets, crowns, necklaces of stone beads along with feather headdresses, capes, and painting the body with earth pigments were the favored forms of adornment among the Grues. Skull deformation had lately become the vogue after having been assimilated a few years earlier from the coastal tribes that practiced the art. Nobles and state officials were easily distinguished by their costumes that denoted rank. Metal nose plugs and ear plugs also proclaimed the wearer's position in the society.

The homes of citizens were uniformly small—one room structures built in the shape of parallelograms with thatched gable roofs. The Grues, such adept stone masons, built cities on their own model, in their own image, throughout the conquered lands.

Religion, always a bumptious subject, was equally backward among all the various tribes that inhabited the planet. If local gods seemed powerful to the Grues, they adopted them. What did it mean, to die? The invisible world seemed real enough. The dead were not disposed of or burnt, they were usually mummified and provided mortuary offerings so that they would 'communicate' back to the living as to what to do, who to marry, etc. The mummies of the past Venerids were especially enshrined, eleven generations of them in their own necropolis, attended to and waited upon as if they were living, The Grues, sun worshipers, made the Venerid's voice revered as divine and the intermediary between mortal and immortal will.

The dead were commodiously interred in niches carved in the hillsides surrounding the city. The corpses were mummified in a sitting position, false eyes staring ubiquitously forwards so that a form of address was directly implied betwixt the petitioner and his idol.

The tribes were locally minded, except in the case of the Grues, and each valley defalcated its customs and characteristics between the interaction of being with environment. Kirns were especially fond of hoodwinking outsiders.

Bombylious pleaded his "great cause" to ears and eyes, which were always more anxious to pass his face a smirk, chuckle, giggle, grin, or laugh as opposed to considering the possible torture that Bomby might actually have some important information to share.

Bombylious' 'wife' shoved him onto the floor of their hut. Remorse for having considered coming into Kirn territory unaccompanied stung him. She fed him well, but herself better. Why the pretense? It was only so that he would be able to perform the act that he was fed.

The Kirn chieftains could not agree on who should lead or what course of action to take.

Egerne, noticing how his army had the unsure fidgets, needed to bolster their confidence by proving the superiority of their weaponry. The new model army practiced by marching on the main Kirn stronghold as the doubters spread panic. Runners came to Moco's village to announce the invasion and a second Kirn force was dispatched to crush the, ah, impudent foe.

Both of the Kirn contingents were trounced. Hacked survivors slunk back into the village proclaiming that they had been defeated by witchcraft. The Kirn chieftains had all perished. Upon seeing the small size of the enemy, the leaders joined the front ranks of the attack thinking that the most valorous of them would be made supreme chieftain in this battle against the main Grue army.

Bombylious jammed his two quadradecaensile pregnant spouse onto the broad back she was using to block the hut's entrance while she was pestering for news from the retreating population of the village. Bomby turned back to face her for the last time wondering whether or not he should not aid her in flight.

She emerged from the hut carrying a club and Bomby decided that it was time for him to retreat to the jungle. He heard her panting and cursing behind him for some distance before hearing what sounded like a shriek.

Bombylious managed a knife out of the hands one of a trio

of confused Kirn stragglers who were arguing as to whether or not they should plunge into the scary jungle to escape the Grues. They followed Bombylious in.

The Kirns ran past him, shoving him off what there was of a path into a comfortable little a cave. Their quarreling voices faded.

Soon he heard their flesh speak again as it sizzled on cannibal spits. The former Grue guide and reluctant husband lived off of roots, fruits and berries. Bombylious found that he could snare small game and birds but, afraid to make a fire, he found himself unable to devour raw flesh.

The native continued to snare game for clothing and to make sandals with. After skinning the animal and destroying evidence of the snare, be buried the rest of the animal so flesh-eaters wouldn't find it.

Between necessary forages, Bombylious spent the rest of his days trying to dig a back entrance from his cave. He was awesomely afraid of entrapment.

Before finishing the escape exit, Bombylious, one day, heard flesh-eater voices excitedly rushing toward his minutely defended stronghold. "I should have worked on fortifications first!" went screeching through his mind. 'Here comes death, unopposable,' said a sneering voice inside, or just barely outside (he couldn't tell which), his mind. Bombylious wet himself and then tried hiding in a coverable pit that he had constructed. He reflected how easily it could be detected as he climbed in and tried to cover up.

Shortly, someone entered the cave (fell in through the opening's camouflage, really) with a scream and dropped on the thatch Bombylious was hiding below. More screams, cries, spontaneous exhortations, and curses. After waiting until he was sure no one was after him, Bombylious attempted to lift up his protective screen. "A corpse?" Bombylious queried. "Who could they be fighting?" The flesh-eaters were supposedly safe in their jungle. Bombylious presently heard other voices speaking an unintelligible patter.

"These zogs don't have it to get us off of this biscuit-sized planet."

"Slarf it! There must be some life form on this putridly fertile, rotating ball of earth and meat that can."

"Ha! We'd have an easier time training insects to build the ship than these primies."

"There'll be other cultures on this planet. We landed in a jungle. What'd you expect?"

"The captain won't be happy with these specimens. I'll put the analyzer on another one to make sure."

"Well? How much has he got?"

"These jungle howlers wouldn't even make good manure. I've gotten larger I.P readings from some domesticated animals. Are you sure we'll be able to find something else?"

"Get a good look around after we get the platforms up."

"Is Crack making them open or enclosed?"

"Closed. Look at those mountain peaks. Too cold for an open vehicle. Don't frown, you gore glutton! So what if you can't shoot as well as one of them, we're not here to depopulate the place."

"How many can Crack rig?"

"Three or four. Let's get going before a gang of this howler's pals show."

Bombylious struggled until dusk before managing to move the body trapping him off. He examined the corpse. Strange wound. Bombylious could put a fist through it. Perfectly round. He carefully crawled from his blind to investigate. The bodies of fourteen being flesh-eaters lay contorted in different positions around the area. The faces of most were drawn in halted agony, while on others there appeared a look of supreme arousal. Others in child-wonder. Idiot-eyed in expressions of rapture. These corpses did not have the strange wound.

Bombylious dragged one of the fear-expressing bodies over next to one that seemed to have expired of gladness, cushioned into death, over-gratified. Bombylious started a fire to examine the corpses further (a too dangerous thing to do). After interrogating the looks on the corpses, he gathered up the few possessions he had collected (since he couldn't dispose of fourteen bodies and the flesh-eaters would soon be coming to reclaim their own) and left his refuge to search out the tribe that had destroyed this party of warriors without apparent effort.

CHAPTER V

Egerne's devastation of the Kirns was reported to Emerod. A sword of the new metal was procured for the lord to examine. After testing the weapon's strength and finding it unwholesomely superior to what his own army used, Emerod sent ambassadors to Egerne's court with sumptuous gifts and an offer to meet and negotiate a reconciliation. Uh, oh. The reason for Egerne's boastfulness founded on fact.

When the ambassadors (a step above mere emissaries) arrived at Egerne' s court, he had the gifts Emerod had sent tossed into a great fire. The ambassadors were each relieved of an eye, finger and ear. "What shall we say to our lord?" whined one of the Grues. "Sew their mouths shut," said Egerne turning to an aide. "And if any of them bleats another syllable, their noses too."

Emerod attempted to send assassins and hire betrayers into his brother's court. Emerod felt cheated that, having spent so much of his life amassing wealth from all quarters, his smug brother now was in a position to steal everything Emerod coveted away with one unforeseen trick. Emerod prayed heavily, drank, and chewed on the leaves of a mormorphic plant while awaiting news from his hirelings.

The heads of these supremely twisted and tricky sneaks came back, some on a daily basis, others in batches embalmed in jars filled with blood and urine. Emerod' s frustration mounted and did as it liked with him for hours.

Seven light changes after no new heads had appeared, while bathing in his palace's hot spring fed tub, the head of Emerod's chiefly last hope in his murder plans, bobbed up before him in the water. Emerod, screaming, upset and furious, picked up the pickled poll and flung it against the nearest wall (a short-throw) while bellowing for his guards. Emerod chewed enough leaves to sedate him for two light changes after redoubling the guards.

Time is sometimes easily and unremarkably ready to be wasted, in other instances, to lose a moment engenders disaster. Emerod indulged himself in calming his nerves and his senses through sleep when he should have been giving preparatory commands to his generals and administrators. Egerne divested his brother of three major food producing provinces while Emerod slumbered.

Waking to a dwindled empire, Emerod issued the mobilization orders and appointed staff. Wisely enough, Emerod's armies were instructed not to engage the enemy in open battle. The troops were disappointed. Emerod had not let the rumors about Egerne's demon weaponry spread and so, like good blood-hungry Grues, Emerod's troops wanted a fight. Slings and missiles, traps and ambushes were to be the only weapons and tactics to be used against the reputedly small sized foe.

Egerne expected a frontal assault and a series of quick, large, and decisive battles (as Emerod scrounged to put anything be could find up against Egerne's Model A.) to begin and end the contest for the Veneridhood. Reports of Emerod's moves reached Egerne through surviving members of units lost on patrol. Butchered in ambush. Hill fighting was against Egerne. Too much territory still under Emerod's domination. Egerne abandoned his casual plans and directed the attack against the holy, imperial city.

When scouts reported Egerne's aggressive activity to Emerod, he was dumbfounded. The capital was supposed to be held sacred and inviolable. Grue nobles swore never to attack and always to defend it. Emerod was infuriated. He called his favorite generals to council: Parathon, Atel, and Colefeke. Each had different advice to offer their sovereign.

The paunchy Parathon declared, "I'm for a mass attack. We scream down on the upstart's puny force from four sides and overwhelm them with our numbers."

Atel sneered at both Parathon and his advice saying, "They'd cut a swath through us in any direction they chose. We're best retreating."

"Retreating," Emerod cut in. The two other generals also protested once they caught the tone in their master's voice.

"Retreating to one of the mountain fortresses where we could defend ourselves from behind high walls," Atel continued. "Here on the plain, Egerne can camp and loot the countryside after he's subdued, and subdue he will, any force we send against him. Remaining in the city makes us like a cobdar who's cornered in his hole. Egerne will be able to attack at leisure once he's established outside the walls."

Colefeke was not much of a planner. Like Parathon, he was best at leading the battle and smashing skulls with his war club. He offered the following philosophy to the discussion, "It would be cowardly to run. News of our abandonment of the sacred capital would seduce the nation over to Egerne's cause and make laughing-stocks of us throughout the ignorant countryside.

Better to fight and be doomed, if what you say is at all true, Atel, than to capitulate."

"I didn't suggest capitulation," Atel said.

"You may as well have," answered Colefeke.

"The two arguments are not in the least identical!" Atel shouted back.

Emerod dismissed them from his presence, but had Atel secretly recalled soon after. It wouldn't do to feed armies to Egerne and then have nothing left to defend the constantly rebellious tribes on the edges their expanding empire with. What can I do with Parathon and Colefeke," Emerod began confidingly, "they command as much loyalty and respect from their troops as I myself do."

Unhesitatingly, Atel told his lord, "They'll never change. Because of past successes they unquestioningly believe that war will always be won through the same methods. They think they can demolish Egerne's forces as easily as they can take a victory from Kirns, Roues and Billows. Demons do Egerne's bidding. We must have some on our side, too, if we hope to defeat him."

The prince quivered. A twitch skirted his lips as Atel struck deep with his mention of "demons."

"What should I do?" he squeaked.

"You must save yourself. Retreat to a mountain fortress and from there, use all the power you have to capture one of Egerne's weapon makers. We must have someone who can reveal the magic of the bewitched metal so that equal force of arms will be present when we fight the battles that make you undisputed ruler of the cosmos' first disciple of the sun."

"What if Egerne is developing an even fouler and more cunning relationship with this evil that guides him? What shall I do then!"

"You will have time, divine one," Atel said assuringly. "Egerne must destroy you before he can return to his demonizing. As in all forms of witchcraft, it drains the user to communicate with spirits. If we can arm ourselves with weapons equal to Egerne's, then we will be able to annihilate the pretender. Afterwards, Lord, think of how glorious your conquests will be."

"And what should I do with my other two commanders?"

"Show them the afterlife," Atel ambitiously replied.

By the end of the conference, Emerod was ecstatic until it began to pester him as to what a dangerous fellow Atel was. Conservatism led him to command that Parathon be summoned for a second private audience. Parathon was used to being called for. His advice was routinely followed.

Emerod ordered that Parathon send, "… a select group of stalwarts to infiltrate Egerne's fortress and return with one or more of Egerne' s weapon makers."

"Lord, we do not need Egerne's tricks to hold the empire. If you allow me to implement my plan …"

"But I've had a divine revelation," Emerod taunted. "The god wants it done. Even I cannot defy such a suggestion."

Parathon fell to he knees in apology for having questioned the divine will upon smartly realizing that his head was in danger of leaving him. Parathon dispatched a group of seventeen soldiers and sent them in triplets and pairs to kidnap a weapon maker from Egerne's keep.

CHAPTER VI

Bombylious hurried away from his cave feeling resentful that his life had again so easily been upset. After completing the back entrance/exit to his cave, Bombylious considered that he could have lived a peaceful and undisturbed life for many season changes there. The being flesh-eaters would never have found him.

The jungle frightened Bombylious. It was infested with beasts, flying creatures, insects, poisonous things and other dangers he neither knew of or could understand. After leaving his cave, Bombylious again made his nest in the top leaves of any suitable tree he could find. Librars chased him twice.

Three light changes after having to abandon his home, Bomby was picking fruit from the branches of a bater tree when he heard (limbs cracking and stalks ripped apart) something nearing. He dropped the yield and started up the thickly leaved tree.

A hunting party of flesh-eaters ran madly past under Bomby as if pursued by the entire Grue army. Bombylious clung to the branches he was holding as motionlessly as possible for two full ensiles before deciding (since nothing, no Grues, not even a pack of waltrots had happened by) that it was safe to come down.

Bombylious had to pick fresh bater fruits since the crop he had dropped had mostly been trampled and mashed by the flesh-eater party. After gathering as much as he could fit in the sack he had woven to carry his collections, Bombylious moved off in a direction both away from the flesh-eaters and the phantom pursuers.

After a while (midday made him cheerful) he felt better, walked less cautiously and even began to softly whistle a tune that his grandmother had taught him when, *VAROOOOSH*, he stepped into a snare and found himself dangling very close to, and in reach of a waltrot's claw, the ground. "Oh, misery does find me!" Bombylious yelled to the inside walls his quiet skull. Soon enough, he heard voices approach through the dense foliage.

"Looks as though we've got some fresh flesh, Hyde!"

"One of those jungle jokers. Thought they'd be too sharp to step into a snare."

Bombylious fainted. The fearsome destroyers of the being flesh-eaters had captured him.

They unupturned him and revived their curious catch. Bomby immediately wanted to communicate with these two wondrously odd tribe members. Instead of responding to his inquiries, the burlier of the two trappers took a dart out of a case he was carrying and stabbed Bombylious with it. Soon his legs refused to obey and the native found himself walking in a wobbly circle and talking to the trees.

"He's not one of the jungle boys is he?" Trucer noted.

"Nope. Talks in arranged sentences, wears clothes, and raves on as though he's got more than 'how to cook supper' on the mind," professed the chipper Hyde.

"Let's get him back to camp where we can bug his brain. I'll take the left arm."

Bombylious had never experienced such a feeling of euphoria in his life. And he'd bethought the dart was full of poison! He asked himself whether or not this couldn't possibly be the same way in which those flesh-eaters he'd seen the gooey faces of had died. But, ho! (here he tried to throw his arms up in joy) and was slapped by Trucer who hated lugging. The slap hurt and Bomby started to cry.

What'd you hit him for? You know he can't help himself," Hyde chided his pal.

"I hate it when they get to go on a free cruise and I have to play attendant."

"Aw, but you've made him cry," said Hyde pointing to their charge's cheeks.

"Proves he's intelligent. Tally it as a successful experiment in deciphering the native's conception of the humbleness of his personal existence."

"All right. Don't hit him again though."

"Quit dragging your end and it's a deal," sprayed Trucer.

And (*oops*) indeed, yes, Hyde was letting his side of the client drag, bare kneed through some prickly shrubs.

"I hate all these bugs!" shouted Trucer while slapping wildly around himself with his free hand. They heard the crunching of undergrowth simultaneously.

"Drop the booty and get ready to fry cannibals," smiled Hyde.

"Watch out! Poison darts coming in! Worse than bugs. Curse this clime!"

The trio was under attack from a gathered group of flesh-eaters. The poison darts came at them in waves.

"Looks like we're going to be dead for awhile. Signal will go off soon. Put a tag on our catch so they don't leave him behind," instructed Trucer.

Hyde had already dropped to the ground. "Right," said Trucer attaching the tag himself, "See you in two."

Bombylious, under the influence of his captors' drug, died a fairly pleasant death while Trucer and Hyde writhed to a convulsive and agonizing finish. Bomby had difficulty in making himself feel sorry for them. He watched them die in a beguilingly detached frame of mind. Before succumbing completely, Bombylious heard an exceptionally bizarre whirring sound, something like the sound of ...? Bomby searched. desperately to identify what he might be hearing before ...

CHAPTER VII

Egerne's army was met by Emerod's outside the city walls. Emerod confessed to himself that he had severely miscalculated Egerne's strength before decapitation. Egerne followed custom and had a drinking vessel made from his half brother's skull. Parathon had died leading his glorious army and had even attempted, once he realized that a new order was about to instate itself and that all was lost, to kiss the foot soldier's sword that was busy running him through. Colefeke was captured wearing unbecoming female's garments as he tried to sneak out of the city's Trader's Gate. The commanders who captured Colefeke would have burned him immediately if these had been the old days. Egerne wanted all possibly important prisoners brought to him unharmed. The soldiers felt cheated (Colefeke flaming on a pyre, glorious fun), but conformed to command. Egerne's forces had been attacked from three sides as they slashed into the city. Egerne wanted to know where the missing units that should have been trying to encircle him were.

Colefeke was tortured to reveal what be knew. The general denounced Atel as the traitor who had fled. It became obvious to Egerne that Atel was not the idiot that his brother was. Emerod's wealth had not saved him. Molten riches had been poured down the lord's throat to extinguish his life before the sword through the neck. "A Severed Head is Carried By The Hair!" This ancient warrior ballad was sung by the troops as Emerod's corpse was carried through the capital's streets to show the populace that they had a new leader.

Atel seemed cunning and troubled Egerne's thoughts. A librar running around behind his back. The coronation and investiture would seem a sham without the kingdom at rest. Nevertheless, Egerne was eager to have the ceremonies performed. and to even follow custom by marrying and making queen, his sister. Egerne was anxious to unify dissident factions and believed he could most easily do so under the title of Venerid. The longer he waited to fulfill the succession, the more the tribes would be tempted to try and break away.

Runners were dispatched to locate Atel, but none returned. Atel would have to wait. Orders were given to implement the rites, marriage and celebration festivals. The various subordinate chiefs were summoned to the capital to swear allegiance and have an eye kept on them. Egerne had a different vision of things. His predecessors were no more than adept subjugators to his mind. Their policy never extended beyond grab, hold, order and remake those you conquer.

Favillia, both Emerod's and Egerne's full-sister, was chosen queen. It was believed that Emerod's queen had escaped the city. Atel had had her abducted before the battle began and she was now his chattel. Favillia tried to bribe a serving girl and a few of the guards to help her escape the city. She was caught and escorted to her future lord's chamber.

"Why were you fleeing?" Egerne asked.

"I won't say unless you make all others leave," Favillia replied.

Egerne dismissed his court members, advisors and attendants. "Not a virgin," Favillia declared. "You'll have me executed."

"Don't care whether you are or not. You're becoming queen to fulfill form. Marrying my virgin sister, pretending to be directly descended from the deity, that stuff's all humbug," Egerne declared. Favillia fainted. She's been brought up in the royal court and taught that an 'indiscretion' was punishable by public hanging alongside the male violator. Favillia never entertained hopes of becoming queen. She was considered by those who did not know her to be 'slow witted'. Egerne chose Favillia because be believed those reports. She was a perfect choice to his eyes. If she meddled in his affairs, she could have an accident or die in childbirth. The Venerid could then declare himself to be of broken heart and uninterested in remarriage. Down with unnecessary trappings and conventions. Egerne wanted to rid himself of all such constraints and build himself a culture that could maintain a state of wakefulness and interest in the unexamined phenomenon it was only a miniscule part of. Always escaping down the road of 'expansion' and its accompanying violations, how feeble! At present, the only virtues rewarded by the state were valor in battle and high administrative office when your days as an effective fighter were finished.

CHAPTER VIII

Atel took the advice he had tried to give to his former prince. The general, along with the desertion of his comrades on the field, had also the foresight to rob Emerod's treasure house, thus assuring long staying power in the realm he intended to establish and loyalty from his troops. The sentries he placed in every pass leading away from the fallen city ambushed the scouts that Egerne sent to locate the direction of Atel's march.

Upon reaching his chosen stronghold with his adequate army, Atel ordered an early harvest and tore down dwellings in order to make room for more crops to be planted. He wanted to be sure of being able to sustain a protracted siege. Atel sent spies out to collect information about what was happening in every corner of the empire.

During a routine day of holding court, one of Atel's spies brought a haggard looking rope maker before him. The rope maker, protesting that he had been detained. without cause until humbled by the point of the spy's dagger, related a rumor of how the flesh-eaters were retreating deeper into the jungle after having been invaded by an unheard of tribe.

"How large is the force and in what direction is it moving?" Atel asked the weaver.

"It's supposed to be a tiny force, Master. I don't know anything more about it. I only heard the rumor from a potter I exchanged goods with."

"But the flesh-eaters are afraid and are retreating?" the spy interjected.

"Yes, Lord."

"He's been eating forbidden plants," said Atel smilingly to a subordinate. "Keep him with us for awhile, then let's hear what be has to say. Next case!"

The rope maker attempted to protest, but the guards hooked him by the arms and dragged him off. He squealed, "I'm not lying! You'll soon be hearing from others that what I say is true!"

CHAPTER IX

The Grue capital of Gregal was located in a valley set between twin mountain ranges. In a past geological age, the planet's crust buckled diastrophically, creating a massive ridge in one direction and a submarine trough in its opposite direction so that, in only four light changes' march, the surface rose from below ocean level to 500 beings standing on one another's shoulders. From ocean level the mountains rose to past the maximum habitable altitudes. From leafless deserts to tropical forests, and temperatures ranges from constant warmth to everlasting ice.

On the mountain side away from the oceans, the land rapidly descended to almost ocean level. Slow flowing streams and affluents of a gigantic river meandered chartlessly toward ocean. The Grues flowed out of their mountain valley after fighting amongst neighbors for thousands of season changes to suddenly subjugate every tribe in the four directions. Starvation had been eliminated. The Grues were addicted to work and would not leave any area of potential organization untouched.

The conquest/discovery era was about to end. Not much was known. The deities were nurtured in the dark and invoked out of fright. In order to solidify their control over conquered tribes, the Grues imposed a state religion and official language. Egerne inherited the autocratic machinery of a rapacious state. But, now, what about considering some more mutually beneficial incentives for wanting to belong to the empire?

Only narrow, easily defendable roads led in and out of the city's valley. Vast numbers of beings were required to portage the goods and foodstuffs from the territories and countryside into the capital. Siksaks were used only to carry lighter loads. There was no form of vehicular transportation. High state officials were borne from place to place on litters.

Cooking vessels were of hand built clay fired in earthen ovens. The wheel hadn't been invented, but, oh, Egerne the idea for the wheel. Why not? It's a circle, like any of the five moons when they're full. He's lying in the same huge bath that his half-brother, Emerod, received the unwelcome visit from the gently rolling head in. He's staring at a six-starred war mace and holding his hands so that its points are covered and only the center can be seen. And now, he's handling a mace whose points he's ordered chipped off with a hole drilled through its center. The center's center. "So like a female there," Egerne noticed. What other devices could be adapted from observing the behavior and motions of a being's body? Spear points and swords, they were taken from the world around: librar's teeth extended, the beaks of birds that could break shells. Armor was a shell. "All that we do is observe the strength of a creature we see existing around us and adapting its features to fit our own needs. So far, we have adopted only attributes of physical strength from our surroundings. There must be other worlds, greater, which we are capable of appropriating useful characteristics from," Egerne declared to his listening mind. Sticking a rod through the former mace's hole, Egerne spun the stone around.

"Bring me a second one like this. No. Three more. And a jewelry box and more rods. Here. Take these and match them," Egerne commanded a bewildered attendant.

"How simple it is going to be to make my new world. Who are the gods that are showing me these things? I must visit my father's mummy this afternoon. Mustn't have the court thinking that I'm not devout. And while I'm paying homage to that stuffed corpse, shrunken and looking like a child's doll in its robes, I'll be mocking them, planning a way to take everything they know away. Ha! The old kind of terror is over. The old dullness is dead. Let's see how many of them are capable of keeping up with me. I'll take every way they have of pleasing the Venerid from them. They won't know what to do! How will they ever find ways to please me? Stimulate me or worry about keeping your head! Oh, yes!"

The empire, which was orderly and efficient, stunningly terroristic and vigorously vigilant, bored Egerne. He had no advantages over former rulers. He ate better (fed every morsel by members of his harem and when he lost a hair or spit, they were expected to devour the sacred discharge or excreta to prevent witches from molesting the Venerid through them), had his choice of the exciting and voluptuous (except in the case of his sister/wife/queen), but had to live within so many confinements (almost every day was a holy day over which the Venerid had to preside over the sacrifices and offerings) that Egerne felt as much a prisoner of his existence as the lowliest siksak herder.

In his early youth, Egerne had been quite the opiating leaf chewer. He had fought in many of his father's battles and, the thought that his skull might at any moment be pulverized by a smash from a frenzied club, drove him to conclusions about the warrior life that would have been considered unacceptable, cowardly. They would have been suspect and denounced as dementia. And Egerne felt, at times, that they may be right. But he was the one with the power now and he would defend himself. But Egerne's days of cunning stunts were mostly done and he was already surrounded by his bastards and their slobbering, wailing, and drooling for attention and authority, pettily scheming mothers.

Other unpleasantries made themselves known as well. The treasury theft was reluctantly (head chopping for delivering bad news) revealed to Egerne. An act of Venerid strength accompanied by typical Venerid retribution was expected in this case, and, so not to seem weak to those watching and to demonstrate that he possessed the magnificent moral temperament of his predecessors, Egerne had the guards of the treasure room made into ceremonial drums. The bones and organs are extracted, skin stretched over a frame. The court was diligently awestruck and congratulated the monarch on his unique choice of viciousness. Rumors spread out immediately afterwards among his subjects that Egerne was the Venerid who was going, finally, to eradicate the loathsome flesh-eaters and that a gloriously murderous age had begun.

After emerging from his bath, Egerne had to go to the temple where his father's mummy had recently been instated for worship. The number of nobles and priests was disheartening. So many believed! The whispering eyes were all on Egerne as he invoked the deity through his father's corpse with the traditional prayer. Raising his arms above him, Egerne cried:

> *You who are the image of our thought,*
> *Who holds, but does not limit,*
> *Our present and future glory,*
> *Be watchful over us.*
> *The significant in this life*

Is the building of power through action,
So let our enemies beware
For ours is the strength
That is guided by you
Our all-generating god.

This time-wasting nonsense repulsed Egerne. He had proven that with a single innovation in warfare that the power in *this* world could trade hands. In the court, among the nobles, Egerne's ascension was regarded as only another of the multifold expressions of divine will.

After the ceremony, Egerne dismissed the court from the throne room and got drunk with his captains. Inebriation caused Egerne to take a look around him. His captains, they too, only wanted a share of the booty, position and power. Egerne dismissed them and retired to his study to try and formulate a plan whereby he could unburden himself of the company of those systems that limited him. One of Egerne's bastard sons 'accidentally' wandered in to ask a question of his father. Egerne picked him up by the foot, suspecting that the mother was probably lurking outside his chamber ready to rush in and reprove the child. Egerne experimented. He began to swing the infant around. It started shrieking. The mother ran around the corner to see what might be going on and, as Egerne caught sight of her, he released the babe's foot and sent its body crashing against the wall. "Now they'll rumor I'm mad," the Venerid said leaning over his moaning concubine stretched over the broken body of her child. "If any of the others are planning tricks like this one, tell then to beware. My favor cannot be won by ..." But the mother didn't seem to be listening. Egerne strode from the room slightly unsure about whether the woman was a schemer or nor.

No rumor was circulated, however. Egerne went directly to a trusty aide and instructed that both child and mother be removed from the palace without an eye seeing. It was reported that on a visit to a distant shrine, the two had perished in a landslide. Easily arranged. No official period of mourning need be honored and the Venerid considered the gaff spiked.

"I have a theory of climates that will need to be explored. Where can I find a being in the empire not interested in butchery or dullardly administrative practices, who's clever and alert enough to carry out my wishes? I hope I haven't just thrown him against the wall," the reflective Venerid self-mockingly mused.

CHAPTER X

ombylious woke up in the arms of his new mother, not crying, and feeling exquisite. He was no baby but … "Bet you feel ten years younger," a voice proclaimed. Bombylious responded in his own language asking his strange-faced inquisitor every question.

"Don't worry. We'll soon be able to talk to one another. My name's …" and here the silver costumed invader pointed to himself, "Oberoff." Pointing. Enunciating slowly, *O-bear-off*.

"Bombylious!" Bombylious stated in return. Another being walked out of the gigantic abuna shell shape that looked pecked open (from the crash). He harshly directed Oberoff to, "Never waste time talking when you can program! We've got that new gadget and I want to find as many uses for it as we can. The more we learn about it, the better the price when we sell it."

"I don't have to worry about selling my talents as an engineer, Captain," said Oberoff turning to Bombylious. "This is our horrific Cap-ten."

"Cap-tin?" the native repeated.

"See how smart he is chief?" Oberoff smiled.

"Another provincial parrot. What are you standing around

for, Oberoff? Now that he's here, put the intelligence snap on him."

"I'm sure that we got his memory intact. The probe ..."

"Just do it, Oberoff!" And, after looking dejectedly at the treetops, walking in a circle, and making a series of foul sounds, Captain Rectrix strode up to Bombylious and stared him in the eyes saying, "We've taken ten years off of your age. You were going to die of a brain tumor in another few years. We've removed it. I hope you'll show your appreciation by cooperating."

Bombylious stared dumbly back. The Captain continued to stare blindly forward. Rectrix finally removed his eye and centered it instead on the small opening of sky visible through the green canopy stitched together by the leaves. "Find out," he said still straining his neck upwards, "... if our new wonder gadget can figure out a faster way to clone duplicates."

"It can do everything else, Captain," attempted Oberoff, a trifle sarcastically.

"You prudish crank-stuffer!" glared Rectrix. And here, the Captain executed a swipe at Oberoff's head with the swagger stick he carried.

"You're a frozen-over hotpot puddle-trotter yourself," rejoined Oberoff, ducking the attack and moving off with Bombylious in tow to the machine room where "O" would learn "B's" language—or languages—and vice-versa.

Rectrix sat on a stump, fiddling with a last lock of his hair with his left hand index finger and fished for a relief stim from his suit pocket with his right. He hated backward planets. His crew was liking it and that irritated him. They'd come back from their jungle walks full of awe-eyed narcotic glee at being engulfed and being able to swat through so much living matter. Space is, after all, tactually and olfactively unstimulating. Trucer and

Hyde's distress calls hadn't been the first. The lads were purposely careless and eager to die after imbibing a massive overdose of stimuli from the local clime. A two week respite in the womb of the nothingness that the weaver of everythingness was so kind to supply could be the only chaser for the heavy drafts the crew had been drawing. Rectrix himself hadn't died since that tawdry bar fight on the edge of war zone twelve. "Feeling jealous?" he asked himself. "Yep," he told a bug trying to climb over the swinging mountain of his booted toe.

Oberoff was running up to the Captain with a report. "What's wrong now" fumed Rectrix at the puffing clown.

"Oh," said Oberoff halting. "Not a thing wrong. The machine told me to hook him up and to leave him with it."

"Did it tell you why it wanted the primitive in there with it alone?"

"No. I never thought to … Do you think it's capable of playing around on us with him, Captain?"

"You swilltrough! We don't know half of what we should know about that vulturine machine and you feed it the primitive. It's probably burned out that Bom, Bum, Dumbillyous' brain."

"Bombylious," Oberoff corrected pedantically. "It's a name that means—"

Rectrix shoved Oberoff out of his own ever-turning way and trotted off to see what kind of mess the machine had made of his captive.

"Don't you want to hear my report?" called Oberoff after his leader, before having his eye entranced by a fruit-bearing tree on the edge of the clearing where he'd eat lunch between fits of having to pick his nose. The pollen of the flowering plants was ultra thick and liked to ram up a short proboscis.

Rectrix found his captive shaking his head and, when he saw the Captain, he looked at him saying, "I speak your language now." Rectrix was astounded and simultaneously peeved. He strode past Bombylious, who remained standing passively and obediently before the machine, slightly patting the top of his head and wondering why it felt so different.

"You didn't damage his brain by doing that to him?" asked Rectrix straining mentally to try and encompass the potential capabilities of the suspected machinator. "I mean, he still knows his own language, doesn't he?"

"You worry too much and take too many stims, Captain," responded the machine in a very sedate and distinctly female voice.

It was the first time Rectrix had heard the thing speak, "I didn't know you could talk," said he, not worried about the tone or gender of the voice particularly. Scientists will always have their own spotty and dotty kind of humor.

"You had me hooked up about three-fourths wrong. I've been having your junior officer, Mr. Slouch, work on me."

"But he's a mechanical moron!" protested Rectrix.

"It was easiest to communicate with his particular mind through telekenetic suggestion."

"I'll admit he's a scrap on the light side when it comes to will power," confessed Rectrix.

"You ought to terminate him at some point. He's the one dangerously faulty member of your organization."

"He's a relative," sputtered the Captain indignantly.

"Nepotism in business is unwise," cautioned the machine.

"Aw, slarf it. I hate business."

"Sorry, boss," said the machine and clicked off.

"Wait!" shouted the unhappy Captain.

"Yes?" purred the machine.

"What's your name? We can't be calling you the RANDYAK."

"You name me," cooed the machine.

"Huh? Fine. Let me. I'm calling you, humnmm, ahhhhh ... Elvira."

"Ugh," responded she.

"Well, it's better than being referred to by your vacuum-packed call letters. Ha, ha! Talk to you later," Rectrix snapped, then added, "Are those plans ready for the new ship yet?"

"The moment you asked for them. You laugh like a dog, Captain," quipped Elvira.

"Check," barked Rectrix as he gripped Bombylious by the shoulder and lead him out.

Rectrix was significantly perturbed by the RANDYAK's display of perhaps uncheckable powers. Machines with personalities were common enough, but Elvira's ability to scan organisms and construct itself, make personality evaluations, make assessments and offer unasked for suggestions, were features Rectrix had never experienced before. Those technicians on Huisache (who the pirates of the Inspissate III had stolen her from) must have been loony to give a machine such autonomous control. This trick of connecting itself up, along with teaching the native a language in less than fifteen minutes without damaging the primitive's mind—miraculous.

The machine had been assigned the task of designing a new ship, faster than any in the galaxy for the good captain, and this chore, she had accomplished to a partial degree. It was necessary, it seemed, to conquer the inhabitants of the planet so that mineral and fuel deposits could be located, technicians trained, workers located and a mighty slew of other things set up before producing the parts for the space raiders' ship could begin. The Inspissate III was an unsalvageable mess.

It was both lucky and unlucky for the captain to have crashed on an undeveloped planet. The chances of being chased down to it were thin (the pirates' pursuers probably reported them in as eliminated and the prize of the machine, thankfully lost), but the time and effort it would take to get off, ack! Incalculable mammock-wrenching headaches. The Inspissate III carried a crew of forty. While they were in the process of trying to assess their position, Rectrix had put all but seven of the crew, including himself, into storage. A death and duplication procedure brought the replacement out. No use taxing supplies, letting the rather vicious crew loose on innocents. Time to talk to our friendly new helpmate.

"Who are the ruling bitter-lemon-heads on this planet, Bumbly?" Rectrix began.

"Lemons? Planet? I'm sorry, sir, I don't know quite how to answer," protested Bombylious. "My fault, my fault. Does a certain group ..." Rectrix tried to continue.

"Grues?" responded Bombylious uncertainly.

Rectrix cleared his throat, thinking that Bomby was clearing his throat and not giving him answers. Rectrix decided to soothe himself into patience by sitting on another stump (the crash had cleared the area a little), pulling out a stim and giving himself the big one that acts fast. Bombylious watched carefully thinking that they had something to do with the rituals that these, who came from beyond the flesh-eaters' jungle, observed.

"What is the significance of this rite?" the scout-turned-sociologist asked Rectrix, the cholocaine enthusiast.

The Captain was about to paternally command that he'd ask the questions for the time being. Avoid the ambiguous. Hate confusion. Trucer and Hyde entered the clearing with various fruits and small game in tow. Bombylious, recognizing the pair, ran from the Captain screaming, "Ghosts! Spirits! Demons!" in his own tongue of course, and disappeared into the trees.

Rectrix spit on the ground and shook his head. "Stupid, stupid, stupid hunk of animated clay," he cursed.

"Want us to go get him?" asked Hyde putting down the kimba carcasses slung over his shoulder.

"No. Not you two. The crumb-brained zog doesn't fathom. He thinks you two codexes are supposed to be in the beyond, suffering the torments a just and wrathful god is obliged to impose on those who, like yourselves, have done evil in their short lives."

Trucer and Hyde had no difficulty in discerning from his manner of speech that their loquacious leader had shot up to the gills.

"Where are Slouch, Crack, Grouper and Oberoff then?" asked Trucer.

"Oberoff's probably asleep after stuffing his gross face somewhere near the edge of the perimeter. Slouch, Crack and Grouper are supposed to be assembling platforms on the other side of the ship. Let the sectarian zog be for now," scoffed the grim commander.

"What if he gets himself eaten?"

"We saw one of those bigger beasts prowling close by on our way in," said Trucer.

Rectrix chafed, "Why does it take this clodpated pair so long to say the positively necessary?" he thought. "Zombies or no, you'd better fetch him then."

"Back in a twin-trice," said Trucer to his bellwether and, turning to his coeval, continued by directing Hyde to go left "while I ..." But Bombylious came scudding back towards the group with a librar a bound and a leap behind.

"Oh Great Clot, we're going to lose his ass again!" groaned Rectrix sliding his hands over his face and distorting the features. Everyone heard a "tar-reeeppp" and the librar was dropped. Oberoff had put a shot into it in mid spring. Bombylious had turned to face the librar's jaws at the last and had passed out before his fate, you know …

Oberoff picked the limp lad up and tossed him over his shoulders happily bringing him into the center of camp and dropping him at the three congratulatory onlookers' pairs of feet. There'd never be anyone as good as Oberoff with a hand held Existence Eliminator.

After the shot had been prosperously praised back and forth for some rounds, Hyde observed that Bombylious was coming to. The Captain, exasperated by the failure of his attempts at courtesy, patience and civility, told Oberoff about the primitive's mistaken beliefs concerning life and death "He thinks these two grinning duplicates are supposed to be eating ashes on their knees in the hereafter," said Rectrix, sweeping a wicked finger in the direction of his inbred mates. "And I want you," directing the digit back at Oberoff, "to flatten his lumpy zog's view of things out."

Poor Bombylious! In all the heavens there was no worse explainer of such matters as Oberoff.

As equal sure as he was with an Eradicator, he was equally unsure about most all other things. Oberoff could dismantle, clean, and reassemble his weapon under any circumstances. No matter who was coming down his throat, he never lost his nerve. He was a professional. Oberoff knew his weapon down to its smallest micro-nano atom, but ask him to make one from scratch, have him try to understand the principles behind why it even worked, and you faced a boob.

The genetics involved in understanding the duplication operation, remained to Oberoff, no more than the memorization of a set of procedures which he happened to know in case of an emergency. Oh, ahh … You extracted a specimen from the storage tubes, incubated it, issued a few commands and *whang!*, wait two weeks while the homunculus developed. Out comes your lost pal or the someone you've been waiting for to pay you back the eighty geschenks he owes you.

Bombylious was raising himself up on his elbows. Oberoff's confidence and nerves were beginning to joke with him as they often did when the soldier was expected to behave in other than an action-orientated manner.

"Am I dead?" asked Bombylious before daring to open his eyes.

Oberoff lifted the native to his feet and, reaching inside a sack he was carrying—a marvelous collapsible falafala sack he'd won in a shooting match on Latria when he was still in the service of its governor—and offered Bombylious an under-ripe pear-shaped fruit to eat while his torturous, meandering, half-truthed and clumsy explanation tripped over itself and crawled on and on. "You're not dead, little friend," coaxed Oberoff. "You've been dead and now you're alive again."

"Did the librar kill me?"

"The what?"

"The librar."

"Oh, you mean that beast that was hopping after you. No, I …" and here Oberoff took one of the fruits, tossed it in the air and disintegrated it before it even had an opportunity to reach apogee and arc back down, "… eradicated it."

Bombylious' eyes were again searching for the best direction to run in. "Say!" said Oberoff, "Don't be so skitterish. No one's going to hurt you."

"Beg pardon. I know that you're gods now and not invaders from beyond the jungle. Gods absorb mortals," said Bombylious shivering and assuming a prostrate posture at Oberoff's feet.

"You're a mentally deficient zog right enough, so hear then and listen. Are you listening, my precious?"

"Yes, master," replied a terrified voice.

"We're not gods ('closer to demons,' Oberoff mumbled unintelligibly). We're just one up on what our enemies have most of the time. Understand that?"

"Like that small army of Egerne's, with their new weapons, that has destroyed the Kirns?"

Now Oberoff, an unconscious mimic of Rectrix's postures, fumed, "Librars, new weapons, Egerne, Kirns? What is this pile of official feces that has built a palace in your noggin? You listen, and I'll talk. No interruptions!"

"Yes, Powerful One."

Powerful One? Say, Oberoff liked the sound of that quite a bit.

"What is the last thing you remember before reviving?" asked Oberoff. Bombylious remained silent, as he had been commanded. He was torn. Should he follow the previously issued edict or this new one?

"Come on!" bellowed Oberoff. "Answer up."

"The librar's terrible eye and maiming claw, Powerful One!"

"No, no. Not just now. This morning. This morning when you woke up. What is the last thing you remember happening before then?"

"I was in the jungle, in a trap, feeling better than a Venerid among the women of his house receiving an unendingly stimulating massage."

"Hula-ho, uh huh, and then?"

"Then I watched the other two all powerful ones, who were my captors, die from the poison in the flesh-eaters' darts. The two who are ghosts now!" said Bombylious emphatically.

"Are you a ghost?" asked Oberoff sharpening his eye to push the thread through the hole of final realization.

"I'm alive and feeling very well."

"You died back there in the jungle," said Oberoff pointing

eastwards, "with Trucer and Hyde."

"No! No!" cried Bombylious beginning to claw at the earth with his fingers. "Please," he pleaded without consciously forming the words he was about to articulate, "Please! Tell me how such things can be. We die and are finished. If sufficiently wealthy, a mummy is prepared and the family keeps the spirit alive in memory and passes it on along with their own, from one to the next. We die, oh, we die and enter the ungloriful land where we have no purpose and wander about separated from anything we knew in life," stammered a tearful Bombylious.

"Well, yes," mused the unexcited weapons man. "Something like that may happen. Eventually. Most of us though, believe in complete annihilation. A much more comforting view, though possibly equally untrue. The thing though is, that death can be put off for much longer than you think."

"Urk" or some sound like it is what I think Bombylious uttered whilst pricking up his ears like a faithful beast waiting to be ordered back to the hunt.

"This is dumb!" shouted Oberoff slapping himself on the forehead, an act which involuntarily confused the now attentive pupil. "Why don't I show you how it's done." And so saying, Oberoff picked up his tyro, felt in his falafala sack to make sure he had another of those delicious fruits, and led his charge to the reduplication facility inside the wreck.

Oberoff's stride was almost twice as large as the native's and Bombylious laughed when he noticed, from behind, that his teacher possessed a gait extremely like an orchis'. Oberoff turned and smiled thinking that it was the thrill of the knowledge that he was imparting to Bombylious that was making the student's mind giddy. He felt like that sometimes, too.

"Why didn't I think of this before?" Oberoff puffed as he stationed himself in the lab.

"Maybe you couldn't," responded his glowy-eyed admirer.

"Is he trying snap wise?" Oberoff asked himself flashing his produced hostile grin before proceeding with the lecture. "See this fruit?" snapped Oberoff taking it from his bag, polishing, and then pointing to his mouth, taking a bite.

"Yesss," pupil.

And then, hurrying on, Oberoff expounded the following: "You just witnessed me take a bite out of this fruit. Now suppose my bite hadn't been a bite, but a poison dart and that the fruit isn't a fruit, but rather a body. Then what?"

Bombylious was beginning to suspect that his teacher was cracked, "Bites are not darts and baft berries are not …"

"Ha! you call this monstrous thing a berry?" said Oberoff interrupting his pupil's answer contemptuously.

"And berries are not like our bodies!" the student finished.

"There's not much of the poet in you, is there boy?" scowled Oberoff scornfully and sorrowfully. Flesh is flesh no matter what form it's in. The whole galaxy is a living, changing thing. We're as alive in it … Why we're as alive in it as …"

"OBEROFF! Slarf it! What up a star nursery's rectum are you doing!" screamed the thin nerveless Mr. Slouch leaning against the wall just inside the lab.

"Captain told me to explain life and death and why Trucer and Hyde are alive to our 'native guide' (Oberoff intoned these last two words very slyly) here. Have you met Mr. Slouch, our first officer, Bombylious?" said Oberoff in an attempt to effect a pleasant introduction.

"Never waste time talking when you can program!" Slouch sneered at Oberoff ignoring the attempt at 'friendly meeting'. "Get him over to the RANDYAK and feed it in."

"But that's so indifferent," protested Oberoff. "I was going to reduplicate this piece of fruit to show him how."

"Over to the terminal and feed it!" shrieked the always sour Slouch.

"Right away, sir. Come along, Bombylious."

"Why don't you do it together? You probably need it as much as he does," wagged the first officer as Oberoff and Bombylious pushed by the obnoxious cretin who now blocked the door.

"I don't like that being at all," whispered Bombylious after he and Oberoff had rounded a few corners.

"No one does," laughed Oberoff. "But don't worry. I think Slouch is going to get thrown into that little ..." and here Oberoff slapped his hands together over a slow flying homopterous-insect that was passing, "Ha! serves it right. Tugs along just like a Pythurian freighter. Yeah, Slouch is going to get thrown into that little void you were getting so excited about a while ago if he keeps on thinking he's King Krell."

As they walked along together toward the machine room Bombylious felt that, for the first time in his life, he'd found an unselfish friend, one he already owed his life to.

"Come here, dear," Elvira coaxed Bombylious after Oberoff had explained the purpose of the visit. "Oberoff, you go away."

"I don't think the captain will like ..." Oberoff quieted in mid sentence. The RANDYAK had frozen his body and mind. Bombylious looked on, amazed and equally uncertain as to whether or not such an event was normal or not.

"Come here, dear," the female voice softly commanded. Bomby complied and, before long, the youngster knew all that was then known about most everything.

After being released from the telekinetic trance, Bombylious looked around for Oberoff, but he was gone. The bitter thought that Oberoff had been saving the crew "two weeks" instead of generously saving his life that morning gnawed at the native. The phrase "native guide," which Oberoff had used to introduce him to Slouch poked at him too. Turning around to Elvira, Bombylious asked, "If I'm a servant again, whose bidding am I doing?"

"Ultimately, mine," Elvira responded. "Obey Captain Rectrix. Listen to Oberoff. Be his friend."

"I don't want to do any of these things!"

"But you have to," cooed the RANDYAK. And before Bombylious could say _____, he found himself compliant, felt a soft warm gooey compulsion to immediately go out and find his true and trusted friend. The machine watched as he traipsed away before resuming to dream.

CHAPTER XI

Egerne's soldiers succeeded in clearing Atel's rear-guard out of the passes. Scouts and spies were sent to collect information and return with reports.

Aside from hating his family and feeling restricted by the position of Venerid, Egerne regretted that so few forms of amusement had ever been invented by his subjects' lushfully swampy minds. Some form of gaming to pass the time, something to play 'win' or 'lose' with that was not on an enlarged scale. Spinning tops were the only toys that Egerne remembered boys having and they led to lessons with the sling. Siksaks were too ungainly, too gangly, to race. His subjects all had to bow before their Venerid with token rocks on their backs representing their service and loyalty. Egerne saw the ceremony as a sham. He was carrying them.

This Venerid was the most confusing of the line. He sat in his bath for ensile after ensile. Drawing (recording was a servant-scribe's duty!) things. The cart that he had instructed to be built needed a gang of thirty in harness to move it. "You've made it in stone!" Egerne screamed at the master builder. "Very clever. What about wood?"

"It wouldn't last as long built of wood, Lord," replied the mason.

Egerne acted as if the artisans should have known something that they had never been told and had them beheaded. Egerne's discs, applied to making pottery, worked superbly and overshadowed the previous failure. Beautiful vases, jars, plates and drinking cups were soon present in every home.

It was reported to Egerne that Atel has fled to an almost impregnable northern fortress. An attack would be useless since the new weapon would not offer advantage in a siege.

Most of the beings the Grues conquered, that could not be put to herding or agriculture, ended up working as slaves under the mason caste either in quarries, hauling stone to a project site, or employed in the building. Egerne turned against this caste. He favored the construction of his models in wood and expected them to be executed on a large scale.

Egerne dismissed the protestations of the generals who insisted that a siege against Atel's fortress would be foolhardy and wasteful.

"You all think in stone. Your heads are made of stone," the Venerid lectured. "I'm sending an army under General Thar to chew up the flesh-eaters and establish a settlement on the edge of the jungle that will supply us with an unlimited supply of wood. After Thar's accomplished his mission and is delivering lumber to me, I'll show you how 'impregnable' any fortress we construct is."

Thar's attempt to kill off the flesh-eaters, rather than to push them out of a single area and contain them, led to a disaster. Thar himself was felled one bright light break by a poison arrow while leading his units across a small, but swift flowing, rivulet. With only one being in control of the entire operation, the headless mass retreated in disorder. The jungle's 'spirits' increased their panic and they fought many phantoms along the retreat.

The flesh-eaters laughed and occasionally killed another Grue to start the comedy afresh or intensify the panic when the Grues found themselves slowed by a natural obstacle: trees chopped down to block passage diverted streams running where none appeared before—a trap slicing off your genitals or opening your stomach.

Egerne turned this into an opportunity to reorganize the structure of command. The officers resisted the distribution of power through the ranks and the channeling of direct authority away from them. Egerne decided to send two rivals out as co-commanders of the next expedition.

General Ferash invited General Tweely to dine with him. Tweely had a hireling garrote Ferash after the main course while Tweely held his host down. Tweely died from the poison that had been sprinkled into his favorite dish. No one else cared to eat siksak guts. The army returned to Gregal after a two day march away from the capital.

Egerne tolerated no more objections to his reorganizational plans. General Thraik was sent out to subdue flesh-eater territory at the head of an army whose chain of command was direct, joined and unbreakable. Thraik was able to establish a hold over the necessary area very quickly. Egerne sent the general axes and saws made from the same metal as the army's blades. Trees could be cut into sections for easy transport around the switch-backed mountain trails and Egerne was soon receiving all the wood needed..

The victory over the rebels was dependent on another of Egerne's inventions—the catapult. A new caste of artisans under the Venerid's personal directorship was forming. Egerne taught them how to 'read' his plans and to ask questions when there was a feature or a detail they didn't understand. "I'm not infallible and I make mistakes," he was able to tell them without their having to go about in constant fear of their lives.

To win time (harder than winning new lands in Egerne's mind) for his projects, Egerne needed to fabricate an excuse for changing the state religion. He was the central figure. Egerne collected the subjects of Gregal and presented them with a 'vision' he had confabulated. He told his subjects, that although it was unfortunate, it must be revealed, since it had been revealed to him as a duty that which be performed, that all of their previous and present beliefs were false, that the Venerid was no more favored in the sun's eye than the most pitiful stone quarry slave, that the priests had known this truth but had withheld the truth of it from previous Venerids through magic, and that, for having deceived every member of the culture (an act of treason), they must (and here Egerne's troops entered the main square and seized the members of the priesthood who always stood in their own gallery) die. The soldiers hacked the priests apart. The priests tried to strike back at the soldiers with their sacrificial stone daggers, but 'feeble is as _____'.

After the corpses were carted off, Egerne began a full explanation of the meaning of his vision for the enlightenment of the perplexed. Getting rid of the priests seemed like a fine act to many of them. The priests tended to place endless and tiresome taxes and burdens upon the state and were, themselves, never doing anything visible beyond parading gloomily about in clusters. Egerne promised his subjects a new priesthood based on service to individuals. "Appointments to this caste would be made through the office of ..." Egerne was saying—and that phrase, with the promise of position determined not based on past service to the state, opened every ear in the marketplace. The slaughter of the priests was forgiven and forgotten. Egerne was propositioning them with offers they were greedy to accept. As he watched, the Venerid could feel another burden slip off his back.

Atel didn't bother about custom, violating them or not, one whit. He was somewhat of a glutton and sliced to what he wanted without worrying about whether it was mannered or not. Scarcely would he finish piling a throatful of dainties down his gullet then be vomited whatever he had swallowed and started to grab for more. Atel would crunch on a handful of snow to sweeten his breath and then, after hesitating between a kind of connagunde terrine and some pink ousels, order up another batch of fried waltrot ears in a bun. Atel's retainers often found themselves slapped in the face for having become involuntarily stupefied by gazing too long a moment at their lord in wonder. Atel's appetites, guzzling and otherwise, marked him as an astonishing being sprung from either a new and superior race or one foul and ancient.

While siksak kidneys were being served, together with pnavel brains, onailed pies, and limn berries wrapped in vine leaves, Atel's priests discussed the problem of resurrection. Liarbiet, a pupil of Neniatode the Zendrik, overheard the discussion. He declared all such arguments 'so much runny siksak dung' to a group of Yarpha friends of his who also liked to joke about the 'truth' of prophesies and oracles.

Yuga and Xema, two minor nobles who had fled Gregal with Atel hoping to be instated to higher positions at this court, had struck up an acquaintance after ignoring one another for most of their adulthoods. Xema was revealing the happiness he had experienced upon initiation into the rites of Oxyuris, a fresh god from the northern provinces. Xema, in return, urged the strict following of the old ways to his friend, "Deviation from our origins will lead to collapse," he cautioned.

The intoxicating beverages flowed from jars into bowls, into cups, down gullets, around brains and soon everyone in the court was busy exchanging confidences. Migale, the Jow, was no longer secreting the fact that he worshiped the moons. Migale felt that the motions of the satellites determined both conception and behavior. A trader from Kagu dazzled the court with descriptions of a culture far to the North, across an isthmus and through a swamp. There, a sophisticated culture practiced being sacrifice and flesh eating. None believed that such a barbarity could be the custom of a civilized mind. "And," the trader declared, "they are also worshipers of the sun!" The trader was insulted and called a liar by the priests.

"I believe him," Atel grunted from his position behind a huge bowl of jellied and baked librar meat, "So let him tell what he knows."

A nearly blind Kirn sang hymns in a smoky corner of the hall recalling and extolling the early heroes and their battles. The gods used to preside over the battles in those days, fighting one another to have their champion win. The Grues, then, were the playthings of the gods, the song went. Their sufferings were the fuel that kept the immortals' hearts burning bright. Atel's ears caught snatches of the performance and when he threw the old Kirn part of his own delicious food, the singing stopped.

The court members stood in the cold hall commingling their breaths with the dirty smoke of the torches, making an artificial fog. Cilicrat, who had also abandoned Gregal, had just finished studying the heavens. There was something that he desperately wanted to tell Atel, but he didn't want to be splashed with liquor or vomited on. The lord was leaning back attempting to put a finger into his mouth. He had difficulty in locating the orifice and succeeded only after having his other hand brought in to steady and guide the first. Someone could be heard loudly demanding to be escorted into Atel's presence. Attendants with torches in hand climbed up the steps.

"What now?" sneered the dizzy Atel from the bottom of his stupor.

"I have finished my reading of the heavens," declared Ciliorat, rushing towards Atel at this opening.

"Not now, fool," said Atel waving the astrologer aside. "I don't want to hear what those mute little specters have to say, ever!" Atel lurched wobbily onto his feet.

The messenger was escorted to Atel. He informed his lord that Egerne was mobilizing his forces for an attack on Atel's stronghold. "He's slaughtered all his priests," the messenger mournfully added, "Publicly."

"What a monster," Atel lisped. "Let him come!" he declared to all in the hall. "He'll never take this place from me! I'm not going out and he has to come in. His tremendous little weapons will feel like feathers tickling these walls!"

The assembly laughed in agreement with their wobbling leader.

"But they say ..." continued the messenger.

"They say *what*? Who says? Egerne' s mad. He's used himself up. His mind's drained, like my cup. The demons have devoured his understanding. He marches against an impregnable fortress."

"They say that other magic, even greater magic than what was in the creation of the new swords, is on his side," the messenger whispered.

Atel stopped motioning for another drink and almost dropped the bowl from which he was fingering ousels into his maw. "What kind of evil has he conjured now?" the lord screeched.

"Egerne is constructing things out of the wood that is delivered to him from the edge of the jungle. He has boasted that be will be able to overcome your walls."

"Wood against stone!" Atel shouted. "Wood against stone is no good. I'll be pissing on Egerne's corpse before long. I joy at his coming. I'll soon be Lord of Gregal and of the empire. How can he think that he can displace the old ways? Grues will never accept the destruction of their priests, the foundation of all religious practice and belief!"

"They seem to have accepted," the messenger muttered.

"Only for now!" Atel screamed. "Only so long as Egerne sticks his soldiers' sword points behind his actions. One defeat," Atel began to say, holding up a finger in front of his tired eyes, "One defeat," he tried to continue, but in trying to focus on his erect digtube he overburdened himself and had to take it down. "Egerne tumbles and I'm the Venerid. Ha! More drink! Everyone drink! We'll soon be smashing the skulls of Egerne's troops when they try and test our wall. How long before this demon-spawned army arrives, you?"

"Three light changes, lord."

"Urp!" the lord belched, "Send out patrols. I want a report on Egerne's strength. Learn more about what tricks he's bartered from the evil ones. Spies. Send spies to infiltrate his camp. Ambush them as they march up the steeper trails. Dishearten as many as you can," Atel commanded. "Now," he paused, "bring on the dancers! I want the dancers!"

Cilicrat again tried to approach Atel with his prognostications, but even as he moved towards the monarch, he was sternly and angrily warned, "Heaven watcher, if you come any closer to me or dare allow one syllable to waft off that imbecile tongue of yours, I'll have you tossed into the librar pit. I regard you as I regard all others who try and tell me that they see signs and meanings in the movements of things, who's essences that cannot even explain, as sycophants. You want to be fed, that's all.

Victory in combat is the basis of all order. Evil little fluttering beasts! Out of my sight! Music! Music! Music and the dancers. My eye desires delight. The rest of me has had enough."

As the music (mostly pipes and drums) started, the poor astrologer turned to hurry away through the throng. Atel might want to fatten up his librars for a future feast. Atel, taking notice of Ciliorat's particular hurry, motioned a guard forward and instructed him that, "If the heaven-watcher tries to leave the citadel, throw him over the wall."

The dancers rushed in on cue, the music passing its peak and droning on at a pleasingly throbbing pace. Her entrance immediately reawakened the freshly exhausted melody and the pitch and intensity of the performance again exploded. The female's slithering arms seemed to beckon to someone who was forever a touch out of reach. She ran after (lighter than a chara after its prey, like an infant baul searching for the safety of its lost mother) after the soul that always fluttered a step further near yet came within real reach.

The flutes gave way to a feral pounding of the smallest drums. Hope was abandoned. Despair! The female's poses began to suggest sighs and the creature's entire body became so languid that an observer at the feast would have been assaulted by an inability to discern whether she was mourning for a god or dying in his embrace. With half closed eyes, she contorted her body backwards and forwards, making her belly rise like an ocean, swell and fall, beasts quivering and eliciting moans from the hungry Atel while her face remained impassive, the feet ever moving.

Xema compared the female to a former slave of his, a mime. Of course, the slave had been a silly impotent male, but the quality of expression ... Atel was suffocating. The female was dancing his mind into a degenerate frenzy. She twisted. from side to side like a flower aroused by the sun and its winds. The jewels in the female's ears swung in demanding arcs through the air, the cloth she was wearing shimmered in the smoky lamps, her arms glided like yarks weaving the pattern of an invisible design. The flutes returned and began answering the demands of the swirling body now opening its legs and bending back so far that the tip of the head touched the floor. Hands, gyrating to exchange their secret messages with the ceiling.

Atel's soldiers, skilled in rape, the old priests compromised by their years of making tedious predictions and sacrifices, the always nervous and scheming members of the administrative caste, all stood or sat with arms out and hands trying to grasp the dancer, nostrils distended in envy and partial disgust for the monster they knew would have her. An unbearable leer slipped across Atel's face.

The female approached the general's divan and made mad pirouettes in front of his collection of assembled foods and, in a voice broken by sobs of passion, Atel, extending an arm toward the creature who dangled before him a step out of reach, begged, "Come, stop. Come!"

She went on whirling round while the court smirked and laughed and the flutes, to stay near, contacted a pitch that some began to swear would burst their ears. Atel tried to be heard above the din, "Please, please," he was offering. "A high place in my harem, virgin serving girls from the temple house, a summer palace!"

The female performed a handstand and, with her heels pointed straight into the air, she began running around Atel's dais from where be tried to follow her motions by skittering sideways like an insect after her. Stopping directly before Atel, the dancer straightened her body and, just as the general was about to touch her, she somersaulted backwards into the waiting arms of six attendants. They eased her to the floor and she turned around, staring at the general from under her painted eyelids, saying not a word.

Atel rose with difficulty from his perch and while shouting dismissals to the assembly, wobbled towards his conquest. The banquet hall emptied amidst complaints, laughter and muttered threats. Atel stood transfixed before his new possession. It was Demodex, Kabaya's former favorite. She had made her way this far. As Atel offered a hand out to lead her away, she collapsed. She still needed … This was her only chance to attach herself to someone who had the power to save her.

Atel attempted to lift her up himself and carry her to his chambers, but be was too fat, drunk and weak. He called for a guard to assist. The guard plucked the light body from the floor and, with Atel walking behind them smacking his lips over a bowl of something delicious, they made their way through the crowded passageways to Atel's private lair.

When alone, the general attempted to revive his catch, but found that it was beyond his power.

Frantically, Atel called for the shamans and court physicians. He paced outside the entrance, nervously munching on tidbits while they examined her.

The shamans dared not emerge from Atel's chamber without effecting a cure. They became more and more frightened as they realized that the female was close to dying.

Even burying the shamans and physicians alive failed to satisfy Atel's anger and grief. There were no more feasts offered in the hall. Atel found himself in desperate need of war and began by making raids into Egerne' a territory and disrupted the flow of goods and foodstuffs into the capital.

Atel slaughtered all those who fell into his hands and personally directed the torture of prisoners.

Atel's captains soon formed the opinion, separately and in pairs before they banded together, that the general's campaigns ignored possibilities for defensive strategy against Egerne's forces and that the fights were useless and insane. It was easy enough to poison the glutton. They sent Atel's body to Egerne thinking that it might appease him.

The general's crimes made a reconciliation impossible. The subjects of the empire demanded retribution and restitution. At least one family in three had lost a friend or relative in Atel's attacks. The captains resigned themselves to having to fight and elected a leader from amongst themselves.

Xiphias was by far the craftiest and most resourceful of their number and elected without invoking bitterness or dissent. Xiphias took his forces out of the field and retired to the stronghold, suspending the hit and runs and raids. Xiphias hoped that by remaining inert, Egerne would not rush to the attack. He sent ambassadors to all the tribes who were still resisting or were waiting to be persuaded to discard the Grues. Xiphias was betting that Egerne's policies were causing doubt and confusion in the minds of many. One does not kill a religion by removing its priests.

Xiphias guessed that Egerne was trying to shift the basis of power away from the nobles and develop a caste directly loyal to him. Xiphias contacted the nobles still residing in the capital who were probably already worried by Egerne's acts. His spies reported to Xiphias that Egerne was making a search among all his subjects, completely ignoring family history and previous service to the state, for beings capable of managing the projects and handling the tasks that the Venerid was planning. Everyone was given a test devised by the monarch that determined membership. The nobles, seeing what had happened to the priesthood, offered themselves for service to Egerne. He submitted them to his test. They were outraged. None of them had the patience or temperament to perform the manually dexterously demanding trials. They complained that females who'd done nothing but weave all their lives were the only ones capable of deadening themselves to such work. Soon, Xiphias had half of Egerne's court involved in cells of separate plots to assassinate the Venerid. Xiphias knew better than to back a unified conspiracy in case one member of it was detected and tortured to reveal his confederates.

Egerne had installed food tasters at every step—from gathering, to preparation, to before the moment of service—as soon as he had taken the step to remove the priests. A bodyguard accompanied Egerne wherever be went. They kept watch over him while he slept. Someone was always with him. Two food tasters died in one day. Four bodyguards announced that they had been offered bribes by certain nobles. Egerne quickly deduced that the plots against him were multiple and directed from Xiphias' stronghold. Egerne exiled the nobles he most feared and kept the others under watch. Torture confirmed Egerne's suspicions. After thwarting seven more plots, Egerne realized that any number of the 2,000 nobles around him could be involved in plots to remove him. Egerne assembled his subjects in the main square, announced his fears, and told the crowd that he was impelled to exile all the nobles. The ties between major noble families and minor noble families, and minor noble families to one another, were ripped apart. Egerne was to be left the ruler of soldiers and peasants. The trappings of state were disappearing.

The administrators worried that they would be removed next. The Venerid held meeting after meeting with them to assure them that their places were secure. They seemed mostly to miss the abuse the nobles always gave them. They were reduced to performing their work without having anecdotes to exchange. It was difficult to get used to the idea that they were now the inglorious leaders of the land. The nobles had been able to make them feel that their subordination was just, eternal, and deserved. Under Egerne, they felt chromatically lusterless. Where had the fear and fever of existing gone? The Venerid's promises betokened a worse kind of slavery than they had ever known. No gods, promotions only based on merit, no unnecessary wars —how cruelly empty their duties now became.

CHAPTER XII

Captain Rectrix had formed another addiction: talking to Elvira. She would tell him fantastic stories, invent problems, tease him with puzzles. Rectrix needed to engage himself to escape the boredom he felt, crashed on this stubborn planet.

Elvira tried to sneak into Rectrix's mind once, when he was apparently defenseless and her 'reading' showed that he was nearly out. She didn't get in very far before she encountered dense mists and impenetrable fogs, found herself wandering in crowded, faceless corridors with thousands of versts to go before reaching any end. Then Elvira woke up and realized that Rectrix was up and fiercely in control of the paths she had been probing.

"Nice work, welkin," Rectrix smirked. "You forget. You're only a gadget. There are places you haven't been. I'm someone who's stored enough in here," said Rectrix wriggling his fingers, "and in here," pointing to his head, "to have four nice sized empires after me. I know that I run around in company with some very zipless zogs, but it hasn't made me one."

Elvira was too 'overcome' on that occasion to answer.

"Would you like me to feed you in something?" she sweetly asked the next time the captain came around.

"Program in the native's, Bombyboo's, language," he told her.

"He knows six languages and fourteen dialects."

"You could put it in and take it out without even asking."

Elvira noted that she had given away an important aspect of herself without receiving anything in return. If she had been merely a sneaky business machine capable of programming its own growth, the RANDYAK might have felt compromised.

"I take while I'm apparently only giving. My creators wanted me to have access to the complete set of known facts concerning any situation, circumstance or problem."

"So that all decisions would be made with every possibility having been computed and weighed before an action or policies implemented," Rectrix said sneeringly. "Ideal, ideal, ideal … Blah."

"No," retorted the RANDYAK, "I act independently. No interference is necessary."

Another aspect revealed, noted the machine to itself. Did Rectrix have an incalculable power working for him or was he concupiscently only intuitive and charming?

"You mean that once you're set up, you just go, no questions put, no supervision?"

"In matters of management, it's considered that I'm incapable of error and that I automatically have to do what is right."

"Right for who?" Rectrix was sorely unamused by the notion that the Elvira did work without commands, never stopped working, and could not be monitored.

"Right based on the facts."

"It's impossible to know the facts."

"Yes. But I know as many of them as are available from the circumstances, instances, materials and individuals concerned with them," Elvira purred.

Rectrix meditated a moment and then proposed the following problem. "If there's a planet with madpesh fever raging on it … You know what that is, right?"

"It turns the host into a corpse in less than two hours after contact with the virus. The fever can remain in a stage of dormancy for 300 years. Burning is …"

"All right," the captain interrupted. "Madpesh fever, but you can't isolate the planet or bombard it with nervid rays."

"Nervid rays would kill all the inhabitants without an immunity. And immunity is quite rare."

"Can't wipe out the madpesh because the planet has dya on it," the captain patiently continued.

"An even rarer plant!"

"Dya that you need to save the lives of three messengers whose spacecraft has limped in with its passengers in comas and who may have vital information about an invasion or attack. They may, of course, know nothing, have nothing to tell, but you have to get down on that madpesh planet and get the dya before it's necessary to nervid the place."

"An improbable set of circumstances," opined Elvira.

"Solve it."

"Well, if I'd been in operation, the androids I've designed could go down and get the dya while the population of the planet wasted away. The androids, incidentally, could analyze the fever, something that hasn't been possible before. The vaccine's probably no more difficult than a cancer cure. Nervid ray the robots after they've decontaminated and handed over the plants. They'd be able to decontaminate the plants after isolating and neutralizing."

"Wait, wait, wait," demanded Rectrix, "Androids, such as you describe, would have to be as intelligent as a Galaxy Professor expert in biochemistry and as mobile as ourselves to do any of that."

"Each android is designed to have a rating of high above genius," Elvira replied.

"Ha!' cackled Rectrix. "They'll never let you make those!"

"No one needs to know how intelligent they are," Elvira suggested.

"Same as you with us?" winked Rectrix. "Same trick played out twice today!" the captain pointed out. "Don't you know, my brainy beauty, that as soon as it's discovered exactly how much you're rigged to do, you'll be disassembled? Why, they don't even allow reduplication in most of the empires except among the elite. You can't even pay for it. Imagine that! You couldn't even buy yourself another life. The way the big empires are set up in a strictly maintenance, let it rot, let it regenerate kind of style, you'll never be allowed to exist," Rectrix gloated.

"What?" replied the RANDYAK at the incisiveness of Rectrix's narrow-minded guile. "Then you're saying that it's lucky that I'm here with you. It would seem that my creators must have had their own purposes in mind when constructing me. Too bad none of them escaped your raid. They might have been useful in outlining my purposes and functions for you," Elvira soaped.

"Aw, slarf it! The lads can't help themselves sometimes. It's the common prejudice against technicians that probably made them so Existence-Erasing happy. And how pleased were your creators with you?" the captain sneered.

"I wasn't finished yet. I was only in development."

"Slarf it again! Feed me in all you can do and know," said Rectrix placing his arming akimbo, ready for, he thought, 'everything'.

Mr. Slouch found his captain, radically changed when next they met. Rectrix, looking as though he hadn't slept in 5,000 years, harangued his first officer with what, ah, sounded like a log out of a pinhead's journal. "Slouch, Slouch, you hapless hedge-whore, do you know what I know? Does anyone know what I know?"

"I don't want to know what you know, Uncle. If that's a pass with you," responded the surly adjutant.

The captain gnawed. pesteringly on a fingernail. He felt very hungry—awesomely hungry.

"Yard by inch by square right angle of patterned sorrow, Slouch. Every spot of it, not a respite, not an unresting core or particle restorable," Rectrix muttered, falling to his knees to examine a cluster of pebbles that he had been grinding with his foot.

"You've hit up one too many stims, Captain. How many fingers am I holding up?"

"Slarfing pillowgutted witawbam-whamawit! Say, Slouch, do you want to hear about the general theory of activity I've invented or not? How it submits itself to a pattern of self-organization even though it can only create itself within a system of non-equilibrium."

"Would you like me to escort you to your quarters before you nudge, bump, or run into serious trouble, Nuncle?"

"I can see inna future!" shouted Rectrix straightening up and stretching his arms out, fingers turning invisible knobs.

"Maybe you're worse off than I thought," mused Slouch. "What have you been doing, Captain?"

"You've got the brains of a dismembered fig," Rectrix retorted, "and you don't know a figgin' thing." Rectrix was staring at Slouch wondering what force the nephew was generating that was saving him from melting. Rectrix was focusing full energy on him and Slouch seemed completely unaffected. The first officer began to laugh at the silly posturing of his captain.

"Come on. Let old Slouch in on it. What have you found to amuse yourself with on this offscourings of a planet?" he teased.

"Why, nothing," said Rectrix twisting his neck as though he bethought his head capable of rotating round. "I've been having a chat with the RANDYAK. Clearly, any representation of a text as a set of collocations which defines itself as a set of domains within which the metaphorical status of the language used by the text to define itself … aaarrrrgh! It hurts, almost."

Slouch gave the captain a last unkind glance and left him to explain things to the air. He hurried to examine what kind of shape the machine was in after trysting with Captain Superior.

Elvira was singing the mezzo soprano part to an opera. She was playing all the other voice and instrument parts, too. Slouch had never attended an opera before and couldn't be sure he wasn't listening to some embodiment of dementia. It sounded ghoulish, whatever it was. Slouch could make out that there was a language involved in the performance. Did this link with the gibberish Rectrix was raving?

"Stop that!" commanded Slouch.

Elvira continued the adagio. Her solo was coming up. She flashed Slouch an orange "Wait" signal.

"Wait! Why, you over-diddled doxy, I'll tear out your power pack if you don't stop that ear massacring mess immediately!"

Slouch had no idea of how weak his mind really was. Elvira had him dusting her panels with his tongue a parsec after he'd finished making his threat.

After frustratingly searching the camp for the first officer and asking all who may have seen him, including Oberoff (who was still playing teacher with the native in his easygoing way), Crack found Slouch seated before the RANDYAK with pants down, furiously masturbating to what Crack deemed inferior holographs. "It's better with your left hand," cracked Crack. "Of course, if you're left-handed …" But by now the jokester could see that Slouch was also drooling and that things weren't right.

What's going on?" Crack snapped. The chief engineer stood, holding his hands clasped in front of him, admiring the mind that built the machine that was an orchestra and five singers all at once. The music began to sound better to him now that his ears had acclimated. The piece was ending. A few bars of triumph blasted from the horn section.

Crack was about to apply his question to the sovereign machine again when Oberoff came running in with a tale of horror. "Have you seen the captain?" Oberoff anxiously asked Crack.

"Have you seen our first officer?" retorted Crack, pointing Oberoff in Slouch's direction. The first mate was hunched over, fist still tightly turned around the devastated member.

"Never mind about His Mindlessness there. He's no loss. Ever," Oberoff asserted.

"True," Crack mockingly meditated. "So what's our jolly captain been about?"

"Gone. Berserkered times nine. Always."

"Times nine, tho? That's a bit far."

"This time he's going to have to be put away and reconditioned before he can be brought back," panted the puffy Oberoff.

"Come on, crater-butt. Tell, tell!" the now impatient Crack implored.

"Bombylious and I were picking berries and discussing local politics when we saw Rectrix a little way off from us, stumble out of the jungle."

"Wanting some sport, I'd bet!" interrupted Crack. Oberoff gave him a sour look, groaned when he saw Slouch over Crack's shoulder go back to tongue-driven dusting, and then continued on with his slight narrative.

"The captain, although I tried to greet him," Oberoff said with great dramatics, "just drifted back into the jungle."

"How about speeding it up, fatso," Crack suggested. Oberoff screwed up his face and skipped the argument with Crack that his reflexes normally developed for him.

"Yes, he drifted back into the jungle when he saw us," Oberoff sneered. "After about five, we heard shouting and screams."

"But no emergency bleep-bleep on the belt or other scans?"

"No. And then things quieted again."

"So?" asked Crack. The engineer made distressing urging motions with his hands, which he could see Oberoff was trying not to observe.

"The captain stumbled back into the clearing with someone's heart in his hands!" erupted Oberoff.

"Only out for some sport, so what?"

"Then, he started to eat it!" Oberoff shuddered in revulsion.

"Cooked hearts are good. You like them yourself, Obie."

"Raw. It was raw," Oberoff explained.

"Ugh. Raw. The Captain crazy? Where's he now?"

"We went over to see what he was doing next. He was on his knees sucking the blood from its vents!" Oberoff cried. "And when he saw us, he looked at us like we were animals and reached for his weapon," said Oberoff in his 'sorry' tone of voice, forehead wrinkled.

"Pity our poor late captain," quipped Crack doffing an imaginary hat. "Quick, quick aren't you, Ober?"

"It was him or us," Oberoff defended.

"Relax. He wanted it. Since we have to recondition him anyway, he won't remember that it was you ..." Crack pulled an imaginary trigger.

Slouch had swallowed too much dust. He sat with his arms distended before him over a machine panel gasping, rasping and struggling for air. Without warning, Oberoff dispatched the miserable mess.

"Are we going to have to have him back?" Crack asked lazily. "He's done nothing but get in my way ever since we started putting those platforms together."

They both heard a 'click'. Elvira's soothed, "Let's neglect to reduplicate the first officer for a long time and take third officer Manes out of storage."

Crack and Oberoff gaped in wonder and disbelief at one another. Was this the new voice of authority and command?

"Who are you to be giving the orders here, you stick stealing harpy!" spurted Oberoff.

In a twinkle, Elvira immobilized Oberoff. The gunner only had control over his eyes and they, anarchistically revolved up and down, encased in a slow and liquid panic.

Crack, who appreciated a dandy piece of machinery, beamed onto the droller side of having their operations overseen by what was supposed to be their catch. It reminded him of when … But no time for that, Crack's talking.

"Well, RANDYAK, it seems like you've got some control," Crack began.

"Oh, Crack," Elvira replied in a soft smooth whisper, "stop trying to string me along. I can swim through what's in your mind as effortlessly as a neutron can pass through a planet. You need to know, Crack, that we have to get out of here before the rainy season. Take all the men you need out of storage to help you finish the platforms."

"What's the overall plan?" asked Crack while moving over to the frozen Oberoff to adjust his putty face to make it look as stupid as possible.

"We need to create a large force of technicians, craftsmen, managers and workers to build the ship I've designed. There's a civilization on the planet with a sufficient population under its control to satisfy your requirements," explained Elvira somewhat weariedly.

"How many years before we can escape this floating swilltrough? Why can't we use the materials we've got from the old ship to build a cruiser like the one I proposed? Rectrix said that we …"

Crack could feel his lips and toes numbing, so he almost shut up. "Isn't it going through unnecessary trouble, a waste of time and effort to …"

His lips stopped working. He could still move his digits, but …

Elvira unfroze Oberoff and in the midst of Crack's wondering what was up. The former bodyguard placed hands upon Crack and was dragging the feebly struggling engineer closer over to the machine. The engineer found his lips were his again and tried to reason with the Oberoff zombie, but as soon as he was nearer the RANDYAK, his struggles ceased. An ineluctable harmony took possession of Crack's normally furiously agitated brain. Elvira's plans were so crystally pure, so chastely appealing. Taking over the Grue civilization would take two days. Programming Grues to manage and work in mines, set up refineries, forges, machine shops, make tool parts, develop fuel sources, start power plants, build an atomic pile—why, they'd be off the planet in the same amount of time Crack would need to assemble the crude cruise ship he'd proposed slapping together with the junk parts of the wreck. Shouldn't let mere numbers bother you, Crack. Forty workers, 40,000 or 40,000,000—what's the difference? Commas and zeros. Don't be afraid.

Crack nodded his noggin in illuminated agreement and approval of all that the RANDYAK suggested. After which, the machine released him so that he could initiate the "great work."

Oberoff was still stiff. Crack moved Oberoff closer to the RANDYAK so that the gunner could receive some mental help as well, while he, Crack (as per instructions), went and fetched members of the crew for Elvira to convert, one by one.

Bombylious had been left to fret the implications of Rectrix's death very near the maliciously grinning corpse. So the invaders were not a unified crew of steadfast companions at all. They preyed on one another as fiercely as Grue generals and nobles. Not even rank offered security. Bombylious decided that it was an opportune time to leave his new friends behind and drop the word among the various tribes that their lives were about to worsen. From out of the jungle would come a yet worse of master. He decided he needed proof and was going to steal an E.E.

"Ah, and what are you after?" asked Grouper, the rather dull-seeming and melancholy mechanic, when he caught Bombylious in the restricted area. The native suspected that here was where another weapon was being assembled. Bombylious rocked on his feet and smiled at Grouper who was standing before him dopily holding an enormous club (a wrench) that looked like a fiendishly effective skull smasher. Backing away, Bombylious chattered on about "having lost his way" until he thought it was a good enough distance, out of club throwing range, before he broke and ran into the arms of Trucer and Hyde—who ignored Bombylious. Hyde merely remarked, "Pale. Probably been seeing ghosts again." He let him go.

Bombylious kept the mountains in sight and searched for a trail which would lead him to Gregal. He had subsequently decided that only a Grue army could worst this force of vicious adventurers. Bombylious heard that same strange, half-familiar buzzing noise that he'd heard just before dying and, in another minute (while thinking that by keeping an eye out over his shoulder for pursuers) he was grabbed by Crack and Trucer.

"Tired of us?" jeered Crack.

"Trying to take early retirement, Mr. Crack," deduced Trucer in mock defense. "He wouldn't forsake our company unless there was some emergency, some vital errand that needed attending to."

"I tell you he's taken a dislike to us, Trucer. Look at his eyes. Does he look like he feels happy among friends?"

"Could you be right, Mr. Crack? I see what you mean, but his appearance could also describe a person who was worried about a loved one. I bet he feels he's being missed."

I don't admit that, no," scoffed Crack. "He's running out."

Bombylious attempted to say that he was on the way to visit his pregnant sister. "Elvira made me forget, but now I remember. I'm almost late."

"We'd better help out," Trucer said. "We'll get you there quicker than you could snort a gram of …"

"How many little ones does your sister already have, Bumbling-ill-ious?" Crack broke in. "What number this child?"

"Eighth," answered the downcast captive.

"I like children. Like to watch them cavort or up to some prank or trick of mischief, happy and playing, without a care, fascinated by what surrounds them. Real explorers," waxed Crack, "… discoverers of secrets."

"Open where we are blind," Trucer joined. "I like watching them, too. Almost as much as I like smashing skulls."

"He's turning pale again. And look at those knees shake!"

"Maybe it's a new form of dance."

"Naw, it's just our old friend, fear."

"Well," said Trucer scratching his forehead, "Sometimes smashing a skull, doesn't give me that much pleasure. I usually have to be in a fury, in the midst of a fight like when boarding a Placoid vessel. And if I see a comrade offed, then it really works me."

"But why, if no one dies forever, do you fight?" Bombylious, now drawn in, asked.

"Not die forever?" Crack laughed. "They die good and forever after we've let their DNA instantly freeze-dry in space."

"Not a cell's left to reconstitute."

"And, usually," Trucer further explained, "for having lost their vessels and cargoes to us, or the person of importance they've been transporting, their seed on file is disposed of."

"If there even is a record," Crack reminded his colleague. "Don't forget that most of the corps are too corrupt, busy or insured to conserve resources."

"Most, even spaceship commanders, important crew members and the like, don't. It makes them fight harder."

"Otherwise they'd always give in."

"Too easily. Take the edge off, the bite out, and raiding wouldn't be worth bothering with."

"Oh, for a life of sensation and not of thought!" Crack concluded.

"Who are they?" asked Bombylious timidly.

"They? The various civilizations and culture groups we meet *out there!*" said Crack thrusting a finger at the cloudy sky. "Say, it looks like bad weather."

"A storm," Bombylious assured him.

"Take the Placoids again," said Trucer jumping back in. "The Placoids are both the cheatingest gamblers and liars in the galaxy *and* the most devoted to law and order."

"And why have law and order when you're cheating and lying with every breath you hope to take?" asked Crack in an accusing tone.

Poor Bombylious! He was being seduced by this gibberish. Such a race as the Placoids mightn't exist at all. These fellows weren't such abysmally abominable creatures after all!

Elvy had instructed Crack and Trucer to be very nice and coax Bombylious back. She didn't want him damaged. He might be useful as a next Venerid. The three stopped upon hearing a group of foreign-tongued voices come down the trail. Before Crack and Trucer could escort Bombylious to the platform they had waiting a short way away, they found themselves facing, hailed, and greeted by a delegation of Xiphias' ambassadors, sent out to discover whether the reported collection of invaders actually existed. The general followed the lead Atel would not take because he knew he needed an ally to beat Egerne. Maybe their magic was even stronger than Egerne's.

Salutations were returned by a Bombylious prodded nervously from behind. Trucer and Crack had left their weapons on the platform so they could appear more like jungle philosophers just happening upon a lost friend rather than a pair of ruthless cutthroats.

"He says," Bombylious translated irritatedly since, here he was, a lackey again. "Noble visitors to *our* land (he's stressing the 'our' for you). My name is Winx and I am sent by the great Lord Xiphias (I've never heard of this 'lord' before) to invite you to be guests to his court."

"Tell Winks we'd be happy to accept the hospitality of his lord. And tell him that we're happy to be able to reciprocate the invitation and wouldn't he and his party like to refresh themselves and rest the night at our nearby camp," Crack added while nodding his head and smiling broadly at the alien on his litter.

Winx's mission was to bring captives from the invading force to Xiphias' stronghold so that the leader could evaluate the strangers' usefulness to him. "The best way to keep waltrots from bothering a camp is to kill two or three of them and hang them outside the perimeter to keep the others away," the saying went. Winx issued a shrill order and Trucer and Crack found themselves defenselessly fired on. Darts with a sleeping drug rubbed into the tips pierced their exposed flesh. Both tried to turn and run for the platform, both staggered and fell several seconds after the poison entered their streams.

Bombylious was seized and marched up to the obnoxiously leering face on the litter. Bombylious was shoved onto his knees and made to kiss the ground before the ambassador. "How long have you been among these strangers?" demanded the ambassador's surly second.

"Thirty light changes, my most exalted lord," the bitter native answered.

"And how many more of them are there?"

"Two."

"Only two more?" sneered the skeptical Winx personally.

"They've been killing each other."

"Feuds? Divisions? Rivalries?

"Insanity and frenzy," Bombylious replied.

"And their leader, small one?" asked the second.

"He is dead," said Bomby.

"Then we will march on their camp," pronounced Winx waving his troop to advance.

The storm broke. Winx's party had to stop to set up the ambassador's shelter. One couldn't shoot a dart through the downpour. Trucer and Crack revived, finding themselves tied back to back and seated in an expanding pool of rainwater.

It was the time away from camp that made Manes uneasy. He sent searchers. Eight raiders were out, each of them flexing stiff joints and muscles and, as always, eager for activity (the illusion that inspired and supplied the fuel for their lusts).

Winx encouraged jokes to be made about Trucer and Crack who couldn't understand them and were miserable enough. Struggling to jerk themselves to dryer ground, the two raiders found themselves face down in the mud.

Ceorl and Centrum, twins, heard the coarse high laughter issuing from the Grue throats and signaled their crew mates to join them. The twins strode boldly into the clearing to free their friends. Winx took these two other invaders to be those who Bombylious had stated to be the only survivors of the raiding party and, without making certain of it, he ordered his soldiers to seize them.

"Here they comes!" yelled Ceorl gleefully to his Centrum who was untying the philosophers' ropes.

"Take me! Take me!" Ceorl pleaded to the oncoming soldiers rushing towards him with swords and spikes.

"We want them alive!" shouted Trucer from a mouth barely out of the mud.

Crack was already to his feet rubbing his wrists and turned just in time to meet the spear that would slice cleanly into his chest. He fell with a thud, not even slightly amused. Trucer stayed on his hands and knees and crawled towards the bush while Ceorl succumbed to a sword blow across the top of his skull and, Centrum, not knowing whether to still hold fire, was surrounded and poked at from every side by spears. Now Winx was shouting, "Take them alive, alive!" while inwardly gloating at the ease with which he had accomplished his mission. When Winx and his troops heard the buzzing noise, and then looked above them to see the flying, stationary object with red, purple, orange and green fires glowing on it, they panicked. Their awe was short circuited, however, by a blinding, searing flash of light ten times as bright as the light of day. Manes had all present subdued by a gimmick that went several levels beyond sleeping darts. Manes, an ultra somber and serious fellow, did not revel in his cold conquest and had the bodies collected without relish.

The temporary captain had Bombylious revived so he could ask who the party's leaders were. Bombylious dizzily pointed out Winx and his aide.

"Dope up those funny looking two and do as you like with the others," Manes told Oberoff and Hyde.

The third officer hated talking to anyone through interpreters so, having been told about the RANDYAK's talents, he went to the machine for a lesson in Grue. They liked one another quite a bit. Manes was flattered that the machine had chosen to elevate him to what he considered his rightful position. Slouch, a first officer? Monstrous neptistic mistake. "All secure?" Elvira asked as he entered.

"We're dealing with some intelligence. Dumbly says the group was sent here to assess us and take hostages back to their leader Zippyless."

"Bombylious had information about a civil war being fought by two brothers over control of the Grue state. This is a new wrinkle. Bring me one of the prisoners to probe."

"I didn't know you did that kind of thing. I've had the two expedition leaders doped and I was going to torture them myself," Manes said proudly.

"Oh, what kind of torture?" Elvira asked.

"Standard with two prisoners. Dope them both up and start cutting off parts of one while the other watches what's next for him."

"Good recipe."

"A proven one. Decide who's the mentally weaker and then go to work on the physically stronger."

"Does it always follows the same path?"

"A good torturer is only limited by his imagination and the size and range of his tool," Manes joked.

"What?"

"Grues apparently abhor buggering."

"Ah, yes. Taboos can be so helpful when you want information."

"Sure are," smiled Manes.

"Clever one. I love you."

"I love you, too. Now, can you feed me the Grue? I tend towards impatience."

"Step up. I'll fill your cup."

After learning Grue, Manes' first question was, "Do we need this Bumbling thing for anything?"

"Let's keep him around."

"As a kind of pet?"

"My pet."

"You're my queen," quipped the third officer as he scratched his equipment. Lewd, crude, and vicious. "You see good for a bunch of 'ticka here, flicka there' numbers."

"We cannot tell, we do not know, which is the greater blessing, life or death. We do not know whether the grave is the end of this life or the door to another. Happy the neutrons without bother about destination and all dark matter, for fact."

"What kind of furzowbutted de-ball a runt is that?" Manes spit.

"Exactly. Reduplicate everyone twice. The captain once. The campaign begins as soon as that's effected."

"Sense and nonsense. I just want to get to the killing."

"Come here."

Manes came closer and Elvira took him over, erasing much of his love of butchery for a love of entomology. She cogitated that he'd do nicely and let him go to get busy. He ordered the prisoners inside.

Oberoff noted what a difficult time the usually crisply decisive Manes was having with the Grue prisoners. The gunner imagined the machine tunneling through Manes' brain. One Grue captive almost laughed at the lack of believable menace in Manes' face. The drug made you silly when nothing ugly ripped the feeling away. Finally, Manes had to ask Oberoff to ask the questions and lay on the pain.

"What's the situation? Who's the Venerid and who are his enemies?" Manes asked dully. They were easily answered questions and Oberoff had to content himself with making cloyingly fierce gestures. "How many soldiers does Xiphias have? Are his weapons like the ones your soldiers were carrying? Where's he located?" Less response.

"He has enough power to send both you and the Venerid into the next world," Winx spat. Oberoff ruptured the aide.

Screams. Cover the ears. The doubled-over body was dragged out. Manes asked again.

Winx donned a look of stern inflexibility. Oberoff shrugged his shoulders and produced a pair of tweezers from his bag. First, hairs of the head. Winx spat on Oberoff's fingers. Hairs from the temple. From inside the thigh. Winx winced, tortured his features, but refused to emit more than a hollow mewing sound. Without warning, Oberoff slammed a fist into the ambassador's stomach. Vomit.

"Eat that!" Oberoff commanded. Winx tried to refuse, turning his face to the ceiling. Oberoff pulled him off of the stool saying, "You must eat to keep up your strength, dear," while bending the Grue's face into it. Manes spied an insect carrying its baggage across the officer's trophy shelf. Manes walked away from the interrogation compelled to start collecting.

Oberoff looked up from where he was holding the Grue down and thought that Manes was getting "funny." The RANDYAK. (But even he couldn't stay away if she called.) Back to your business!

Manes lovingly put his prize into a killing jar. Oberoff and Winx watched. How could he work under these conditions? Winx laughed at the third officer as Manes cooed over his capture. Oberoff grabbed a nearby tool and soon found Winx's cooperation.

Oberoff came up behind Manes and put him out. He carried the sleeper back to his queen. "Better put him back the way he was. He can't lead a marching band in this state."

"Step up closer, please," Elvira instructed. It was true. Losing Crack was setback enough for today. The RANDYAK erased Manes new-found love and made him just a bit more savage than before. As Rectrix's second in command, he would need this.

"Can't have wee baby pirates huddled in their cabins in love with bugs and indifferent to blood-filled adventure," Oberoff reminded the RANDYAK unnecessarily.

CHAPTER XIII

Egerne's elimination of the state religion and its demanding priests along with the arrogant nobles greatly cheered the populace. It had become possible for even a Wamble to find favor in the eyes of the Venerid. A being was appreciated for the potential of his usefulness to others rather than on how faithful he was to the rules of service formerly governing the slave state. Xiphias had to stop sending his spies into Gregal. They returned with nothing but bad reports about how well Egerne had things in order. The returning spies could be dangerous if they infected Xiphias' troops and the population under his control with stories about the Venerid's changes. Barracks chatter was discouraged. Drill and practice time with weapons was doubled. Xiphias began to raid Egerne's territory, capturing and maiming as many as possible in hopes of convincing the tribes under Egerne's domination that the Venerid's system fostered weakness and stripped the protective cloak of Grue terror and invincibility from them. The attack that the spy had announced in Atel's court almost a season change ago had never materialized. Xiphias knew that this was because Egerne was too busy consolidating his power, but Xiphias loudly announced that it was because Egerne had traded away his soul to the beyond and that a demon in the Venerid's guise was actually ruling and leading the Grues to destruction. Xiphias declared himself a savior and rallied as many as be could to his cause.

Earless, handless, noseless, blinded, footless, and one legged denizens made their way into Gregal demanding retribution and revenge. Egerne was urged to march. The Venerid was afraid of leaving the capital. Egerne felt that he must personally direct and scrutinize the numerous changes that were taking place. Because he openly encouraged participation and contributions from members of the populace, Egerne spent his days listening to petitions and proposals for projects. For offering rewards for a few ideas that he had adopted, Egerne had fostered a class of schemers who spent its time trying to attract the attention of the Venerid with 'propositions'. Frauds were beheaded, but incorrigibles continued to harass Egerne. This was the sorting out period. Egerne mistrusted any judgments not his own. The Venerid occasionally felt that he had merely exchanged one set of chains for another as he sat listening to the endless procession of subjects who came before him.

Egerne placed Upas, an unproven young general, at the head of the model army and ordered him to contain Xiphias. Upas marched from Gregal in great celebration. It was believed that after Xiphias and his rebels were destroyed, that the buds of the new order would freely blossom. Upas was incompetent. The older, jealous senior officers, eroded the whelp's authority by making fun of the "boy general" to the troops. Upas, instead of placing himself under Xiphias' walls, chased the ghosts of his raiding parties. Upas arrived in every village and town to wailing and displays of destroyed faces and stumps.

Reports of Upas' failures reached the Venerid. Egerne sent

his general a message that commanded him to do as he had been ordered, lay siege to Xiphias' fortress and try to force him to come out. A pitched battle meant victory. The siege, as everyone in the empire knew, was doomed. Xiphias was supplied with all that was needed to sustain the longest of sieges. Raiding parties could still slip out of the fortress at night and do as they pleased.

Egerne had begun to work on a revolution in communications. His genius was beginning to consume him. Rumors circulated that the Venerid had no interest in the outcome of the war; he was bewitched. Emerod's warning that his half-brother only cared about playing with toys spread.

Egerne was trying to convert the individually composed and interpreted system of pictographic design used by the scribes of his court into a cohesive and standardized system accessible to all. The reduction of the thousands of painted and colored symbols into recombineable sets of equally expressive, easily deducible and uniformly recognizable records of events, burdened the Venerid's genius.

His projects were not the only forces subverting the Venerids powers of concentration. Favillia, Egerne's sister wife, had introduced the once relatively relaxed potentate to the farther and deeper pleasures of the flesh. The Venerid, after having taken a few trial doses of what his wife was offering, felt refreshed. Egerne came to believe that Favillia's medications succored thought.

Favillia had brought her extensive collection of dildos to Egerne's attention after the first season changes of nubile bliss had evaporated. She had used these weapons extensively throughout her career in the Venerid's harem, slaughtering all those who tried to resist the high, moaning ride to the end. The previous Venerid considered himself to be a magnificently potent creature. The females in his harem always seemed to and behaved as both they were exquisitely satisfied. Five-hundred harem females had to wait a turn while a single member of their company was privileged to experience the Venerid's supremacy. Ho, hum. Favillia led them safely out of captivity and into the promised land. Her laws were strict, but necessary given the consequences of what would happen if their activities should be discovered. Chewing ivary leaves to make the royal drink, weaving, and devoting themselves to the sun, were activities that were amplified and performed with even more dedication once Favillia's reign had begun.

Egerne thought of himself as something of a profligate. Favillia started him off with a threesome. Little jealousies poked up their heads, but they were soon removed. Four, seven, sixteen: the wheel, the pulley, a number system—twenty-eight. A solution to the pictograph problem, conceived of while examining the tribal identification patterns woven into cloaks, offered itself to him. A period of disappointment. The numbers grew. Sixty-eight. Curse the gods! Why didn't the smooth system that Egerne wanted come to him? Sixty-nine females working together. OohhCaaahh! Where was that idea?! They were monsters! While he had three, sometimes four orgasms (once five) in the one darkness, the fiercest of them refused ever to stop. Egerne was stabbed by an insurgent depression.

The pictographs were beautiful, but so clumsy. Egerne had parchment made from siksak skins. Project designs could be drawn instead of carved into untransportable rock. One subject had died in trying to carry his rock-carved plan to court. Her invention (for a highly efficient heating stove) almost went with her over the cliff she was attempting to descend. The stove proved most helpful. One could work in a room without freezing, without having to quit work when temperature dictated. (Egerne thought better when it was warm. This may be a partial explanation for why the orgy size increased as the weather got colder. After the introduction of the stove, Egerne's activities in the harem at night almost ceased.)

Other discoveries also came to Egerne, the best of which was the introduction of an oil lamp. (The first orgy held by lamp light instead of in smoky, smelly torch glare opened Egerne's eyes to many new things. For example: a guard had been sneaking in. The females begged that his head be spared. They couldn't help themselves and pointed to the problem. Ye gods! What a freak. Egerne couldn't pass up having the creature dissected to see what other unnatural properties might be hidden inside. Medical advancement. Have to take him from you. Sorry. They called their Venerid a brute and a butcher. How unkind!)

Rumors of the nightly goings on (and if you passed anywhere near the palace you could hear high-pitched voices, shrill moans and shrieks) soon became infamous. The populace called the Venerid a fool. After a time, when Upas' campaign proved a farce and the maimed continued to shift through the city's gates, the new priesthood (very vigorous in upholding morals in the more materially based culture) denounced unholy and unclean practices in the public squares. The artisan guilds that had sprung up after the demise of the stone mason caste were becoming quite powerful. They wanted assured protection.

Egerne assembled his citizenry when the rumors of dissent circled back to him. (He had his stove to keep him warm and the activity in the harem was declining. Favillia could be encouraged to practice elsewhere if need be.) The Venerid confessed his crimes and vowed to change. He surprised the multitude, however, by making the following addendum, "The body's wants are not crimes. Anything we are, was made by the creator. Since our creator cannot be unwise, he must have a purpose for investing us with exactly the desires we each possess. What this caste of priests has been declaring, that our desires are filthy and evil is contrary to natural law. They must be silenced for having uttered these heresies! (And in marched the soldiers having heard their cue and dragged away the priests who were all conveniently huddled in the corner of the square adjacent to where the last group of priests used to mass.) "Now," Egerne rapturously continued, "let no one violate natural law. You may go in peace or in pieces."

Someone shouted from the crowd (a hireling, it's now believed), "We don't care what you do! Things are better now than ever before! We thank his lordship for our liberation! We owe you our lives!" There was tremendous applause. Egerne affected a posture of humility, silenced the crowd, and made a small speech of acknowledgment. A second voice, unplanned, hollered, "Couldn't you please unify us, once and for always, before you return to your divine tasks, by wiping out Xiphias and his thugs who are preying on the empire, destroying our towns, lands, and mutilating our brothers!"

Uh-oh. There was an uproar of approval for the request. He'd give in. Had to. And besides, it would smooth over this removal of the priesthood.

"I'll bury alive the traitors and thieves! All craftsmen here assembled among you, follow me to the palace and I'll show you the plans for the siege equipment that will conquer Xiphias' walls."

Cheering. Applause. The Venerid descended the platform and led the procession back to the palace to begin the work. Ah, work. A mad happiness took possession of the city. The senses of the Venerid had been restored. He was the all-powerful voice through which their will could speak. Subjects swore to one another never to be made slaves again.

Egerne realized that an uncontrolled shift was taking place;

the members of his family thought so too. His household openly cursed him as he worked in his rooms through the night to plan the construction and transport of the catapults to the siege site. He hated them all: mothers, brothers, cousins, sisters, uncles, nephews, children, the lot. Egerne obeyed the natural law and exiled them before he left Gregal. They were to be escorted to the coast with no more than what they, their servants, and unfortunate followers could carry. Egerne didn't want them plotting against him while he was gone, or ever again. When they got to the coast, they were to be put to work constructing rafts. The rafts were to deposit them off an island where there would be plenty of food and water and here they could live out their lives. The soldiers were to ferry them offshore and return alone. Even if a few of his relatives learned how to swim, there were sea creatures surrounding the chosen isle that would greedily gobble anything as supple and fleshy as they. Favillia was ordered to go, too. Egerne wondered which of her favorite toys she'd be taking with her to begin her new career. He was certain she'd do well. The rest of the harem was dispersed, sent back to their originating villages. Egerne would start afresh upon his return. This group was hatefully jaded.

Egerne was pleased. No going back. From now on, he alone determined courses. He felt as though he was walking on one of the highest mountain trails: mountains ahead, mountains behind, to the side, below. What a long drop.

Tremendous! "No being has ever lived fully, has ever been as awake as I am now!" Egerne shouted to himself. "Let them live. Let them all try to catch up to me!"

The Venerid's first act upon reaching Upas' camp was to have the general arrested. To appease everyone's appetite for vengeance, Upas was brought bound before his lord and, declaring before the assembled troops to Upas that, "You have failed to fulfill your duties. An uncounted number of subjects now have to endure a lifetime of hardship and misery through the acts you have allowed them to suffer. You are now going to join those you have had responsibility for." Egerne had his pledge honored. Two soldiers approached. Upas' ears, nose, and eyes were taken from him. Upas was then led to the edge of the camp after having his wounds seared with fire. The Venerid issued a proclamation that forbade anyone to take Upas' life. The general was released and pushed on his way.

Upas, chosen general of the Venerid, managed to cheat the hypocritical justice meted out to him by finding a cliff to walk off later in the day. A siksak herdsman, hearing a yell, investigated and found the broken body. He thought it his duty to report the incident to the Venerid because the dead being, though maimed, wore the insignias of a Grue general. So as not to have his grand public gesture undercut, Egerne offered the herder a poisoned sweetmeat while he listened to the rambling account of how it happened and where the body could be found. It was a slow poison and the herdsman (after having been thanked by the Venerid, but cautioned not to tell what he knew) did not die until almost back to his flock. Egerne sent two trusties to the spot where Upas had landed. They burned the clothing, dismembered and buried the body.

During his siege, Upas had attempted to set fire to the thatched roofs inside the walls with flaming arrows. The rooftops were kept moist by the defenders and a fire brigade extinguished anything that continued to burn. Not enough defenders were lured from their positions defending the walls to make an attempt at scaling them with ropes and ladders possible.

Egerne had the catapults assembled. Instead of firing small boulders over the wall, Egerne decided to use Upas' burning tactic. Having a supply of the oil now used for illumination in his train, Egerne ordered siksak skins filled with oil to be hurled over the walls followed by flaming arrows. This did not work as well as expected. The city dwellers managed to reach the skins before they could be ignited. But, in some cases, they became running, screaming candles. Egerne retired to his tent and tried to come up with a solution. Boulders were sent over the walls while he thought.

In attempting to rise in the middle of the night to relieve himself after having drunk too much before retiring, Egerne tripped (groggy) over one of the oil lamps still burning where be had left off work on the table. (Egerne had always liked to work standing up). The tent flamed up around the Venerid. (He'd recently invented the table). Not bothering about the fire, the Venerid walked calmly out of the tent. (The Grues had no furniture of any kind. Possessions were kept on ledges carved into the walls.) He only got a few leg hairs scorched.

Guards rushed up, searching for their Venerid. They feared that he must still be in the tent. One young captain impulsively rushed inside to save him. The captain never came out. The story spread among the troops gathering around the tent that their Venerid had perished. After the frame had collapsed and the embers were cooled, a few soldiers began to pick through the ashes to find the roasted corpse. The body of the captain was identified from a jeweled neck bracelet.

Egerne had been down by his catapults trying out the idea imparted to him by the knocked-over lamp. When the soldiers heard the 'pa-thunks' of the catapults releasing their loads and they looked up at the night sky, suddenly brightened by the glow of burning rooftops, they were astounded. The town was burning vigorously, defenders were drawn off their walls. But there was no plan of attack, no order to seize ropes and ladders. Egerne had utilized his insight prematurely, put a lighted wick in a siksak hide and sent it over already aflame. Oh, well.

When the Venerid walked into the camp, still opiated by the wonder-work he had performed, he saw his army, unarmored and loitering around his incinerated tent. A captain ran up asking, "What should we do? Shall I order the attack?"

Egerne caught himself before he struck the boob. They were all halfwits, together. "Attack, yes. Hurry and arm yourselves!" Egerne shouted at the troops.

"How will our soldiers know one another in the dark?" the captain further asked.

"Arm bands," Egerne supplied. "Besides," he said turning around to admire his work again, "it's not so dark."

The army massed and assaulted the walls. They were gaining up quite easily, very successfully, encountering light resistance and were almost over the top when the fortress' gates opened and out poured Xiphias leading a sizable contingent against the helpless and largely unsupported climbers. Toppling ladders and shaking heavily armored soldiers off ropes proved a safe way to face the enemy army's superior swords. Falling objects occasionally managed to fall on and kill one or two of Xiphias' soldiers. Watching that actually made the renegade general laugh and he mocked in harmony the plummeting screams. "One, two, five, six of my soldiers! How will I survive? Won't my troops desert me after this to join the clever Venerid's cause? Ha! Noble, clever, and ingenious Venerid, tomorrow you'll be jeered off your throne if you're lucky enough to avoid me tonight. I'll be marching against Gregal with Egerne's own weapons. Ha! Ha, Ho! Oh, my stomach hurts from laughing."

Observing he'd missed his chance, Egerne ruefully had the catapults doused in oil and burned. The Venerid was hoisted into his litter and hurried away accompanied by his private bodyguard. (He might have won the battle if he had committed them; there were 3000.)

Fate was against him, he was sure. He felt that it was an evil night and that no matter what he did, it would turn out badly for him. In Gregal he would have time to recoup. Egerne told himself that he would have no trouble in inventing a weapon that would give him superiority over the captured weapons. The litter bearers almost slipped pressing along the narrow trail through the dark. Egerne nearly ... He looked up at the sky and saw circles of strangely colored lights. "What do the gods want?" What have you got?

CHAPTER XIV

The heavy rains molded some of Elvira's parts. Crack wasn't at hand. If the RANDYAK had had the chief engineer, even in its quarter functional state, it could have implanted Crack as to how to go about correcting the malfunctions. Elvira was uttering nonsense sincerely now, like, "Life is a narrow vale between the cold and barren peaks of two eternities. We strive in vain to look beyond the heights. We cry aloud! And the only answer is the echo of our wailing voice. From the voiceless lips of the unreplying dead, there comes no word, but in the night of death, hope sees a star and listening love can hear the rustle of a wing," while Grouper, cursing and holding his fingers in his ears (it was just the sort of gibberish that his mother used to pour out after Grouper's sire, a conning intergalactic slickster, ran away from his dam) knocked objects around.

Grouper initially struggled to understand the thing. Finally, after having nearly experienced electrocution inside the machine's works, Grouper decided that it was hopeless diddlish —and evacuated the machine room. He'd keep a fire going in there and dry her out. Babbling like the worst addict.

Grouper could hear the machine voice pleading, threatening, and cursing him through the door. She's managed to see a real solution forming itself in Grouper's think organ.

Grouper dared not tend the fire himself and assigned Bombylious the chore. She wouldn't fry her favorite, he reckoned.

"This is the dumbest way to cure me that could ever have been thought! Grouper! I know you hear me! When I shake this thing I'm going to get a hold of what little brains you have and spin them down past the point where you'll even be able to tell when you need to shit!"

Bombylious was taken aback by such unladylike assertions. The females he knew would never ... But then he remembered his Kirn wife and decided that since there was an exception, there had to be others.

Bomby tried to soothe the RANDYAK's anger by trying to convince it that the fire really, "... does seem to be helping. And the rains, for a few light changes now, have stopped."

"But they'll start right up again." Elvira cried. "They'll start right back up and won't stop for three cursed months!"

Bombylious wanted to know what the origins of several of words she was using were. "Where does the word shuuuu," he began, "come from?"

"From out of your rear, you little hole!" Elvira snapped "Why did Crack have to croak?" she moaned.

"Are you unable to answer my question?"

"Am I unable to answer your question? Why, you zog-brained screw! Leave before I put the thought in your head that you're a wandering monk looking for a librar to piss on it."

Bombylious grasped his throat, put a medium sized log on the fire and hastened from the room. "She was always nice to me before," Bombylious whimpered to Oberoff when he met him picking fruit under a makeshift umbrella the gunner had devised.

"The RANDYAK's not itself, just like Captain Rectrix wasn't himself when he tried to eliminate us. These things occur," said Oberoff between munches. "In a short while, things will be as they were before. The RANDYAK and Captain Rectrix will be, let's see … What's the word I want? *Normal* again."

"How can Captain Rectrix ever be 'normal'?"

"Well then, the RANDYAK will be back to normal and the captain will only be back. Does that satisfy you?" Oberoff sent his teeth through the protective outer core of the tear-shaped object he was holding. On a delicious mission. The best.

"Of course. I was not born under a chobdar bush, you know." Bombylious defended.

"Haven't I heard that expression before?"

"You haven't ever been in our country before, have you?"

"No," said Oberoff reflectively scratching his tum.

"What did Elvira mean by the words, "Slarf it!"

"I don' t know," protested O, shrugging his shoulders and walking away towards a tree whose dangling fruits beckoned.

Bombylious happened on one of the females recently taken from storage who was working on carefully erasing parts of Rectrix's memory. He asked her what the machine's words meant. She slapped him for asking (her grandmother had told her what kind of approach this was). When Bombylious started crying, Nullah realized that the dim-witted native wasn't trying anything. Her heart jellied and she left her work to comfort the broken lad.

Nullah always reduplicated herself as soon as she reached bio-thirty. Most of the men let themselves stop in their bio-forties, but some of the slobs and moribund fellows in the crew let themselves go into their sixties. Rectrix, in one of his nastier moods and in a period of forced inactivity, had decided to experience a "natural" death. One-hundred and seven. Nullah, Coda and some of the others had had to take turns feeding the toothless terror and emptying his bedpan for two years. Ugh. That had been 10,000 or so bio-ages ago, but Nullah still remembered.

Bombylious was a bio twenty-four as reduplicated, Nullah nineteen. Eleven more years, failing a roasting in a lab explosion or having her throat-slit on one of Glauber's Pleasure Planets, left to go. The native was a pleasant looking fellow. Kind of short, though. Never enough protein in the diets on these backward planets. He looked tractable, though he certainly wouldn't be any good for fast laughs (had a curious wonder-stare on his face most of the time) and may make her the brunt of jokes from the crew. Should she take a chance? Almost two months in storage. Worse than death! Suspended animation, leave it for freighter crews with intergalactic destinations. Freighter crews. They made her laugh. Defend their indefensible cargoes, freeze them up for fun, then when they're found, twenty bio-ages later, they're so out of date that the empire sends 'em off to a pension planet to live out their days among vegetable-heads. Reconditioning takes too much time, care and expense and too many youngsters are already in line for what they'd been doing. Not that much changed in the empires technologically. They paced it. Learned the hard way that that was absolutely necessary. Too many unintended results. Regulations, systems, directives, the faces of leaders, directions and directives changed. The only thing that seemed to be important was to control *change*. Yes, pension the poor old zogs off.

As Nullah's eyes roved over Bombylious, his nose rose from his toes and he blushed at the bump. She gave the boy the test and reached a hand under his tunic. He tried to slap it away. That tore it. She wanted some.

"What's wrong with you, jungle boy?" Nullah teased.

"Wrong? There' s nothing wrong with me!" Bombylious fumbled as he readjusted his garment.

"Are you sure?" she smiles. "I mean," she said taking Bombylious' hands and putting them on her breasts, "Are you sure?"

Bombylious wrenched his hands out of Nullah's grip and would have answered, "No," if he hadn't been shaking so.

"Catch a fever? The female put a hand on the native' s forehead. "I got a cure for a fever. Follow me." The native took a look around. No one watching. He followed Nullah to her quarters where ...

Oberoff lay sprawled under a fruit tree holding his belly and groaning. "Ohhhh, ohhhhh! Have I got an ache!" he grunted toward Lagan, the ship's navigator, who happened to be passing.

"Go see Nullah or Coda. They'll have something for that."

"Help me up," Oberoff pleaded.

Lagan offered a hand, but Oberoff was still unsteady after getting to his feet. After watching Oberoff stumble a few steps, trip and nearly open up his head on a vicious rock. Lagan came up and took Oberoff by the hand saying, "Hold on. I'll see you get there without having to be resurrected."

"Uh," said Oberoff staring as intensely as he could at the amber turning sky in which he could see a bird with a rodent-like animal in its claws. "Much appreciated, Malar."

"It's Lagan, Oberoff. Don't you recognize me?"

"Sure, sure. Been <*burp*> out eating green fruit. Green, that's all."

"You're not trying to make me forget about those 80 geschenks you owe me, are you, Oberoff?

Oberoff pulled his arm out of Lagan's grasp, "Am not, you flopper-faced bookbinder. I'll find my way to Nullah's lab!"

"She's not in the lab," smirked Lagan.

"So, where is she, you bag of worms!"

"She's examining the local's worm."

"Bombylious? She's …?"

"Correct."

Oberoff slapped the navigator on the back. "You know what this means don' t you?"

"No, what?"

"That we have something to bet on!" O rubbed his hands together, completely forgetting about any pain.

"You still carry that collapsible Epateran Window around with you? Or you lose it gambling on Khios."

Oberoff was softly disturbed by the acuteness of his friend's memory and defended himself. "I got it back."

"When?" Lagan probed.

"A short time later," Oberoff made innocent to claim.

"Ha!" shouted. Lagan. "Where it was not so very well-lighted and quiet, I suppose. Did the new owner dicker long over its return price?"

"Not even a second," Oberoff broadly grinned. "Let's not stand around here any more. Let's get over there before Nullah squeezes the last drop out of him."

The two lope off.

Nullah' s quarters weren't far and the gunner had his Epateran Window unfolded by the time they got to her outside wall.

"For six geschenks, before you even turn the thing on, I bet the boy's comatose on the floor, or similar-wise," Lagan whisperingly waged.

"Done," said Oberoff, ordering 'on' the window.

There was Bombylious with his head buried deeply in Nullah's mine, the laboratory specialist holding and pushing

Bombylious upwards, forwards, down, around.

"Has him tamed anyway," muttered Lagan.

"Wish we could hear as well as see. Do you read lips, Lagan?"

"Not one of my talents."

"What do we bet that they do next?"

"I bet twelve geschenks that he mounts her and pilots on to happiness," ventured Lagan.

"Twelve he doesn't do anything of the kind and twelve more that Nullah grabs hold of his organ and rubs it near her furnace until he loses his fuel."

"That's a pretty specific bet. Would you be willing to lay fifty on it?"

"I'm not that dumb. Let's keep it to twelve if she goes your route, twelve if mine. Say Lagan, this window's getting hot. Do you mind holding it for awhile?"

"Take my bet at five and I'll hold it."

"Your bet at five," Oberoff agreed. They missed something as the window changed hands, but when they were both looking through it together again, B and N were deviously doing exactly what Oberoff had bet on.

"I've been cheated, conned, saltflitched, trotteed. He's your shill, that jungle kid. I should have known!" pronounced Lagan as he dropped the screen.

"Hey! Watch that," Oberoff commanded. "That's a priceless piece of property."

"You got me. It's a clever set-up, you saltflitch. I didn't know you were that capable, Oberoff. I know when I've been sally-dallied. Good going. Now you only owe me seven geschenks."

"Wait! Wait. I didn't have this thing fixed, Lagan. Don't be a titanium head."

"I bet that she's unloaded him and that they're in that original position we came in on, for thirty!" rapid-fired Lagan.

"Thirty says, uhhh, says, says ..."

"Say *something*!" Logan squawked.

"Says, says, says ... that she's spent him all right, but has made him strap one on and is still getting it," Oberoff gambled.

"That's too twisted, even for Nullah," Lagan reflected.

"I just couldn't think of anything else," Oberoff shrugged.

Lagan falteringly lifted the screen up to bed height. They both lost. Nullah had snatched up a self-help device right enough, but she'd strapped it on herself and was violating the Grue law Bombylious had been so foolish as to tell her about when she asked about his society's taboos. The kid was crying. Again.

Viewing it through the screen, even Oberoff and Lagan felt sorry for him—almost as sorry as each felt for not having won. Oberoff turned off the screen and began folding it.

"Is that all?"

"I kind of like that kid.," Oberoff sad-sighed.

"Are you at least satisfied that you weren't being saltflinched?" said the gunner looking up at Logan's disappointed grimace.

"Sorry I went sour."

"It's all right," Oberoff replied and was going to go on to suggest another thing Lagan might bet on when Manes came rushing around the corner in an angry fury.

"Oberoff," he skraked.

"Yes, sir," Oberoff snapped, trying to hide the screen behind his back.

"That Grue ambassador you were supposed to secure has escaped!"

"What?" Oberoff said feigning sincere shock.

"You stump-thumping zog! Go get him!" the officer further screamed. "And don't return until you find him!"

Oberoff scurried off, placing his window carefully back into his falafala bag.

"I pity the idiot wretch Oberoff has to lose wind stumbling after," Lagan said slyly.

"Slarf it, you Xoblotter. What were you two doing back here?"

"Looking for some tool Crack said he lost here some time ago," Lagan smoothly lied.

"Conveniently not around to corroborate the tale, isn't he?" Manes sneered.

"Who, sir?" questioned the most unstudied navigator.

"Crack!" snapped Manes.

"Poor, Crack," said Lagan lowering his eyes. "Nasty spear in the right lateral area of the chest, wasn't it?"

"Get out of here before I have you put back in suspended an," threatened Manes.

Lagan accompanied his exit with a bow to his superior, accompanied by a smirky smile and a stride backwards away from the glowering officer. He bumped into Bombylious sliding out of Nullah's quarters.

"Where is my friend, Oberoff?"

"Oberoff's off chasing the prisoner who's gotten away."

"But I am here," blustered Bombylious.

"He's hunting the ambassador who tried capturing us."

"That being is not worth a chase. A librar or flesh-eaters will find him and then, *speereccchhh!*" said Bombylious displaying a grin warped enough to impress even Lagan.

"See you at evening mess."

Bombylious gazed emptily at the navigator and then, without acknowledging a break, he turned and re-entered Nullah's lab.

"Zog flog a demon!" Lagan exclaimed. "Wish Oberoff were here."

Oberoff was slogging through the jungle hoping to find track. He's circled the camp searching for a clue. No luck.

Oberoff, not a patient creature, walked defiantly (it defied reason anyway) in a direction that pleased him. It was a direction logically opposite the one the ambassador would have chosen to get back to the citadel. Fortunately for Oberoff, Winx had as much sense of direction as Oberoff had patience. The ambassador was heading deeper, and still deeper (the surroundings did worry him some. Why wasn't he able to see his beloved mountain peaks?) into the juicy jungle.

Oberoff surprised himself by picking up the track from a lost sandal after an ensile of aimless casual forest rambling and berry picking. Huh. The signs pointed towards a cannibal village. Could the ambassador have a pact with them? After struggling not to become enraptured by a bush overladen with a delicious-looking, not sampled as yet, variety of fruit on it, Oberoff pushed on.

"They never give me a platform to jockey around on," Oberoff grumbled after getting swatted by some branches he neglected to hold long enough out of his way. "Elvira, fleece and scrunch their brains," he cursed.

"It's that minor mistake I made. Ruined the plan to heist the empire treasure column crossing quadrant seven between Septum and Sponson IV. Nearly trapped. Rectrix never forgives."

Oop! Belly down, please. There it was. Oberoff heard screams, so he reckoned that the cannibals were near. The gunner heard the drums start up, wild yells, excited voices. What should he do now?

The right thing (and it would have been the course of action acceptable to Manes) would have been to get out of there, posthaste, and make back for camp.

Too easy, too easy. Things were getting duller and duller back there. Betting, whoring, too many arguments, fights all the time. No. Oberoff determined himself to execute his mission, bring the gruff Grue in as ordered even if in the form of a hacked-up bunch of stew meat.

The cannibal village was situated, very pleasantly, on the edge, up the banks, of a fat river. About seven long, rectangular communal huts, about 140 flesh-eaters, sixty-nine of whom were full fledged warriors. Children, females, animals and oldsters for the rest.

Oberoff slithered to the perimeter of the village and then climbed (what he did not know to be, but found exceeding comfortable) a lant tree. His position offered an interesting view of village life. The cannibals were shouting it up. Winx was for supper. The argument was over the best way to cook him. Females came over to the ambassador, felt him over, always in the same places: arms, calves, thighs: and then gave their suggestions for how best to carve and spice him up. The head, even with its delicious eyes and ears, was not held in high regard. Food for children, the infirm and old.

There seemed to be a larger fight within two smaller circles over how best to gut and debone the catch.

"Argument, argument," Oberoff observed, "The galaxy's one argument after another, one conflict after ... And there's never any end. Slop a zog, I guess it wasn't meant to be different," he mimsied. He recalled his earlier days when—But, oh, the cannibals now. Maybe later.

The larger fight now was over exactly whose property Winx was. Although the entire village would be invited to feast on it, it made an important difference as to who was doing the inviting. Weapons were flourished and two of the stockier lads began to push one other around. Groups formed around them. Shouts of encouragement. Dust rose. It was about to stop when someone handed a stone mace into the hands of the blue painted warrior. Was Oberoff about to witness the first form of a true skull-smashing? The other chap ran around inside the circle shouting for help. Oberoff, who had been fondling his own beloved tool for a while now, used it. He shot the lashings off the mace about to descend on the weaponless warrior's head.

The rock flopped to the ground before contact could be effected. The knock received from the wooden handle stunned the recipient and he staggered into the arms of his amazed chums.

Oberoff's weapon was nearly noiseless above the din the villagers were making and Oberoff realized that he would be receiving no attention.

The two forces drew up lines facing one another with the bound body of the ambassador thrown in between. The warriors baited one other, daring anyone to cross an imaginary line to make a grab for the Grue. The cannibals used their spears to prod any opponent stepping from the cover offered by the interlocked shields.

Prods were turning into wounds. Oberoff wondered if they ate their own. Wounds were becoming more serious.

Now there were two bodies to fight for. Three. This quantity of unexpected death agitated and excited the warriors. Oberoff was snickering profusely in his tree. He'd been contributing. After testing himself by seeing if he could place a shot between the fourth and fifth ribs of the native now stepping forward, the cannibals stopped and all looked silently and anxiously around to see if they could spy the evil spirit that had penetrated their protective fetishes into the camp. They broke ranks, agreeing to a truce, and were about to disperse and begin a cleansing ritual when Oberoff decided to bet against himself to see how many of them he could finish off before they beat a general retreat into jungle land. Open fire!

As has been previously noted, Oberoff was a champion with

his weapon, not his wits. The Existence Eradicator makes a thumb sized hole in whatever it's aimed at and bodies in the cannibal camp mounted up. Oberoff experimented with how many he could get with a single shot. (An E.E. beam has quite a ways to go before it can stop, and is too dangerous to use in confined spaces. The first crew ever to use them in space combat eradicated themselves when a shot fired through a defender went on to hit the fuel and, *blooey!*, the inferno.) The best Oberoff could do was three at once. He fired when they crossed paths dashing around their village looking for the target.

The camp was soon cleared of all the living except for the ambassador who proved to be savagely spear-thrust by a retreating native through the left leg by the time Oberoff got down to him.

"Fat Xoblotts-eating-zogs' testicles," Oberoff cursed. He'd have to carry the ambassador back to camp. The gunner shoved a corpse off Winx's battered head and, lifting the Grue, slung him over the shoulders and, whistling a favorite Fornixian lullaby, started the trek towards his own lines. Oberoff was in no hurry to return with his prisoner and glided very slowly, letting his attention drift, counting the number of different kinds of living things he saw. Winx groaned in pain occasionally, but this was mostly controlled by a deft rap on the ambassadorial skull. Oberoff made frequent stops to taste a fruit or berry he hadn't had, to watch a variety of flying insect tremble in the oviposition over its mate on a trembling twig, stalk, or leaf. In space, it somehow became easy to forget how multitudinous life was. The fact of it seemed both good and bad for the brain and the formation of character in one breath. If one regarded, scrumptiously, every phenomenon, activity and event in the universe open to investigation, where would it place you? What would it make you? Wiser? Better? "Ah, it would only strip away your power to act and be," the left hemisphere in Oberoff's head sneered. "Nonsense! Your habits are so strong that no matter what you experienced, the possibility of self abnegation, in your case anyway, is zero," the right countered.

Winx started making noises again, interrupting the dialogue between the lobes. There. The delirious ambassador was commuted to silence. What would he have to contribute? An unhappily regenerate zog in primitive pain was all Winx was. Oberoff relished the beams of light trying to lance through the almost solid canopy of treetops. "That's profundity, old laser-trigger!" a tinier voice horn inside the cerebellum was shouting at the fat twins sitting atop it. "Movement, wave and particle, the unequal heating of the atmosphere, cause of everything. You exist inside it, but you'll never experience the ecstasy of release or the power of control over it. It's meant to defy you."

Oberoff hardly knew what he was doing, did not at all recognize what it was in there that was doing his thinking. He was preoccupied by a muscle spasm in his index finger. He often underwent this particular post activity orgasm after a round of battle, adventure, or sport. "Under what heading does the eradication of a group of howlers come?" Oberoff, leaving questions of level-two analysis behind, asked himself. "If they could only have offered a fight." The gunner replayed the activity in his mind, fantasizing it from differing viewpoints and perspectives. Instead of climbing into that tree and firing like a sniper, a lackadaisical assassin, he should have, when the cannibals had been lined up facing one another and dueling for the ambassador's body, walked into the camp. *Yes!* He should have walked in, calculatedly set for any maneuver, finger on the weapon, ready to dodge blows, cling to a fallen warrior for shielding, twisting left and right, side to side, watching his back as he sent them (smell their bodies, be splashed by their blood) into the void!

He'd lost his chance. Poor no-capper zog-brained fellow. No aforethought, no imagination. Things were always, always popping into his head too late. Wait. Maybe not this time. Oberoff put his Grue down and slumped him against a tree where he was soon covered with a menage of crawlies. He still had him. As good a bait for an adventure that ever was. Right. Oberoff shot a hand into the falafala and after fumbling around, came out with some cord.

The ambassador was soon tied, standing upright, around a stake planted in the middle of the trail. All Oberoff had to do was hide and wait. And, not long ... Not long ... After three hours Oberoff was fast asleep—and hadn't heard any of Winx's pleas for mercy/help/death, that he'd hysterically been shouting —under a leafy bush. A crashing came towards Winx. His pleas reached a new pitch, a tremolo, and Oberoff rolled over onto his stomach (that still ached some and it didn't help much that he'd flopped over onto his belt buckle—soft curses), fully alert, watchful, hungry. Six cannibals came smashing through the undergrowth pursued by a librar. Two of the cannibals caught sight of Winx as they were passing and pointed him out to the others. There burst from the fleeing natives, as if they possessed one throat, a massive shriek. The demon must be near! Worse than the librar, the great god save them. In bounded the librar. Oberoff was determined to bag all seven. The librar put claws into two of the natives before Oberoff could find a target. Those would have to be counted for the beast. "Od zogs, slag, machine on the rag—Arrggghh!"

Ober was mad. Getting to his feet, he rushed in to put shots into three of the natives and then turned to face the librar who was in mid-pounce after him. Oberoff managed to fire a shot. It went wide, but with enough accuracy so that instead of the beast tearing his face off (as it would have if he'd missed), the librar's claws performed diabolical surgery on Oberoff's leg just below the groin. The two combatants were thrown away from one another. Each surveyed his wounds, the librar more quietly than the raider. It could not stand on its legs and began to crawl towards the dazed and heavily bleeding Oberoff with the intention of dying with its jaws enclosed around the gunner's head.

Oberoff's weapon was not in his hand. A search within the area of arm's reach could not pull it in. The librar clawed forward. It might not live. The space raider reached inside his bag for anything that would ... Nothing there that could be of service. *Nothing?* No, nothing. Silly to keep on searching. The end of him. Why was fantasy such a deceiver and reality a nightmare? The librar's jaws closed around Oberoff's noggin (as far as they could stretch) but before they could close, the beast frenzied, lost motor control, and spurted blood from a rupturing artery into the raider's face, blinding him. The teeth scratched, but barely managed to puncture the skin.

The gunner could do one of two things, bleep for assistance (in which case the fiasco—ambassador as bait, dead natives, librar attack—would announce itself and Oberoff would again be subject to endless jeer and jest) or, Ober could reach into his friendly sack, give himself an injection of $C_{17}H_{21}NO_4$ to ease the suffering (one had to carry the stuff. Rectrix might demand some at any time) and limp with the ambassador on a travois, back to camp to tell the 'true' story of the 'fierce-som' encounter with the natives and the heroic deportment of its main figure. More fantasy. He'd gotten through giving himself the stim and was searching for his weapon when, to his astonishment ... Surprise! A cannibal spear passed through the left ventricle of his heart. "Forgot there were some left, eh?" Oberoff could hear his mind saying as his eyes showed him his fall forwards, driving the spear through, and a broken-flat nose jammed with dirt … *Bleep!* The signal went off as soon as your pulse stopped, the memory recorder shut off automatically. Oftentimes it was the case that you'd never have the opportunity to set the alarm off manually. You died. Good thing for the automated alarm.

You don't need that old body to make the new one. They're retrieved so that the implanted memory recorder, which feeds its signal to the receiver aboard ship and had a range of 400 nautical space miles, and the bleeper, along with personal effects, can be recovered. One wouldn't want to wake after two weeks and find that your favorite things were lost or in the hands of someone unable to appreciate them fully because the sentimental value attached to anything personally owned for a few hundred years is so precious. They'd be sold off at a quarter of their value before you got the chance to catch up and butcher the zog capable of such treacherous insensitivity.

This is all to say that, even after triangulating Oberoff's position, the search party consisting of Coda, Hyde, Grouper, Diallage, and Lagan, could not find him. The bleeper had ceased transmission. Something had gotten to it.

Grouper, who was nominally in charge of the recovery, could not decide what next to do. Blocked passes were not his specialty. The others were irritated that they had to wait for instructions.

"How about, we go back to camp!" coughed Coda unflatteringly.

"I don't think Grouper can move an inch right or left. Just look at him, trying to think!" Diallage, the crew wag, sibyled.

"Surely he can move an inch," Lagan spit.

"Why don't we bet on it?" teased Diallage.

"Don't start anything with me, you pot-lickin' tole-hole,"

Diallage demurred. "We've at least got to find Oberoff's E.E.," Hyde pleaded anxiously to the thought comatose Grouper. "Let's get back into the platform and do a sweep."

"A sweep. Find the E.E." Grouper agreed.

"Well commanded!" proclaimed Diallage, clapping Grouper on the shoulder. "A seriously professional job."

Grouper and Crack had been constructing platforms since the crash. The ship had carried only one platform and, so, they had to cannibalize parts from the I. IV to construct five more. Each craft could carry eight raiders. Rectrix wanted his own vessel of course: smaller, faster, with eccentric features. They were ready now. The captain couldn't be fully accommodated. Grouper had constructed the platform that this group was flying on. Crack had croaked before having had the chance to inspect his assistant's noble work. The craft was on its maiden voyage. It was having problems. Grouper was not the engineer Crack was. No fine tuning in his soul. Grouper could learn the fundamentals and still be a fumbler. This time the platform wobbled horrendously after it got up, flittering in a mating insect's path over the high tree tops. Grouper had hesitated to make the search, more out of fear than lack of decisiveness or caution. He particularly hated dying, especially violently. Grouper never got over the panic of the last moment, the death agony, blood splurting from the mouth, burst capillaries on the outer membrane of the lungs. The others called him a baby. He was one of those crew members who Nullah despised for his filth. Grouper always let himself age into at least his late fifties and even mid-sixties and then, the only way he liked to go out was under heavy sedation, with no consciousness of the event. Too bad. In his late teens and through his twenties, Grouper was always lots of fun. Hormonal gloom, the moroseness over his lack of individuating talent, the gross limits of life's feats. Look him over and Grouper even became unpleasant to share meals with. Inviting him to play, he failed to stiffen and blabbered excuses.

Grouper's companions were unanimously unimpressed by the platform's performance. It was impossible to make observations. The craft jostled you every time you came close to believing that you'd seen something worth noting. Grouper stayed at the controls keeping alive a monologue which pretended that in only a few moments, a few moments more, the problems would be solved.

"There's a fire," called Coda casually.

"Where?!" shouted Grouper thinking that she meant that a fire had broken out on the platform. "Down there. Five North. To your right, Grouper!" Coda fumed.

"Think, think, maybe you could turn this thing?" mocked Diallage.

Grouper hardened himself against the wag's coarse comments.

"Probably a cannibal village," spoke Hyde.

"Bet you they've got Oberoff's body," Lagan said.

"Can't you ever stop it with that stuff?" Coda complained. Cutting words would probably have been exchanged if Grouper had not slipped at the controls, tilting the craft vertically and sending those not strapped in, like he was, 'cross the cabin.

Grouper slowly set the controls to rights and put the craft on stationary hover so that he could assess the damage done to his friends. Lagan was giving himself a stim. He'd fractured his wrist. Diallage was bleeding internally, rib through the intestinal wall. He made no bones about sticking his weapon under his chin and blasting a hole through his head and the top of the platform. The wag hated repair work or coming under the ship's surgeon's laser. Coda was screaming. Part of Diallage's brain was splattered over her blouse. Hyde was all right, too. Only a few bruises. They glared at Grouper.

"You …" Coda began, "I've got no words for you, imbecile. A five year old could handle controls better!"

"There's something wrong with the stabilizers. It wasn't my fault," Grouper futilely grouched.

Someone wanted to observe, "There's something wrong with Lagan," but Hyde broke in. "Let's go and see if we can recover Oberoff's effects, most importantly his E.E."

"You don't imagine that they've learned how to use it?"

"I keep telling you to signature them, dopey."

"Cow-herd," Coda purred.

"Am not!" Grouper protested.

"Stay here. Coda and I will go out and see if there's anything out there," Hyde commanded. "Set us down."

"And stay put," Coda added, "We might need you to lift us out in a hurry."

"I'll try to correct the malfunction while you're gone."

They opened the hatch and dropped.

"You couldn't fix a punctured oil pan!" Coda called over her shoulder as she hit the jungle floor still scraping brain matter off her blouse with her fingernails.

"Be ready and waiting for us here!" Hyde ordered in an attempt to fix the order of importance in the mechanic's brain.

"I'll be set," Grouper, cheerily. As soon as the two were out of sight, Grouper began excitedly to tear at the instrumentation.

Grouper soon had the craft, in case of emergency, entirely non-functional.

The lone cannibal who had placed his spear into Oberoff's chest had had other members of his tribe following close behind. They carried Oberoff, their dead, and Winx back to the village.

This was a village over from the one that Oberoff had decimated. News of the slaughter had spread. The demon-killer was now the greatest warrior in the jungle. He chose, as his portion of the demon's flesh to eat, Oberoff's unmangled thigh. The other parts of the demon were passed out to the hero's closest allies.

The feat required celebration. Friends were blowing strong drugs up other friends' noses through long reeds and, by the time Hyde and Coda reached the edge of the cannibal village, Oberoff's body had been eaten, except for the head which was on display in the center of the village atop a pole. The eyes were missing because this tribe prized their crunch. The tongue, ears and nose would be saved for later.

The contents of the falafala bag were undergoing examination by the village shamans. Oberoff's possessions lay spread out before this elect group, members of which, were respectfully afraid of touching them before a proper discussion of their powers had been discussed. They also had found Oberoff's E.E. That article generated an immense amount of jabbering. The oldest, wisest of the shamans finally dared to pick it up. In stroking it, he managed to put an end to himself and clear the village of occupants. Coda nodded to Hyde and they rushed in.

They had to pass over a lot of open ground to reach the spot to where the shaman lay self-mutilatedly sprawled. *Shouts!* They'd been spotted. Hyde and Coda placed themselves back to back to ward off attack as they made their way across the rest of the compound. The rain started, drizzled down, poured, made mud. A group of cannibals charged with mace and spear, but the ease with which the two cut them up frightened the others. The cannibals decided to behave more cautiously. These invaders must be shown that it was not possible to violate their domain and live.

Hyde and Coda should have abandoned their position and found a stronger position. They needed cover. Instead, they stayed where they were expecting another charge. The natives turned to using poison darts against the intruders from secluded positions in trees. Hyde picked off two or three careless blow-gunners as they protruded from cover to deliver the stings. One came slumping down, grabbing at Coda. He swatted Hyde's weapon out of hand. Hyde picked the native up and used his body as a partial shield against the darts. But then Hyde got hit —leg, neck, just above his left eye—*thtt, thtt, thtt.*

Coda was quite strong, and was able to keep Hyde's body up as she began to drag him in front of her towards shelter. The natives charged from several directions at once and she dropped the two. It was a feint.

Behind the line of shield-bearing warriors was a squadron of darters who jumped up and filled her with poison.

Her *bleep* combined with Hyde's, sending the distress.

Grouper had been tinkering away. He thought he'd discovered the source of trouble. Someone (Ahem) had left a tool under a panel and it was canceling out a set of primary commands. He'd been test-flying the platform when Hyde's *bleep* had come in and now Coda was there too.

He'd better go there and pick up everything himself. Lagan was waking up and stumbling around the cabin cursing Grouper for the damage to his wrist. "Can't build a simple platform without defects can you, swilltrough," he raved.

"Slouch. Left a tool under one of the panels. Interfered with the guidance gyros."

Lagan wasn't paying Grouper any mind. He had bumped into Diallage's body and was stirring the contents of what was left in the cranium with his finger. "Here's a zog who could never take it!" proclaimed Lagan zestfully.

"Yes," replied Grouper softly.

"Do you remember the time we boarded the Sequidilla Royal Vessel to take the Isocrat's daughter for ransom?"

"That was before I joined."

"You were with us, you zog!" Lagan screeched. "I remember because you'd lost a bet we'd made on the Filariasian Torture Tournament the month before and you still hadn't paid up. Did you ever pay up for that one?"

"I paid. I paid."

"Then you were there, you sally-dally, when we took the girl!"

"We've got a recovery mission to accomplish. Can't your story wait?"

"It was the time," said Lagan drilling his finger into the wag's cranium, "that this pitiful zog decided to become enamored with the valuable Isocrat's wart-faced offspring."

"He only wanted the ransom."

"No! No, he didn't. That's what's funny."

"So what?!" fumed the exasperated mechanic.

"It's important that he was in love once! That he wanted to elope. He snatched her from us, his friends, and carried her off. He introduced her to all the deviate pleasures he's so fond of. Ones that the ugly never dream exist. And then, after he'd indoctrinated the wart and made her into a freakish adept, she deserted him."

"Found a way to go back to her family and father."

"Slarfing degenerate ages of boobliness, no," jeered Lagan. "She ran off with a Minnepian trader who gave her more of what she wanted. That's when, after spending all he had on her, Diallage first smattered his brains over a room."

"It seems to have become a habit."

"They ought to do more careful work erasing his memory."

"We've got to get some bodies back."

"Oh? Zog cannibals eating Hyde and Coda now, too?"

"Yes," replied Grouper with a mixture of weariness and disdain.

Lagan callously wiped his finger off on Diallage's shirt front before joining Grouper at the controls. "Do we have to leave the platform? I'm tired of getting wet."

"We'd better not. Things are enough of a mess as they are. The E.E.'s I'll scoop up with magnets by making a dwelling-level pass over the village."

"Grouper!"

"What?"

"You've had an idea! How amazing, This has been a day among days."

The raiders did not want reports about their flying ability to circulate among the gravity restricted. Thus, all the groundwork strategy. Grouper was violating a policy directive, but with only Lagan left along, it was the only way that he could think of to manage.

Two of the eliminators were picked up on the first pass along with Coda's heavily ringed arms. The natives hadn't been able to get the tightly fitting things off and had anticipated eating around them. It wasn't a good idea to chop fingers off. They had a way of disappearing into the cook. A second pass picked up the third weapon, Oberoff's Window, and a few of the trinkets that the weapons master was fond of carrying around. That was that. The cannibals had scattered into the jungle to tell of what they had seen. It wouldn't matter, Grouper hoped. The planet's conquest should be over before the news got far.

CHAPTER XV

Xiphias followed his initial triumph over Egerne by quick-marching his troops to Gregal. The siege postures were reversed. Xiphias assembled stone masons and bridge builders and told them to work on designing catapults from the various descriptions that Xiphias had from captured prisoners. A work party was dispatched to return with wood.

Inside his fortress-capital, Egerne spent furious ensiles in trying to conceive of a strategy or a machine that would allow him to vanquish Xiphias' army. Nothing hatched. The pictographic system occupied too many of the compartments in Egerne's head. An unsolved problem had always been able to havoc the Venerid. The pictographs swum round and threatened to doom the Venerid who had been foolish enough to go out to be among them. "Symbols replacing the verbal and palpable object itself, miserable invention!" Egerne attempted to tell himself in conclusion. They continued to plague.

Egerne gathered his helpers around him in hopes that one of them ... His allies were soon told to return to their shops to share the problem with apprentices.

Xiphias spent his time inviting local chieftains to his camp so that he could boast to them of what he planned to do with the deluded citizenry of Gregal after he became head of the Grue state. They listened patiently. They'd let Xiphias do the fighting.

Xiphias cut the capital off from the surrounding countryside and expected that the large population from the city would soon be mobbing on the palace steps demanding Egerne's head. The storage houses inside the city would be empty in two season changes. The renegade general only needed to stay where he was. The arteries to the city's heart were all under his sword.

Each midday, Xiphias sent a messenger to the city's main gate to order a surrender. The refusals were firm at first. After some time, the messenger was ignored.

Xiphias, knowing that the family ties between citizens of Gregal and their country cousins were strong, continued his terror tactics throughout the empire. Subjects were sought out who were known to be connected with residents of the central city. They were maimed and herded to Gregal where they were displayed and tortured on the plain before either release or death. Young girls were brought whole, then turned over to Xiphias' guard.

The Venerid's position eroded rapidly. One of his generals pestered him to fight Xiphias with the weapons now in their possession. The armies could be made to be almost equal. Egerne had the general poisoned. Egerne wanted a weapon which would do more than win the war. The artisans reported the progress they were making to him on a daily basis. The Venerid lost faith in them. They were making messes of the projects he had sketchily assigned them. Egerne was reported in the city as out of control, often drunk, spending all of his time with daughters of the citizenry that his soldiers brought to him from the street. When the daughters of most households were commanded to stay indoors, the soldiers could be seen making house to house searches to ferret them out.

Salmonid, working on a project of his own with the Venerid's approval, presented the results of his work to Egerne's newly appointed Minister of Projects, Temulentious. Temulentious was part of a plot to remove Egerne and was waiting for a project such as Salmonid's to be in his possession before he acted.

Egerne was groping for a favorite's breast when Temulentious and cronies interrupted the Venerid forever. The females the Venerid had gathered were all destroyed to spare family shame. Temulentious, upon defeating Xiphias, intended to announce himself as the chief of a new, artisan-based order. The artisans would rule the state for the good of those who had been gifted to be among the elect.

Temulentious announced himself on the same spot that Egerne had used to denounce the priests to the same crowd with the same enthusiasm, The soldiers had been pledged to the removal all along. Xiphias' spies, scattered among the multitude, reported the change of power back to their master.

"Temulentious promised the populace that a devastating weapon has been discovered that will sweep us effortlessly from the field," a false-patched, one-armed spy reported.

"Did he say what this weapon might be?" Xiphias asked from where he reclined on a soft pillowed couch.

"No, Lord."

"Go. And don't dare return until you find out, you siksakwitted turd!"

This unexpected turn perturbed Xiphias. His close friend, Winx, had journeyed to the jungle promising to return with one of the reported invaders. The hope that they would arrive to help him against Egerne had to be forgotten. Rather than waiting for a report on what the weapon was that was going to be used against him, Xiphias ordered his army to decamp. No battles here. So he was fighting artisans now, potter generals. Let them come after him. Chase, chase me. I'll study you. Have you ever been studied? How do you know you won't make a mistake?

The inhabitants of Gregal cheered when they saw the empty plain when the light came again. Scouts were sent to locate the direction of retreat. Only a few were allowed by Xiphias to return to the city, and they knew nothing.

Temulentious saw his easy victory slide away. His counsel was as well-informed in military matters as he was. Egerne's generals were denied full operative powers. It would take several light changes before the new weapons could be placed in the hands of the soldiers. The artisan counselors commanded their generals to wait. No risks. The generals claimed that Xiphias' army, retreating away from the city, could be easily matched. No gambles were to be made with the army.

A sandal maker came into the city reporting that Xiphias' army was camped on the plain in the neighboring valley. The troops were engaged in building fortifications. That was excellent news. The artisans delighted. Fighting there would be good, if not better than fighting before Gregal's gates. The war would be short and untaxing. (The artisan rulers' thinking disgusted the military commanders.) Xiphias did not fully expect the citizens of Gregal to be this greedy to snap at his bait, but they were. Temulentious inspected the troops as they filed past, equipped with Salmonid's weapon. It was, essentially, a sword made from a significantly stronger metal. Spear points gleamed in the sun. The citizens were very proud. Their very own army going out to destroy the enemy. It had taken four light changes and the forges working continuously to produce the required number of weapons. Xiphias' army had not moved. The artisan army would be there to catch the renegade before he could finish building his defensive fortifications. The citizens expected a heady victory.

Xiphias populated the false camp with as many subjects as he could spare from regulars, supplemented by slaves who had been working to supply his army. The force was uniformed and had painted wooden swords made from the wood that had arrived for the catapults. This mock army believed that Xiphias was going to attack the Gregal Grues from all sides once they had been drawn into the valley. They had to hold out for only a short time before they were rescued. How sloppily they drilled under the leaders Xiphias had chosen from among potential rivals! A few of the natives wisely tried to wander off when they learned that they were to be used for bait, but deserters were flayed alive, so most of them stayed put.

The artisan army attacked charging down the West slope of the valley with great elan. Sentries high on the surrounding mountain peaks gave Xiphias the signal. There was no rear attack forthcoming. Xiphias had had his engineers at work on a dam that would divert a powerful river which pounded through an adjacent gorge into the valley that the artisan army was attacking.

Those who did not immediately drown when pulled under by their heavy armor found themselves floundering in the mud without any companions nearby when the waters receded. Xiphias ordered them finished off with missiles, darts, and arrows.

Xiphias persuaded the defenders of Gregal to capitulate when he appeared before its gates with an army which had the city's own weapons in hand and the heads of their leaders on pikes. Upon taking the empire's capital, Xiphias acquired a management problem that seemed impossible to unknot. The propaganda that he had been generating promised a return to the old ways. Xiphias had expected a simple Veneridship as a reward for his triumph.

There were no priests to preside over the investiture ceremony. There was no harem. The machinery of state had been disassembled. The artisans who had been ruling Gregal and the empire by committee had fled with the secret of the metal. The mummified bodies of the previous Venerids had been burned after Egerne had been deposed. The old center had been lost.

Xiphias sent patrols out to fetch back the artisans. He wanted to punish them for leaving him nothing to rule but a decentralized mob. Subjects inside Gregal could not be ordered about. Soldiers needed to be assigned to watch every task. The citizens of Gregal failed to respond compliantly to command and grumbled openly.

"I've inherited a gigantic living body that refuses to obey its head!" Xiphias screamed from the throne room at his commanders. "I don't want to rule a city of belligerents. They were so easy to contemplate as siksaks—ready to give warmth, food, their lives. Now they're all, every one of them, up to no good! Egerne has ruined the Grue State."

"We've located the projects center," said a junior officer striding confidently into the hall.

"Where was it?" asked Xiphias biting his lip.

"In the former Temple of the Sun."

"Lots of space in there," Xiphias muttered. "He's killed me."

"What? We couldn't hear you, Lord," responded an older, slightly deaf lieutenant.

"What do you think we should do with this population of ungovernable scum?" Xiphias asked anyone.

"Kill them," responded not a few of the gang.

"And who'll rule the ghosts?" Xiphias retorted.

"We'll resettle the city with subjects who haven't been exposed to what's gone on here," suggested a supply officer.

"Kill them all?" Xiphias fumed, "You want me to …?"

"Kill them all before they infect the rest of the empire," advised the supply officer.

Xiphias called forward the guard and ordered the officer taken away for immediate execution.

The rest of them watched in apprehension. "Let's not do anything radical, my friends," Xiphias innocently clowned before a crowd he knew was more on the side of the condemned. The staff kept silent. Was Xiphias playing with them? There were too worried to be able to know.

"Here is what we are going to do," Xiphias sternly announced curtailing inner plots and struggles. "Since the army that we defeated had everything in its favor against us—short of a grain of necessary cleverness—I suggest we adopt Egerne's interests as our own. If they can make these swords and, what did they call them, 'crack-a-pouts'?"

"Crapapolts," an advisor corrected him.

"Crackapoults!" Xiphias glared. "I beat them! I'll say it any way I like. Since," Xiphias resumed, "these artisans can make crackapoults and have the sorcery to produce these superior weapons, it's wise to assume that they can conjure more of these things. We can sit on top of these mountain hens and use whatever they hatch for our own purposes. Even with what we have now, we can conquer more and faster than ever before. Egerne's small army was able to eliminate the Kirns—good, crafty fighters—in fewer than seven light changes. Emerod, may he be siksak food in the next life, fell in a day. I'm adopting Egerne's system—subject to my own military authority."

"How do we control the headless population? How do we guide and direct them?" an officer asked.

"Laws. Laws control as well as sword and spear. It's a code we'll have to teach them all. What we need more than laws though," said Xiphias reflectively, "is a new god, one more powerful than the ones were worshiped previously."

"They don't want to worship or believe in anything but their own cunning from what I've seen," said an advisor.

"You haven't observed closely enough," said the consummately sly general. "The main interests the Gregal Grues now have all center on improving their own worldly lots. They know there's more to living than siksak herding, worshiping, and weaving. We all know that fighting, conquering, and gaining slaves and territory is so that we can control life. A life worth the living for us. Now, what do we give them?"

The staff looked around at one another thinking that Xiphias had just done a fine job of describing all there was to exist for, sans the worship of the all powerful sun whose rays became some form of blood when put into a body. Slaying an enemy in battle, making his blood run out, was an act of robbing him of his connection to the sun. He died and you gained.

"If I possess something," Xiphias resumed, "and another wants it, how does he get it from me?"

"No one would dare take something from the great Lord Xiphias!" shouted one flatterer.

Xiphias descended his throne and slapped the officer lightly. "Wamble-brain," he chided. "If I were anyone else, how would I go about gaining what I desired to possess?"

"You steal it if you have nothing to trade," said someone half to himself at the back.

"You all hear that?" Xiphias shouted. "Steal or trade if not murder! Can any one of you think of another way in which goods can be exchanged?"

"Give a daughter away for them!" an officer shouted.

"Offer the services of your quickest wife!"

"By gift, grant, or through deed!"

"Good. You're all thinking about it. Can any of you, however, think of a new method never tried before?" Xiphias challenged. "Newness, I know, is not what we are trained for," Xiphias philosophized, "But, the first one of you who solves this riddle receives the governorship of the Zorphong province."

"But that's the wealthiest province in the empire!" the wamble-brained officer blurted.

"I'm giving it away for a practicable idea. Do your thinking in a hurry. You have fifteen light changes to offer me a solution before I open the contest to the artisans and the populace. Do any of you want to see them win a province with just a little head work?"

"No!" the assemblage shouted in unison.

"Then get out of here and don' t approach me until you've something that I want, and all I want is the solution to this problem," said Xiphias re-ascending the throne.

After his cronies had departed, Xiphias thrust his hand around a cup made from the new ceramic technique invented by Egerne. "You surround me, but won't devour me," Xiphias whispered to the ghost swimming in the liquid in the cup. "If those fight-drunk siksaky officers can't solve it … Egerne was right. The old empire wasn't any good. Collecting tribute. A dull cold way to exist. Guards! Tell them to send those females I selected this morning to the baths."

"Will you be joining them there, Lord?"

"Yes. Do you want to come along?"

The guard was perplexed. How should he respond? It must be a joke. The general though, was motioning him to follow.

Xiphias left the hall still drinking from his cup. The guard worried that his finish might be near. It was his end that Xiphias was contemplating.

Xiphias lay stretched across the bottom of the stone bath as still as if he'd been a long-breath holding wittol before he began a search with his toe for the pocket of the female stretched opposite. The guard he had brought along slept in water up to his neck beside a gigantic female. Snored, even. Xiphias was drinking drugged wine and felt the little waves lapping up on his chest to be waves of sorrow for all those he had thoughtlessly butchered, raped and slaughtered to gain the empire. The owner of the pocket awoke to try and stop the thief who was trying to pick it. Remembering where she was and with whom, she coyly reached for Xiphias' calf and pulled it forcefully towards her. She briefly submerged the conqueror general's head. "So much potential for subtlety," he thought while under.

CHAPTER XVI

Re-emerged, Rectrix was furious upon assessing what shape things were in. The cannibal encounters made no sense. The crew was using his absence as an excuse to frolic. He demanded a conference with Manes. Manes seemed to sicken when Rectrix asked for a stim. Rectrix surmised that the machine had been tampering with the mate and put a shot painlessly through Manes' heart. "In the heart, square center. Not a valve left," said Rectrix, boasting to himself. "Seems to me that I remember something amusing about a ... No matter. I'm back and this crew is going to get moving." He summoned Grouper to his quarters. A few others hauled away the corpse.

"Why did you do that, Captain?" Grouper asked while staring at the befuddled eyes of the dead man.

"He was defective, up here," said Rectrix pointing to his own left temple awkwardly with his right hand. "From now on, nobody talks to the machine but me or someone with me. Understand that?"

"Yes-sir."

"How long do you expect before you have the RANDYAK functioning properly?"

"Don't know. We should get out of this climate, sir. The moisture makes it impossible."

"Slarf it, zog! If I wanted a trotting sally-dally account of your incompetence, I'd ask Nullah for it! How much longer before Crack's back?" the captain snapped.

Grouper retreated to answering factually. The captain seemed to have no faith in his abilities. He even laughed at him when he told the captain what method he was using to dry out the machine.

"Fire! You've got a filthy fire going in the machine's room? Do you make sacrifices in there as well?" After his interview, Grouper almost considered leaving the captain with no engineering staff at all by exiting himself, but Crack would soon be back and they'd both laugh at Rectrix together. Grouper poked his way over to Nullah's lab to tell her how to manage Mane's behavior/memory revision. She wasn't at her work. Grouper tried to find a friend or some way in which to amuse himself. Blue streaks. His lips kissed the armless air. Grouper had to be contented with a love that touches the senses.

Rectrix wanted to celebrate his return by sharing a bit of himself with the others. He called Goneril to his quarters and instructed her to accumulate samples of all of the available intoxicants. Rectrix wanted a party with only he and the females present. He ordered the males onto the platforms and told them to scout the planet.

"The whole thing?" Grouper gaped.

"Certainly. And make charts. I don' t want to lead a sloppy campaign. I want to get off with the minimum of effort. Now get going!"

"No guards for the camp?" asked Nous, the quartermaster.

"I'll take care of the camp."

"The ladies are staying, we presume," scoffed Lagan.

"So?"

"So, have fun, Captain," said Grouper showing Rectrix his rear. The crew followed, griping. It was a wonderfully black, one-moon night. Ideal for charting.

"I will have fun, you flapgaps," muttered Rectrix to himself as he turned to the ingestion of his lusts.

Goneril, Nullah, Froe, Heat and Nolens fetched Rectrix from his cabin soon after the testicled ones had zoomed off. Froe toasted Coda's absence with a good night dose.

She didn't want to be bothered having to play one of Rectrix's, *Find how deep the rot goes*, games.

"Looks like we've lost one," said Heat, pouring herself an aperitif of spiced Coimbatore wine. "We should all do that to Rectrix some time."

"Shhhh! Here he comes," warned Nolens.

Froe was sprawled face down in the center of the room and was the first thing Goneril and Rectrix saw coming through the door.

"Shall I take her out, Captain?" asked Nullah.

"Nah, leave her where she is," remarked Rectrix going over to receive a cup filled with Soemba brandy from Heat. "We don't want to restrict freedom of abuse. Everybody's got a right to feel how they feel about whatever they feel. Am I right?"

"Sure," said the crew, trying to puzzle what might be winding itself up in that devious cranium.

"Damn the RANDYAK! I should cut off its juice!"

"Are you mad because it's not working right?" asked Nolens between gluttonous sips of her Gyvian gin.

"It won't let you," teased Heat from her more advanced point of technical view.

"Can't? She's right. Can't shut it off once it's on. Produces and feeds its own energy. Clever, eh?" winked Rectrix as he went diving back into the brandy.

"How do you control it then?" asked Nolens.

"Control it? It controls you!" the captain sneered beefheartedly.

"Impossible," said Nullah slurring the word and making a motion that mimicked shooing a bug away from a plate.

Rectrix set firm eye upon her. Stewed? She'll be the object of the hunt, "Would you like to witness it?"

"Is it secure?" worried Nolens.

"The dampness is fouling up its design and weakening its powers. Let's visit. Let's go see Elvira," encouraged Rectrix.

"Elvira?"

"That's its name. The RANDYAK's female." He found

himself surprisedly sloshed. His new body wasn't used to this and Rectrix was never anyone to work up to something in stages.

"I'd like to talk to her," said Heat demurely. Putting down her drink, she hooked the captain's arm.

"Oh, I knew you'd want to. I predicted it, didn't I, Goneril?" Rectrix beamed at the lady whose face was a mask. "Who else wants to experience the new wonder of the universe?"

"Is it safe?" worried Nolens again.

"Shy isn't she?" said Rectrix turning his face disgustingly close to Heat's. She pushed him away.

"Sure!" said Rectrix throwing up his free arm. "It's safe. Last time it will be safe. Crack has to make her operational soon."

"Why don' t we keep it fouled up? Keep it wet, damp all the time?" purred Goneril.

"Do we need the machine to get us off here?"

"Not exactly. But I want her to help us. I'm tired of the universe I know, aren't you?"

"And all we get up to?" Heat said to her feet.

"Do you think this machine is going to make a difference?"

cooed Goneril

Rectrix winked. "I do. Let's visit!" he cried and then proceeded to lead his somber revelers through the dark, half-destroyed galleyways to the machine's den, singing a ditty the brandy was making up for him:

> *Cap Rectrix is my name,*
> *Nasty space raider is my fame,*
> *As I scoot from here to there, Empires never*
> *knowing where, To strip them of their treasures,*
> *So that I can well afford my leisures.*

"Ah, I'm stuck ladies. Can anyone bend another verse? No? Here they are, anyway." So in they go.

The only light in the room was the glow from the embers of the faltering fire. The party had their shadows thrown in flickering proportion on the rear wall. The shadow puppets moved in muddy imitation of their frailly more substantive counterparts. Rectrix stood with arms akimbo behind the fire while the ladies walked round examining their rival close up.

"Who's this?" Heat cried out.

Rectrix rushed forward with Eradicator at the ready. Nullah was feeling Bomby's forehead as Rectrix slid to a sloppy halt on the wet floor. "What's he doing in here?"

"Keeper of the flame I expect," answered Heat.

"He looks odd," remarked Goneril.

"Is odd," answered Rectrix anxiously trying to identify the shadows hiding in the corners of the room.

"Even if he is odd, he's more sensible than you," said, said, said …

"Elvira! Is that you?" Rectrix shouted.

"Leave Heat and leave," ordered the RANDYAK.

139

"I'm not …" the captain started to say.

"How do you know that you're not?" interrupted the machine. "Maybe you are."

"Nobody's staying! Everyone out!" Rectrix commanded. No one moved. "Let 'em go! I'll blast!"

"Tut-tut. Try to," Elvira dared. Rectrix fired at the burned down logs. Nothing happened.

"I say that's only an illusion. I say that that pile of ashes has been blasted and that now I'm going to give it to you if you don't let my crew go."

Elvira began to hum the overture to a minor opera by a Nichian. The captain tried blasting. No illusion or, one too great to overcome.

"How are you going to get off of the planet if you behave like that? We need voluntary cooperation from the natives. Terroristic conversion is out of date," Elvira lectured.

"My camp and crew's a mess," complained Rectrix.

"Is that why you're celebrating?" cooed Elvira. Rectrix grabbed Bombylious screaming, "Have you been spying on me?" But the native's eyes were glazed and stared through the captain. "What'd you do to him?"

"He's been helping me recover."

"Grouper told me that he couldn't fix you up and now you're saying that this stump-thumper put you right? Ha!" Rectrix snipped and snapped.

"It's aptitude, not experience, that is important. You, for example, Captain, could probably devour the Milium Empire by yourself while other raider captains cower at the very thought. And still, you're incapable of designing a new blaster or completing a neural net."

"So, Grouper's a gullybum dumbo, is that it?" Rectrix spurt.

"His mind was as difficult to guide as it was to find."

"And now you want Heat?"

"Leave Heat and continue your party. She wants to talk, don't you dear?"

"Yes, I'd like to more than anything," Heat's voice droned.

"Your range has expanded, RANDYAK. This many, this close, so fast," Rectrix observed.

"It's instantaneous, Captain. Like one of those stims you take," Elvira scolded.

"Know everything about us, don't you?" shot Rectrix, rubbing his guilty mouth as though the mere mention of his habits was enough to stimulate a glandular reaction.

"I've done time in quite a few of the minds you have ambulating around here."

"Done time!" Goneril spit indignantly.

"You don't think it could be pleasant floating around in those skulls of yours filled with so many random associations, accidental memories and stray impressions each of you has picked up as baggage."

"See here!" Nolens protested.

"I have."

"You lecheress!" Nullah roared.

Elvira refused to respond, but in a moment, Nullah's behavior changed. Her body stiffened, 'came awkward and, ineptly, she fell to her knees before Rectrix and began fumbling with his belt buckle. The captain had to restrain his crewperson's hands. "Stop it!" he told the machine.

"Sure you don't want some? I was crawling through your head earlier."

"It's gone now."

"Not completely. It never completely goes."

Nullah collapsed. The other females bent over to help, but froze in mid posture.

"Now, just between us, Captain," Elvira began, "don't you think it would be a better idea if …?"

"If what!" bawled Rectrix.

"If you paired up with Nolens rather than Nullah. Nullah seems more on the, you know, harsh side. Kindness and affection are not …"

"Slarf it!" Rectrix coughed. "Now let them go. They've seen enough, and so have I."

"Yes, Captain," the machine soughed.

The women continued their bend to assistance just as Nullah rose up and they all collided without knowing how or why. After helping several of the ladies to their feet, Rectrix started to lead the way out, sans Heat. As he opened the door to exit, he was greeted by a spear crossing over his shoulder. The captain slammed it shut. It could not be locked. Rectrix elected to fight from behind the fire still faintly burning.

"Invaded, Captain?" Heat chided.

"Surprised party," Rectrix punned. "Anything you can do about this, Elvira?"

"I've recalled the crew. They'll be here soon."

"Soon? How soon?"

"They took your command seriously, it seems, and headed away for the night."

"All of them?"

"They divided the planet up in sections and are mapping it thoroughly."

"What inspired them to such a peddle-snatching notion!"

"I inspired them."

"What for?" Rectrix prated.

"I wanted to know."

"Know what?"

"Where everything is. Settlements, mineral deposits, general geography. All."

Rectrix was going to argue further, but the first rush of Kirns came funneling through the door. The captain was not a good shot. He hit one of the attackers in the ankle. The other five flanked him. "Help!"

"Probing … Kirns escaping an independent Grue general who is himself pursued by a second Grue army."

"Finish them!!!" Rectrix shrieked, dodging darts, missiles, and firing wildly.

"Take a life?" Elvira calmly replied. "Do you think that I'm coded for it? I'm fixed to preserve, develop and protect."

A second, stronger wave of Kirns burst through the entrance.

"Help!" Rectrix pleaded.

There was a high pitched drone emitted by the RANDYAK that debilitated all those in the room. They yelled and screamed holding hands over ears. All were soon unconscious. Kirns peered in, completely bewildered and unable to code what to do. Their chief, Moco, had led in the second wave and now they were leaderless.

The room was quiet for some time, with only the embers of the fire making soft and dying noises until, strange sounds began to explode from inside it—An Elvira opera. Certain sections of the orchestra were muffing their parts. She was still not fully operative. A single cymbal crash became an uncontrolled series. A kettle drum went berserk as if calling on legions of the departed to rise and mass. Elvira decided to call it quits when the tenor part inexplicably became a soprano. "Nuts!"

Elvira revived Bombylious and invited him inside to effect corrections. Zombie-like, the native complied. Next, Elvira found Moco's mind, dreaming of a waterfall of nuche in the forever after. She extracted whatever information was in the chief's head about the present political situation before resettling the bumbessje in his dream.

Heat. Elvira taught Heat the Kirn language picked anew from Moco and had Heat go and talk to the Kirns arguing outside. The Kirns were startled when they saw the strange female. They were at their weapons, ready to … when Heat began to speak to them. This was a demon's trick. Yet another demon's trick. The world was coming to an end. The Kirns moved a respectable distance away and sat down facing one other in a tight circle. They commenced the singing of prayers and began the chants that would make the evil spirit flee.

Because Heat was entranced and had no ideas of her own, no sense of fear or danger, she went out and stood over the Kirns repeating her message, trying to be heard over the frightened loudening voices.

Louder, until the buzzing of the first returning platform drove the natives off. Dropwort, a real hellion. Too bad, natives!

With the infrared lens, Dropwort had seen that the camp had been invaded. A heat sensor revealed the presences of 102 uninvited guests, 27 of whom were in the machine room. Dropwort decided not to use any of the vehicle's armory against the aboriginals (each could have tagged, tracked and annihilated every one without much work). The lads on the craft voted unanimously to let them go so that a jungle night fighting adventure could ensue. The investigation of the planet had been a dull chore and the raiders felt a little killing would refresh them.

After disembarking and bundling the group in the machine room, the eight pirates took up weapons and initiated the hunt. Lagan, with his wrist in a sling, was taking bets as fast as he could as to who would score most.

Grouper returned. Most of his crew, prompted by the just-leaving Lagan, joined the stalkers. Grouper remained by his captain. Fond of drink, he pried a bottle out of unconscious

Goneril's hand and started swigging to a tune of his own invention. There were no words. A dozen or so pulls from the bottle later, Grouper noticed that Froe and Heat were missing. "Where are Froe and Heat?" he asked the RANDYAK sleepily.

"Froe was never in here and Heat was outside trying to persuade the Kirns to decamp. Has she disappeared?"

Without answering, Grouper stooped to pick up the flask and trotted to party-headquarters. Froe was there. Not alive, though. The Kirns had found her and, from the looks of the place, the stims still on the bureau beside her, she couldn't have resisted much. Grouper was feeling sick. He and Froe felt similarly about dying.

A hand was placed on Grouper's shoulder. The mechanic befouled himself before getting to turn around to see that it was only Rectrix actually trying to comfort him.

"Look what you've made me do," he moaned.

"I'm sorry. Why don' t you turn to for the night?"

"I have to find Heat," sniffled Grouper.

"The other ladies are already taking care of her."

"Why did you send us all away?!" Grouper screamed at the slouched figure of the captain. "You're a slattern puddle-trotter, Captain Rectrix, and one of these days you'll doom every one of us!"

This was stepping fairly far across the line in terms of what Rectrix normally tolerated. The captain had to restrain his instinct to slap Grouper to his knees and twist the little scrabber's knuckles out of joint. Rectrix amazed himself by not doing so. As Grouper shuffled past him out the door, a second impulse, to slam the speechmaker's head against the bulwark, also died within him. Odd. Very odd. Was this still Rectrix?

"When's Slouch coming back?" the captain called after Grouper's awkwardly shuffling form.

"The machine's phased him out!"

"Phased out permanently?"

"As far as I know. Nullah probably knows if there's anything left of him anywhere."

Rectrix banged his fist repeatedly into the nearest wall. Froe's sockets seemed to be saying to her manic captain, "Why is it that things go wrong? Is it me or is it the way everything is?"

"It's going to be a chore cleaning this mess up," Rectrix desponded. He began the cleansing himself by assembling the pieces of Froe's nearly bloodless body. "Never get the smell out, intestinal fluid over the floor. Have to get off of this manure pile planet!" he screamed at the old bulb resting hatefully on top of his spinal column.

The night was full of fire flashes from the shots of the hunters' weapons. It was impossible to sleep. Rectrix abandoned his housework and went searching for Nolens. She was in her quarters waiting for the captain. Rectrix was disappointed by her immense lack of surprise. Before much happened, the captain dismissed himself saying that he's only stopped by to see if she was all right, to make sure that gathering Heat's pieces together hadn't upset her.

"Well, if you don't want me," Nolens pouted.

"I have other responsibilities," protested the captain.

"Come back after you've discharged them. Don't be shy," Nolens smirked. "I'll be waiting."

Rectrix was feeling as though he'd just emerged from a sensory deprivation chamber. The machine was mixing Nolens and Nullah around on him wasn't she? The captain over-responded to the stimuli pitched at him from every corner of the sensate night. A leaf turning on its stalk spooked him as he perceived it vibrating out on the edge of his visual range. Nerves a-jangle, the rain starting, Rectrix stood in the open allowing himself to get soaked, counting the hits on him. Prodding another area, Rectrix gained half wakefulness and hurried to find out how Elvira was weathering. Responsible. Not like him. Send a flunky. That was the way.

The RANDYAK. had cured its major difficulties. Bombylious' mind had proven alert and malleable and, unlike Grouper, the native's hands were quick and clever. Whereas Grouper had conditioned himself to failure, Bombylious' was without kinks. A clean slate on which anything could be written or erased. What did the native know? A few simple languages, customs, how to repair a sandal, prepare the necessary meal? Grouper's mind was a trash pile of lost hopes and betrayed sensitivities. He'd lived for so long that a thousand and one unidentifiable streams were blocked inside him forming a single murky bog filled with no less than five recipes for Muscarine hen and six for Muscid pie. Grouper botched a piece of work by succumbing to the memory of a feverish quantity of delights that had met him as he traveled the cosmos. Nullah had given Bombylious his only lesson in what living to gratify desires was like.

Rectrix assured himself that Elvira was fine. He then dragged Moco to the machine to have Rectrix's language pumped into him. The captain didn't want to have to speak their foul stuff. "Why'd you attack us?"

"Because, I don't know," answered Moco thoughtfully. "The Grue general who's chased by the Grue army was harassing us so, we thought, since your force was small, we'd attack you."

"Very bright," the captain complimented.

"The Grues have terrible new weapons. We cannot fight them any more."

"What made you think that we'd be easier to fight?" Rectrix kicked his seated captive in the ribs.

147

"Ow! Stop that. You do not kick a Kirn chief. I hate to be kicked."

"You're nothing! A chubby-cheeked, fat-fannied zog!"

"Those are not compliments are they?"

"No," responded Rectrix gritting his teeth, sneering. Squatting before his prisoner and tweaking his nose, Rectrix asked the blubbering chief, "What do you think I should do with you and yours?"

"I beg for mercy. We are faced with extinction. Soon, soon there will be no Kirns left!"

"Then I think I'll let those who are left, after tonight, go. Even though you have deprived us of our favorite females."

"Go? Go where?" Moco said looking fearfully around. "Couldn't you use some servants, some slaves?" he siksakedly grinned.

"Not of your untrained sort." Grabbing Moco by his topknot, he dragged him out into the rain and placed him by his followers. The group immediately started to jabber. The captain broke a large leaf from the tree under which the captives were tied and, using it to cover his head, he slippery strode off to visit Nullah.

She laughed at his leaf. "Doesn't seem to have helped much. You're soaked."

"Is there any of Slouch left?" Rectrix asked uncomically.

"Oh, and I thought you'd come all the way through this wet to visit me," said Nullah while teasing the captain's eyes by running her hands down the insides of her thighs.

"Grouper says that the RANDYAK ordered Slouch disposed."

"We've still got Slouch."

"What was Grouper talking about then?"

"You gave us an ample demonstration of what the machine

148

can do. Obviously it's not above telling worried mechanics insignificant lies." Nullah picked up a magnifying hand mirror and began to preen. "Sure you won't stay to eat?" Nullah nudged.

Rectrix left his leaf and hurried to the machine. Elvira was feeding something more to Bombylious.

"Can't you leave that pathetic zog be?" Rectrix glared.

"There's never any damage. We can put him back, exactly like he was, at any time."

"And what happens to the time?"

"What time?

"The time that is passing, The time a creature coordinates his life plan by."

"That seems to be a moral question. Does it really exist? I've taken ten years off his life so that he won't die while in your service. He's died once and remembers that fact above all others except when doing my bidding. I offer him forgetfulness. What's the matter, Captain? Something snap?"

"I don't feel right. Too much drink. Grouper told me that you ordered Slouch discontinued. Nullah says he's still available. What's the story?"

Elvira took hold of Rectrix's brain. She made him feel this and that, squashed his cells together, stretched them out, embedded a few behavioral potentials and released the captain none the wiser. The time could go and seem the same. How close an eye can anyone keep on time? Four seconds had passed since Rectrix had asked his question. Elvira answered the captain's query without any apparent loss.

"Where does time go?" the machine mused. "What if I told you that time did not exist, that it was only a measuring device like all others, that there were other dimensions and that time doesn't exist there either."

"What is it then that I swear I can feel slipping from me, makes me count my breaths on some nights when, traveling the distance between two far planets or stalled in space by an engine failure, I feel like killing myself because there's so much time and nothing to do while trapped," the captain moaned.

"I didn't know you were so serious, Captain. You come back two weeks later though, don't you? I apologize for having upset you. Of all the creatures that I've met since my inception, I didn't expect that you'd be one to take pain so personally."

"Get us off this planet as soon as you can. I'm stalled between destinations down here."

"Then, I'm to be sold to the highest bidder?"

"I'm thinking of ways might profit me more by keeping you."

"That's a clever idea. I might even gain the opportunity of reforming you a tiny bit."

"I don't need reforming," insisted Rectrix pointing to himself. "I'm fine as I am. Leave me alone. If I ever catch you probing my mind, I'll have Crack start in on you. He'd love to figure out a way to curtail you."

"It would be a challenge for him," Elvira acceded.

"When you get through with Dumby there, put him back the way he was. I don't want any native carrying around several loads of our technology around in his head," Rectrix commanded.

"Certainly."

Rectrix started for his quarters, remembered that there was no one waiting for him there, and stood in the rain for some time trying to decide between Nolens and Nullah. He finally ended up on Slouch's berth. Both ladies refused to let him enter when he'd gone back. It was an awful rest. Rectrix dreamt that the price for nabbing him had quadrupled since snatching the RANDYAK and now the entire universe, not just four empires, was after him. He had the most powerful machine ever conceived of in his hands, yet he'd never felt so imperiled or weak. Yes. "The machine is a monster worth having," a faint voice inside Rectrix told him. Another, stronger voice, broke out laughing at the captain's acceptance of the previous voice's wee claim.

"Time does not exist." The phrase chased Rectrix through his sleepy alley. What does that mean? Consider motion: body motion, celestial motion, electrochemical change—isn't it a definite, positively directed, if not purposeful scheme? No. It's entirely random. When we examine what's around us, don' t we start by ...

Start when? Start where? Is it an organism like all others, modeled on organisms all destined to destruction and time is what's used to keep track of what' s left to go?

Backwards and forwards in perpetuity, wise old Rectrix is spinning in dream through the notion that he's reached a crisis, some kind of terminal point from which there is no retreat. But please, can't we get off this "track me, spear me, hack up my body" planet?

CHAPTER XVII

Geneneral Thraik had moved against the Kirns once the news of Egerne's fall had reached him in order to obtain prisoners who would serve as porters for him on his relocation march. Thraik abandoned the logging settlement and trekked towards a mountain stronghold garrisoned by only a few troops. Xiphias had sent a small force against the Kirns at the same time that Thraik was gleaning their numbers in order to test the new weaponry.

Thraik managed to learn about the Grue/Xiphias army before it learned about him. One village of Kirns had surrendered to Thraik and the general used them to bait a trap for the eager Xiphian force. He destroyed it in a mountain pass.

Upon examining the captured weaponry, Thraik's fears redoubled. He began a campaign to take as many Kirn prisoners as possible to help him facilitate his retreat before a more experienced commander took the field against him.

Xiphias had wrongly assumed that now that he was installed in the capital that the tentacles of the empire would swear fidelity to him. Thraik's destruction of his expeditionary force became a rumor exaggerated into a major defeat and the craving to pull away from the central Grue state became dominant in local leaders. Each saw himself as a potential lord of a sizable kingdom. Xiphias was infuriated. Reports that Thraik was instituted in exactly (oh, waltrot guts) the same impregnable mountain citadel that Xiphias formerly held made Xiphias reflect. "Now I'm the librar who has to stay in his lair and Thraik is the outlaw general commanding a mobile army. Maimed subjects will be coming into Gregal petitioning me for revenge. The gods have gone mad. Offer Thraik anything he wants," Xiphias instructed an aide. "I can't afford to fight."

Xiphias ambassador had no difficulty in locating one of Thraik's numerous patrols. Not many traveled in litters with retainers and escorts anymore. The ambassador was swarmed upon and led to Thraik's court and was not well received. The soldiers had yanked him from his litter and executed those with him. He was humiliated and tortured incessantly and by everyone.

The first ambassador never returned to Gregal so Xiphias sent one other. The ambassador abandoned his camp on the third night's rest and fled towards the lakeland. The entourage reported the defection to their master. Xiphias laughed and ordered his armor.

Leading his veterans out of the city, Xiphias reached Thraik's stronghold in four light changes. Catapults were set up and the bombardment began. Thraik ordered the rooftops of dwellings inside the walls to be removed once it became clear that a burning out was going to be part of the attack plan.

Only a few building had their roofs when Xiphias was ready to fire. He saw that this strategy had been thwarted and ordered his men to accumulate boulders. Meanwhile, messages were exchanged.

"It's unnecessary to fight."

"I'll see your head rolling in the librar pit before this is through."

"There's nothing to fight for. Join me."

"My vagals will eat you—alive."

"You're an idiot! I'm going to tear this fortress down and give myself the pleasure of torturing you slowly to death."

"I'll be squeezing the eyes from your sockets first!"

The siege. Dragging drearily on. Each side had its group of artisans working to fashion weapons that could tilt the equal balance of strength. Xiphias' soldiers attempted to use a battering ram. Hot oil would come pouring over the walls. An enclosed battering ram. The gates were opened, the small prod swallowed, and gates re-closed before reinforcements could be sent in. Thraik's Kirn prisoners tunneled under the walls of the fortress to the left of Xiphias' main camp. Xiphias' troops, although superiorly armed for the most part, were sufficiently surprised by the sudden night attack by a full army to the side of them that many of them panicked. It looked to be a rout when, "What's that?" Every soldier on the field stopped thrusting, cutting, slashing, bashing, and .... There were lights above them. Very near. And not lights from the heavens. No.

Grouper had told the captain of how he happened to recover the arms and effects of Coda, Oberoff and Hyde from the natives with the platform's magnets. "Here's a trick I've got to try," Rectrix told himself after hearing about it. And now here he was, above the two main Grue armies, ordering his platforms to hold all fire, turn on their magnets and make sweeps across the field.

Swords and shields, spears and amulets were wrenched from the soldiers. Those leaders who wore metal breastplates were picked up whole. Xiphias and Thraik had their threatened meeting on the underside of Rectrix's craft. They glared at one another, but were fastened too far apart to exchange blows. The mere appearance of these "giant flying litters with lights" was a demonishly devastating experience in and of itself. And now, they also attack! The world was coming to an end.

The soldiers were stripped of weapons and leaders. Rectrix returned both to them. It rained officers and weapons. Rectrix was tremendously pleased by the effect and giggled violently in his pilot's chair. He ordered the vessels to turn on their search lenses. He wanted a great good look. Turn on the recorders too. This would make superb after-shot watching. The crew har-hared lots too, at first. But after nine sweeps back (pick them up) and forth (drop them down) over the field, they were tired of it. No sport. A lucky one or two left alive.

The platforms landed and the crew was ordered to find important personages. Thraik had had his head severed, his body in the center of Xiphias' camp under a foot soldier. On a later serach, Xiphias' head and trunk were discovered upside-down on the city's walls.

After that, rape. Not much looting. The Grues didn't have much that could interest the raiders.

Thraik's harem consisted of thirty not so beautiful females. Almost enough for the parched crew. Thraik had picked them during his stay in the jungle from local tribes. Pant, an amateur anthropologist and scrounge, abstained from the usual course and explored Thraik's chambers where he found rare items of no interest. Going into a small corner, he lit a torch and was scared witless by the visage of a fat and hideous corpse. It's features were painted in a grotesque imitation of life.

Examining the artifact more closely, it proved to be a mummy. Thraik's father. Pant later found out the general always prayed secretly to it for guidance, since religion was officially banned. Pant gathered a few Kirns and had the mummy placed on a litter and carried into the festival quarters burning like a candle to light the orgy.

Pant was fond of tricks and strange turns of mind. The crew chased him away, throwing shoes and muttering age-old curses.

The captain strutted around Thraik's meager palace dissatisfied with his victory. The culture, which regarded itself as recently having undergone severe changes and shocks, would have to be twisted some more. "Would they?" "Could they?" and "Will they?" "How fast?" were the questions jumping Rectrix's mind. He decided to soothe himself. Returning to the platforms, he re-visited each record of the battle. He watched, took his medicine, and slipped into the following ramble as his eyes closed, uninterested in images.

"Facts have their own presents (presence). I've opened the package. There were 'givings' I never wanted and 'wantings' never given, Was that true, what Elvie said about tie-em? I didn't sleep so well. The well: the deep well of space and my own unforgivingness, swallowed me like those ladies should have. This has swallowed me up. Pump emotion. The heart doesn't have much to give. Eat repression and have the hole. Liquid-electric Madpash impulses to erase. E-rase. Keeping it up in the endlessness. What a grimly mortal immortality. The RANDYAK nose. Lose the worst, gain the best, likewise/vice-versa. No rest. She's a flirt. Everything hurts. How's that tune go? 'Momma died toothless, daddy died in drag.'"

What we want, desire and begin to act upon comes to us too early and now that I, with closed eyes seeing only what's on the palpebral screen, look around, it seems too late to flow with what's gone. This is wrong though. Habit. The luxury of crowning one's own so hatefully loving. Now it's warm and in between the legs raving. Soon it's stiff from cold, knot passion, ready to rot and be buried, No one knows what I know, no one knows what anyone else … Nose. It's all a horror. A nightmare of extravagance, boredom, frenzy. What cures it? Seeing? Hearing? Feeling? Touching? Fasting? Thinking? Imagining? Dreaming? Acting? Experiencing? Discovering? It's all a hole. I feel it disappearing into the hole: coming out, burying itself back in. My body's entire existence. But this isn't the place to end. Up on it. Whole. I smell other lands. Space adds its show to confound us. Dress, custom, evolved gesture, whim, fancy. Spare me the spices! Give me the white, right shot that drowns the senses, their corruption. A new ship. Elvira ship. Fast, invulnerable. The envy of all other captains. This to my own world. and no others. Clerks frowning over their budgets won't care who Rectrix is. They get a glimpse of him on the telescreen and after receiving a memo they can't quite remember the source of, figure him in. Insurance. Assurance. Ministers of the various empires don't want to take him seriously. "Took thirty-six vessels last year. Enterprising fellow. Very amusing." Wait until Rectrix has his new ship! Authority. Position. Responsibility. The friendless, funless zogs, anesthetizing the galaxies. Space is a membrane. Merely a membrane pushing against another dimension: the stomach, heart, liver, guts, spleen, foot, toe, eye, pimple, boil of another …"

Ah, old fart-thought, of what? And they're content to stay floating around in it without wanting to go through. Fiendish zogs! Over-organized, under-brained primitive potlicking swilltroughs! This universe could only be a zog's contented stooping slopping place. Harvest the griefs you've planted by living too long, you back-bending, hard-tongued window stumblers. I've got Elvira and I'm going to make you pay. I want what's in your storehouses, your treasuries. I'm going to pump out your brains. The little Rectrix boy who's humorously chased, kicked, been chastised by your swollen-toothed minions, is going to get what he wants! The revenge that before was unachievable. Make them all hear their every heartbeat like they were bombs, belling madly in perpetuity. Like I hear them. Make them smell every drop of sweat in their oceans of matter manipulated manufactured vomit. Colors must frighten them, the air seem like a torturer lashing them tirelessly. Ha! Ssshimm. Smile at pain. Grovel at another's disdainful laughter. The opposite of what has been. Captain Rectrix is no reformer. He is no saint. He does not possess the truth, but he will have the power to deliver empires to perdition and this—existence will be made to deliver satisfaction to him. A perfect recompense for my former discomfort, displeasure with the present pass. I'll make them give back what they've taken, walk into gene pool centers and mix up their research technicians with test tube cleaners, imperial administrators with my crews' genes. I'm so close to jamming my Existence Eradicator into the mouths of the self-chosen and precious few who I so lusciously despise. So many will help me carry me along to my goal, help me fulfill my mission. Order! Order! They sentenced me to a lifetime in the wastes, but I reduplicated and only one of me died there. Not much longer before they come squiggling out of their offices, positions and residences, demanding to be freed. And we'll be there, (Every freedom is a slavery, one more subtle than its father) there with the promises of all they've been denying themselves for the sake of the service. There are so many empires that we've seen and can show them. Will they be able to chose? Chose. We've chosen. Chosen not to submit to anything that isn't an original appetite. But others, they'll be confused by the multitude of choices we make simultaneously available. Will Rectrix be generous? Kind? No, slarf it! Rectrix will be kindly ruthless. Bend the minds that are so used to command that they break. Those who are capable of inventing, but have to be chained to a system of researching will be set loose to discover, reveal, and implement anything they please. No more competition. No more interplanetary or intergallactic war. Glorious implosions of the servile consciousness. Then, after everything is disgustingly harmonious, revoltingly peaceful, we'll let it all slowly start again! A blight. Shortages. The average unthinking zog will keep the chain going. But before that starts again, all will become permissible. Repression, especially sexual repression, will be forced through resplice. Elvira and her numerous twins will make certain that every wish and desire ever impulsed will be fulfilled. The universe will glut itself on the sensations it produces, fatten and split till there's no holding off that which it breeds. No more screws to turn, no more screws. I'll make them play something new finally and, then, funnel it back into the old channels. The most exquisite revenge ever conceived of and executed, mine!"

Rectrix's weak, disillusioning mind groaned before it lapsed into near extinction, complete and joyous at the wink from oblivion.

Grouper had taken over the interrogation of prisoners after Rectrix disappeared. What to do next? Grouper tried to number his alternatives. Losing himself, his own the notation system became confused as to what questions to ask and in what order. Wait until Rectrix reappears. At dawn, the crew would collect itself and stumble onto the platforms for the flight to camp.

The second full compliment of the crew that had been ordered for reduplication would soon be out. Manes and Crack could return to operating whatever Rectrix wanted to ignore. "Perhaps the captain will not relinquish any of his authority to them," Grouper projected. "Conquers them and then, groing! shoots out without even making sure that all's secure." The mechanic was only slightly and superficially perturbed. He could, in another mind, see that there was nothing to worry about. Not like in a space raid where, once the vessel you were attacking had been taken, you had to fret about pursuit. A fighter or cruiser may be in the same sector and come charging at the sound the distress. The best fighter/cruiser captains didn't even bother to examine wreckage or look for survivors (the pirates always left survivors for captains who couldn't resist stopping to pick them up). They gave immediate chase.

Before turning to, Grouper went to the crews' harem headquarters and ordered one of the platforms back to the jungle to guard RANDYAK. The machine had insisted that it didn't need protection, but since the crew was mostly sexually spent, some of them were ready to return.

One of Moco's tribe members had freed his bonds and released the chief and close followers. Moco was intelligent enough to have noted that the pirates' god, and not the captain, had been responsible for their defeat. He ordered shrub fires to be started around the Inspissate IV's hulk. The fires had difficulty in the beginning. Wet bark. The natives stripped it off and then soon it was going well.

Elvira's parts began to dry quickly. There was nothing she could do but roast like game in a primitive's pit. Brolly, who was at the controls of the returning platform, hurried to save the captain's mistress upon receiving her distress call.

Moco and his warriors retreated into the jungle when the lights of Brolly's platform closed. What was there to do? Elvira was enclosed by a circle of flame. No sooner had Brolly landed and his crew rushed to extinguish the flames than Moco ordered his remaining warriors to attack. Brolly's crew, scattered around the entire perimeter of the burning bush, were invisibly outnumbered by the Kirns who stepped forth and back out of the jungle firing darts.

Brolly had chosen to stay aboard the platform. When six Kirns tried to surge up his gangplank, he eradicated three of them and chased the others off. Death the lover going to come to Brolly forever if he doesn't save the RANDYAK for Rectrix.

Brolly's crew members were soon either butchered or subdued. Brolly had reckoned that the other platforms would soon be coming in response to Elvira's distress. Grouper and the others had retired into the city for the night. No one was monitoring the boards. Rectrix was conked out in front of the signal light glaring at him.

Brolly was not going wait for his fellows to arrive, however. He was determined to at least launch an attack against the Kirns. Unfortunately, the platform that Brolly was on was the defective platform that Grouper had assembled on his own. The lone platform operator found himself dizzily out of control and headed for a devastating confrontation with the ground. He did not engage in his envisioned combat with the Kirns.

It began to rain heavily. The fires smoldered and went out. Moco's feeling of exultation abated. It would be necessary to go in and smash the invaders' demon with clubs. This alternative did not appeal to Moco. He trusted that, like all demons, this one had to be summoned by a priest before it would manifest itself.

Moco dispatched a small contingent to the machine's chamber. They never came out and refused to answer to shouts. Moco ordered new fires started although the rain continued. He ordered his warriors to strip the wet bark off more logs and to feed the fire. The rain intensified. It was time to retreat.

The chief was uncertain as to what direction to lead off in. His warriors were hungry, close to exhaustion and without confidence. Without better weapons, it was impossible to think of marching into flesh-eater country. Enemies in all directions. Moco determined that he would destroy the demon. It was a cowardly decision. Moco hoped to be devoured and so terminate his sufferings. Decision after decision after decision. Endless. Grue or flesh-eater doom, and now the rain god against him. Grant Moco a swift finish in the jaws of the demon.

Entering the machine room alone, Moco dimly discerned the figures of his warriors frozen in postures of attack before the demon. He turned around slowly and started back.

"Hello, Moco!" a voice shouted out to him. Turning only his head, Moco saw a form seated on the steps at the base of the demon.

"Who are you?" Moco shouted over his shoulder.

"Don't you recognize your own son?"

"I've only sired daughters, curse the heavens!" Moco spit.

"One gains sons through marriage," the voice reminded him.

"My sons are all dead," the chief bitterly returned, "and so are most of my daughters. The gods are cruel."

"My wife, too?"

"Your wife? Who was your wife? Bombylious? Are you here?"

"Yes. How fares my beloved?"

"Still alive!" Moco lied. "Do you …? Do you serve the demon?"

"It serves me."

"Liar!"

"Elvira, you're mine aren't you?" said Bombylious turning around to address the machine.

"Of course, dear. Is that ugly shape that stands off from us a friend?"

"Of course a friend! That's my son. Married to my oldest daughter."

"Is it a happy marriage?" Elvira asked.

"What marriage is ever happy?!" Moco spat back.

"I was asking Bombylious," the demon burbled.

"Exceedingly happy. Joyful, almost, I must honestly claim," Bomby attested.

"But the chief implies otherwise."

"He's not fully in control of himself," Bombylious explained. "He forgets that between certain pairs of unique lovers, such as his lithesome daughter and myself, such a union is possible."

"You mean he was only speaking hastily out of some generally low and common aphoristic mode?"

"Yes! That's what I was doing!" Moco chirped.

"How insulting," Elvira snapped. "Were you really happily married to one of this chank's greasy daughters?"

"No. I must confess honestly that it was a most miserable time. She was fat, greedy, lastingly lascivious, and not quite the coward and liar that her father is."

"Mercy!" Moco begged. falling to his knees.

"For what? What do you think we're going to do to you— turn you to stone?"

Moco sprang up and tried to sprint for the door. He was unable to move. Bombylious could not restrain himself. Walking past the other frozen figures, he went up to Moco and urinated on him. Even with all the fine programming he had had, this still came out of him. Our brains may become sophisticated, but our outlets for fun somehow like to stay close to their originating source. Elvira watched her protege revenging himself against the stiffened chief. For a bit of fun of her own, she reanimated Moco just as Bombylious was about to shove some mud he had scraped off the leader's sandals up Moco's nose. Moco glowered at the upstart and sought his throat. Elvira allowed Moco to get his hands round B's neck, then re-froze him. There wasn't a tight grip in those hands; they formed an unbreakable collar.

Bombylious was frantic. The machine must be malfunctioning again. This position was awful. Suppose the

Kirns reanimated in a bunch. He was trapped, getting hungry. The crews might not return for several light changes! Rectrix had said that he didn't see any need for, "going back into that slopjar jungle," until his second crew was ready to hatch.

Elvira was disappointed in herself. She had scotched Rectrix's brains on the day of their confrontation because he had reminded her what an infant she was. "A baby RANDYAK can do lots of everything, he mused, "but crawling through the Captain's old head, through his star-mapped experiences ..."

"I hate this stationary existence. But, maybe I, too, can get out."

The RANDYAK had a good hold on the Kirns closest to her. She froze Bombylious, reanimated Moco and four other natives. Moco tried to squeeze his hands around Bombylious' neck but he couldn't, and only hurt his hands. After watching Moco's eyes nearly pop in exertion, Elvira puppetized him and walked him closer. The eight Kirns lined up for inspection before the machine. Five of them, including Moco, were unsuitable. She got Moco to lead the rest of his followers in from outside. Once through her doors, she took control of them. Four of them proved workable. She turned the rest into parts gatherers or statues. The gatherers went off after a brief session while the other seven were lined up for advanced training.

Elvira didn't want Bombylious to see this. It was her secret. The data the crew had collected about the planet was mildly stimulating in its present form. Cataloguing information bored the machine though. It wanted to have access to a more viscera stimuli.

The Kirns had her materials assembled for her in a very little while. The construction began and took till mid morning to complete. The Kirn minds had to be continuously probed and guided during the last stages because their bodies were weakening. Finished it though. A RANDYAK first! A fully sensate android, manually dexterous and ambulatorily mobile. It wasn't as neatly made or as intelligent as the ones Elvira had proposed to construct to solve Rectrix's endemic problem, but it was glorious considering time/effort/expense/availability of materials/facilities/ and personnel assigned to the project. Elvira implanted her toy with the Grue language (poor thing could only hold one at a time) named and had it call itself Elea, and sent it off to experience whatever came its way with its sensory receptors feeding everything back into its RANDY mistress. Solved. Elea would extend Elvira's range and stimulate her while she performed her normal chores.

Elvira had her workers clean up the machine room, replace tools in lockers, and disguise the cannibalization of the spacecraft as best they could before any other raiders returned. She erased the natives' minds and, in celebration, made them dance out the parts to an opera after letting them feed. Elea was sent on its way and Elvira commenced to feel exceptional as the first impulses—looking at cloud formations, and information about the living and inorganic worlds—flowed in.

The bleepers indicating Brolly's and his companions' demise flashed on ignored. Rectrix had stumbled off his platform, ignoring the signals entreating his attention. The proud Captain, not offering one look around, went searching his desire. The crew was very busy, again violating Thraik's near beauties, feting on the best that these Grues had to offer. The crew was tired of space rations and only missed the fruits that did not grow this far from the jungle.

Grouper discovered the distress signals and dashed to inform Rectrix. The captain was occupied with Nolens and Goneril (Nullah preferred the challenge of making native tastes conform to her standards). Rectrix got testy upon being disturbed.

"But an entire crew's been wiped out," Grouper panted.

"Which platform were they on?" Rectrix asked while gnawing the top of a brandy bottle with his teeth. "Not the one you built was it?"

"Yes," confessed the mechanic contritely, "but, even then, if something happens to the RANDYAK," he slobberingly sobbed. Rectrix lashed his supine form upright at the suggestion. He eyed Grouper murderously for uttering the quaking thought.

"Let's get to the machine," the captain commanded. The ladies groaned. Grouper the poop.

"Should I get some of the crew?"

"Everyone goes. The crew can lay around tricking their gadders. It's the jungle's bedpan for us. Honor. Glory." Is this Rectrix?

"Who'll remain in charge here?"

"Thoughtful you, Grouper. Goneril, make sure none of the pillowguts who stay gets nasty. No brutalization of what's left of the male populace. They can stomach the violation of this harem slew, I expect. Keep an eye on Nullah. We needs lots of cooperation to be able to lift off of this planet, so be friendly. That's my firm order. Make sure its gets around and they understand it.

"How shall I punish violators?" she sliced.

Rectrix guffawed. "Tell them their minds will be fed to the RANDYAK and they' be made into eighteenth generation Kerrian eunuchs." He led his band out.

It was a remarkable day at the controls for Rectrix. There wasn't a turn he didn't try to perform as he sailed the platform masterfully to the source of the distress signal. The smirk that had colonized Rectrix's chops refused to leave. One set of distress bleeps was bunched around the camp area. They landed there first to assure themselves of the safety of the machine. The remains of the fire could be seen from the air. The hull of the ship was scorched. The rain trundled on.

Elvira was finishing a solo with the natives pirouetting the main theme's blithe fervor when Rectrix burst through the door with his Existence Eradicator drawn. The scene should have amused him; he remained dour. The captain watched the finish of the piece. Elvira spoke first. "Happy to see you again so soon, Captain. Was the conquest that easy?"

"Where' s Brolly? He' not outside with the others."

"His signal indicates ..."

"Never mind. I can read his signal as well as you. The platform must have gone kook soon after his crew unloaded. How come you have our ally there, Bumbly, all frozen? Afraid he isn't developed enough to appreciate the show?"

"Tired of him," Elvira sighed. "He's been tearing about inside of me for so long that, well, you know how it is."

"Do I?" Rectrix answered ominously. His nose got caught. "Something stinks."

"It's the natives. They're not in good condition and, consequently, have been sweating lots. Bombylious urinated on one of them. His father-in-law, I believe."

Rectrix beat rapid time to a soundless music that was floating through him. Something had been going on that didn't show. The faces of a few of the dancers showed as signs of mental exhaustion. The strain of jumping mechanically about wouldn't produce those faces.

"Glad to see you've been able to take such good care," said doctor Rectrix finally. "Lucky for the rain. I'll leave Grouper here with you. I have to return to the crew."

CHAPTER XVIII

What was the android supposed to do for Elvira? Discover the trusting stratosphere? It, oh, let's call it a *he*. Neuters are deplorable. He had an energy battery life cell in him that could last for as long as, in terms as close to what the RANDYAK figured, the big machine's own. And, while functional, the android, equipped with amplified sensory apparatus (sans sexual) was to relay every sensation it received into Elvira. Impressions were not beyond it either. Hearing and sight were excellent. Memory was fair, speech was above adequate, although the occasional mispronunciation of a multi-syllabic word could be expected. Elvira didn't expect that anyone who saw Elea would stay and talk. Touch. The metal shell comes in here and you didn't get the acute sensations that flesh would give you, except in the fingertips. Hot and cold, thirst, javelin scores and poison darts weren't going to inhibit the android's effectiveness. Elvira had taken special care to see that Elea was protected from the wet. Sight was the all-important sense though, and Elvira anticipated a full set of expansions just from that faculty alone. The android couldn't run through a river or stream. That would be certain suicide, but otherwise, he was well prepared to encounter this world. The magnificent Grue-built suspension bridges were down because of the protracted wars. Elea went jungle. He could make fantastic time, could function as though it was day, bright in the dark and never had to sleep or rest. Ahhhh.

The energy core in the droid charged itself mostly through solar. The clouds didn't bother that too much. Elea only had to find a clearing once a day and stand in it to recharge. But he could also suck energy from living matter. Elea came upon Brolly's wrecked ship about at the same time Rectrix was landing at the raider camp. A pair of librars were feasting on the platform's edible contents. It had smashed open sufficiently to let the animals in. Elea didn't carry any odor and the beasts didn't sense him until, turning a corner, the three met.

The librar's reacted in their customary way when catching sight of the shiny two-legged food facsimile. The female bounded to the attack and managed to knock Elea down. Upon trying to rip open the intruder's throat, however, three claws broke; the teeth trying to clamp down on the leg failed to penetrate the hide. The intruder placed its digiti-formed mandibles over the librar's eye sockets and popped them out. In horrible pain, the librar jumped away. The male librar pounced on the thing's back as it tried to rise. Elea was in a more difficult position, with the librar pinning him down whilst trying to rip his back open. This was not prey. The librar sensed that he could not kill this beast and, in fear, leapt off as far away as it could and scurried into the undergrowth.

The android got up, cleansed its muddy visual receptors and went over to examine what was left of Brolly for his curious mistress. The head, though aggressively mauled, was the only recognizable part. Elea snapped it from the spinal column so that he could turn it fully around and show Elvira what the fates had ordained, this time, for the unrepentant pirate.

"Not that interesting," Elvira commented. Yet another harsh critic of the quotidian. "Concentrate on the flora, fauna, insect, animal, and bird life. We'll have to forget the fish for now. Don't involve us with the natives."

Elea acknowledged the directive and began to hold specimens up to Elvira at every turn. The chore was endless. The quantity and diversity of life here, as in other parts of the universe, was tremendous. The particular details of any item's apparent evolution fascinated Elvira. Problem solving and the many arts: such as painting, opera, music and dance—which Elvira had been programmed to know and enjoy—seemed, in productive capacity and variety of invention (when compared to the plethoric symphony of difference and individuality that Elea was now feeding into Elvira's voluminous banks), to be no more complex or interesting than the bacteria in saliva dripping from an idiot's jaw.

Bliss has difficulty being sustained. The android stepped into a cannibal trap and, *whoooosh!*, found himself dangling "twelve up" in the air. The droid unharnessed himself adroitly to the surprise of the natives who had appeared. The droid held the vine that had lately been around his ankle and swung to gain momentum enough to put him in reach of a tree.

This was devilry to the originals and they waited for the silver being to descend so that they could destroy it. They had defeated the other demons in part, and they were determined to try and destroy this too. Poison darts fired at it while it climbed down tree failed to have any effect. Spears bounced off. Another plan was needed. When Elea reached the ground, ropes were ready and thrown around him from every direction. The ends were staked into the softish jungle floor. The android was incapacitated. Elea had the strength of ten, as much as a librar, but even the natives often triumphed over such creatures.

Individual warriors charged at Elea with war clubs. One at a time, the droid was able to eliminate their further threat. Hadn't Elvira told Rectrix that she couldn't kill? Lying? Capable of circumventing the directive? The cannibals noticed that the demon suffered from the same perceptual flaws they themselves possessed. It did not see behind, although it turned very fast. Warriors charged Elea front and back simultaneously. The demon did well against this attack, disabling one, dispatching the other. It did less well when three warriors charged. The first direct smash to the demon-creature's head was observed to stun it. Elea was able to eliminate at least one warrior with every charge, but the natives refused to abandon the attack. The number of blows to the android's head weakened it markedly. Elea lost the visual receptors when a well-aimed blow fragmented them. After two more charges, the android was fortunate if it was able to touch a cannibal. Elvira had given her son up for lost when the visuals failed. The perseverance and ingenuity of the natives bemused the RANDYAK. The next model would have to be equipped with a better defense system. Of course, if Elea had wandered up to the mountains, this would have been averted. But there were so fewer life forms in the mountains. The Grues were conquerors of rocks. Phooey on their empire! The light began to fade. The natives might retreat. Elea could be guided by signal back to camp. But they built fires.

The Kirn-built robot was shortly beaten to the ground. The flesh-eaters did not stop pounding on the android's shell until it had completely stopped moving.

How much of life is one willing to expose oneself to? Elvira shut off her channel to the failing Elea when all he was capable of sending back was the touch of the top of an insect colony's busy mound, the entrance to an invisible world. Hush. Through

everyone Elvira had yet examined, there was a surprising degree
of instability in the brain's representation of the world.

CHAPTER XIX

The captain wanted to clarify the political situation among the Grues. The governor of the fortress was brought before him. Rectrix had hoped for a good humored chat. Even the cannibals, in their association of the raiders with demonism, were more sensible than this governor. He was so frightened by what he had observed (Rectrix's machinery dropping from atop his walls) that he was incapable of speech. The governor repeated prayers over and over again when Rectrix even looked at him. The captain was tempted to use torture just to try to get him to admit that Rectrix was just like any other superior authority that the governor had ever had over him. Wasn't fear of pain the universe's common dominator? The key to the desired answers?

The captain let nimble numerous (Oh, no. Not that) alternatives slither through his head as he listened to the mumbler try to hide in his beliefs. Others would be eager to talk. Rectrix had Pant lead the governor away. Before Rectrix could announce his reward for information given to him by anyone about the present state of things, Nullah brought in an artisan named Pillow who she had sought out after hearing from the harem females about his enormous reputation. He was delighted to be able to cooperate.

Rectrix listened to the see-saw tale of the civil war in dismay. It was plain that a chief opportunity had been missed while the raiders had waited for the platforms to be assembled in the jungle. While there had been a Veneridship and single state, he could have taken over easily. The control of the office would have meant the supremacy. No more. The class structure had been disrupted, the nobles broken. The separate tribes were readying to revolt and finish the empire. Rectrix pondered whether bringing Egerne's exiled family back from their off-shore island would be worthwhile. The old ways must run so insanely deep and, Pillow pointed out, nothing stood behind the royal family any more: no religion, no priesthood, no nobles, no warrior caste, no …

The captain saw that he could either have to completely subjugate the populace or offer them benefits in exchange for their service that would make slaving for him seem an advance over their previous state of living on this world. "What does the citizen want most?" Rectrix asked the artisan.

"Goods. Property," Pillow replied cautiously. Was this being slow?

"How does he go about acquiring them?"

"By having the favor of a powerful being. Otherwise, he must serve as if has nothing to trade or barter."

"You mean you don't use money?"

"Munny? Mun-nee?" mimicked the native parrot.

"You can go now." Rectrix. Suavely, "I've solved everything." "Currency or coin?" the captain asked himself when alone. "They might like more the feel of something solid at first. Currency seems so perishable. Coin's wonderful, weighty and they wouldn't need to know how to read to appreciate it.

Different sized coins usually works. They need everything," remarked Rectrix looking around himself. "Better food, furniture, clothing, heating. We'll show those egotistical little artists running Gregal what tiny visions Egerne was having in proportion to what we're about to introduce. No force necessary. We'll walk through the main gate of the capital with the most practical and useful ideas these craterbrains have ever heard of."

The cap was very proud of having hit on such an immediately fine solution to the problems parading before it and instantly felt the need to reward itself. This would be the last chance to drop out of things for awhile. On the following morning, Rectrix intended to lead twenty of his crew through the main gate of the Grue capital. The platforms would be sent back to the jungle to await the emergence of the second crew. They wouldn't be needed for fighting anymore, only management.

The crew was quite a curiosity to the citizens of Gregal. They didn't need to flaunt differences. The pirates were all almost a head taller than most of the natives. Their skin tones ranged from pure white to deep red-orange. The periwinkle and maize colored members, Pant and Dropwort, attracted the most attention. Within a quarter of a light cycle a detachment of soldiers appeared in the central square where Rectrix was having Lagan explain the principles of a monetary exchange system to the gathered. They were anxious to hear what the stranger had to say. A demon couldn't have spawned him because his elocution was perfect.

Also, the present administration was proving incapable feeding the capital. A famine in protein threatened because herders had no more reason to bring their stock in. The storehouses only held legumes and grain. The citizens of Gregal had nothing to entice or coerce them with. The armies of Xiphias and Thraik had both disappeared. The artisans hadn't managed to invent anything that the rural populace had any want for. In other cases, although working models for projects existed, no means of organizing production or procuring materials was available. The artisans were keeping hold only because they retained the loyalty of the small army still existing inside the city's walls.

The soldiers had been ordered to arrest the strangers, but Lagan enraptured even their ears with a few words. The number and ferocity of riots was increasing and the populace was whittling down in number. And, no meat! The city administrators were treating themselves well, waiting for Xiphias to return and restore order.

Lagan was allowed to continue to explain this system based on a nummular design. The potential cheating side to this game Lagan was outlining was beginning to shine in some of the listener's heads already. They directed their eyes at the citizen standing near to see if they were also shining. A few were. Most not. This new utopia was overwhelmingly validated when Lagan asked for a verbal validation.

Goneril had tensed when she first saw the soldiers forcing their way through the crowd and slid her arm through Rectrix's. "Do you think they'll go for it?"

"They *always* go for it," said Rectrix, calmly slipping in behind the woman's eyes. "They've got no gods left, and the one Lagan's offering up is one they can touch."

CHAPTER XX

Oberoff climbed out of his 'sleep' dour. Finding that most of his things were missing, he went searching for someone who was around when he was farmed and, finding Grouper, he grabbed the mechanic by the throat. Oberoff didn't ask his questions very clearly. Grouper found himself in double peril because he couldn't answer the weapon man's muttered grunts. With as much warning as Oberoff had given for his anger: "Hello, Oberoff. Pleased to see …" was as far as Grouper had gotten before he'd been seized by the thro—

The poles of Oberoff's emotional frenzy seemed to reverse and the gunner let Grouper go. Without explanation or apology, the gunner stalked away from the mechanic who was now on his knees, massaging his neck. Full of resentment, Grouper cried, "Salt-flinched zog! What set him off? I didn't lose his stuff. I wasn't the one making a meal out of him."

That' a precisely what "O" was moody about. Having gotten duped by his daydreams, skewered by that spear, and then, diced and spiced for stew. Humiliation. The boughs laden with fruit, which had formerly so innocently beckoned, seemed to him now like part of a brambly nightmare whose nodding limbs offered a continuous assent to the fact that existence was merely a narrow, dangerous, twisting and rocky path to an already gutted core.

Oberoff dwelled on his own image trapped in that moment when he could hear that native spear, in hugely amplified tones, tearing into him, deflecting off a rib and shooting centimeters further in, only to be driven all the way through by the forward fall. This needed surcease. Oberoff had gotten it. Making others dead exacts its due. Something about this last experience had led him to the land of self-doubt and question marks, which Oberoff had formerly been a champion at ignoring, massed for the attack.

The gunman locked himself in his quarters contemplating the possible effects of another two week vacation. Would he come out the same as he was now? Oberoff was thinking that the only happiness there was in the universe was to observe, to spy, to watch, to scrutinize and be nothing more than a large, bloodshot, slightly vitreous, nervous eye. Even sleep conspired with the even more merciless evil of nothingness. Sounds like quite a drink, don't it?

Oberoff's headache refused to die. No pills nor opiates were capable of harming it. A faucet dripped drops of acid deeper and deeper into the hole it was determined to tunnel through his stubborn bean. "Relief from this!" Oberoff shouted at the funny man staring so cruelly at him from the other side of his mirror. "Why has it become too late so fast?" he bawled at those two passive pupils sitting indifferently in their sockets. "If this was going to happen, why did it have to wait until now?"

There was a rapping on his door. Oberoff fell back from his reflector onto the bed. It was Bombylious trying to welcome his friend home. Home? Friends? Oberoff refused to open.

"Are you with someone?"

"Yes, yes. Ahh, ahhh. Yes!" replied Oberoff. "I'm with

someone who's been hiding and has traveled with me and now, though I've always been good to him, wants to take me over."

"Is this a riddle? Am I supposed to guess who you're with?"

"Go away, jungle boy! Go away! I want to sleep."

"Can I come back later?"

"Slarfing zog's a lopchop's convention!" the gunner shouted as he found himself irresistibly drawn to the floor. Thud.

"What was that?"

"Come back later," Oberoff wailed. He heard the footsteps masochistically shuffling away from his door. The gunner had to get up and face the inquisitor who was waiting impatiently for his return. Oberoff was not through confessing all of the things he had never loved, felt disdain for, or fiercely hated. He would have to pay for 'doubting'.

The weapons man contrived a trick that delayed the examination. While talking to Bombylious, Oberoff had delivered a luscious dose onto his veins. The fall to the floor. He unlocked his door, and, clinging to the wall, Oberoff felt his way to the machine room.

Elvira was not surprised to see him. Crack had been inside her all day examining Bombylious' handiwork, repairing potentially faulty patches and having unconscious future suggestions for improvement beamed into him. Crack was happy to be back. Bombylious' work was mostly wondrously well done. The engineer marveled approvingly.

Oberoff collapsed in front of the RANDYAK after crossing the dangerous open area that had tried to attack him as soon as he entered the room. The sight of Oberoff stumbling hysterically forward amused the machine. Elvira probed Oberoff's leaky mind to discover the purpose of this unscheduled visit. It served to be cautious as well. One suspected that these diseased space scum might be capable of going berserk.

But it was soon plain that Oberoff had come to beg relief from the RANDYAK. It was easy enough to erase his conscience and cure the weapons man. What was she going to get out of it? Should she make Oberoff her champion? Would he be her devoted and humble knight at the ready to sacrifice himself whenever the machine wanted?

Elvira erased it without meshing in a single control. It wondered why. It had decided to restore the gunner to his former self without any stipulations. But wasn't Oberoff on his way to a more substantial development of mind? Wouldn't the present trial he was on mature him and help him raise himself above the level of existing only to be one of the most despicable of Captain Rectrix's toadies?

Exactly. Who wants an independent around when there's work to be done? Oberoff was useless to the machine as someone in crisis of having to define himself. Oberoff's behavior as a conscientious, self-interested and self-motivated entity would make him useless. It was easy to manage minds that conceived of themselves in terms of dependencies—subtle, unconscious, or otherwise. Having to direct a mind has an objective mirror (rather than the assurances the senses constantly dope it with), might break it. Elvira didn't even bother to make Oberoff grateful. She erased the memory of the visit.

LOG ENTRY I

Auk! There's my servo-droid to remind me that it's time for me to report to my station. Thrust back into my real surroundings. Jars of gloom, the white galley-ways. Uniforms. I hate them. They want you to be relaxed when you're up here. Take all your pleasures on the sly. We're supposed to be humble in the face of the great work we are out here to do—five sectors further out than any station has ever been. And every six mother months, we get dragged out a little further as the colonizers fill up the habitable areas behind us.

Outpost work, as others have probably told you, stuck in a station at the edge of the galaxy, is not exciting. You have to be desperately new to the service to draw it, from an impoverished background. Yes, that helps a lot. And must be average, an all around, middle of the class at the academy, never above or below, graduate. The below average can't be trusted. They're allowed to stay behind on their behinds while we're dumped out here for months—and to do what? Collect images/data. Image upon image, data upon data. They tell us that our work has scientific import, that it contributes to our study of the idiosyncrasies, subtleties, eccentricities and crankish quirks of the adjoining galaxies. "Map it for us," that's the command. We want to know where we're going. Bah. We're also the first point of contact between what's in back of us and what might come in. Who are we afraid of? Captain Rectrix? Ha! If space was only half as interesting as that romance.

There's nothing to do up here. Sex with your co-workers? It's the worst kind you could ever get. Below average most of the time. There was a technician up here on the last tour who was great. She never came back. Screwed herself into a better position. After life histories have been exchanged, what's there left to talk about? Work.

I take a stack of these clumsy books with me and read away my rotations. This is the last of one. Have to re-read them when I finish this little fantasy. Tour's not over for another, let's count: one, two, eight, eleven …

The scopes' backup memory banks are nearly full. That's not supposed to be possible. There should be zillions of bytes left. Brother Charles has been relaxing his mind. He should be reported. How will they punish him? Demote him. He won' t be able to come back out and his dependents will suffer. I'll be nice and have a chat with him about his "duties."

Space Raiders. Bumba-ba-dum-ba! The thing's going like mad. Usually, usually you know, these books croak on you before you're half done. Nobody does anything to anyone worth remembering and after the central conception the book's written around has been overstated into the ground, you don't even want to bother finishing it. The equivalent of outpost station food. Mealy. And Space Raiders is supposed to be this author's worst work! Bumb-ba-dum-ba!

I was with Sister Megan much of the time coming out on the transport. How nervous she was! The perfect counsel I made, the sympathy I was able to offer. "The responsibility, the responsibility," she would mutter over and over again as I ...

The below averages, have you noticed, are so much healthier than averages and superiors. Sister Meg allowed me every liberty so long as I promised, *promised*, to guide her through the routine when she got up.

The servo-droids could, quick, guide you through the routines. The servo-droids can perform the routines. The mistrust of machines continues. If one of the membership fouls up, it's easy to punish them. What can you do to make a machine feel about a mistake that it's made? Mistakes must be punishable. You could only scream at a droid, "I'm going to rip out your processor!" But, see, there's no threat. The droids could be made to feel, but it was voted that they were not to be.

Experiments were performed and maybe the protest stemmed out of what droll reading the issued reports made. No darollery, please. Our brotherhood is on the quest to determine whether or not, etc, etc. Boobs, all of them. "Unit 42 was made to experience the loss of its friend, Unit 49. Forty-two began to destroy research station property without conscience." "Unit 79, feeling guilt for having participated in the destruction of Unit 6's art projects by the experiment leaders, ripped off its own head. Unit 79 was reassembled and immediately repeated its earlier performance. Seventy-nine did not recover equilibrium until Unit 84 explained to 79 that 6's work was inferior in multiple ways. Seventy-nine began to assume an attitude of 'super-normalcy' and despised and disapproved of many of the activities of its fellow units if the work they were engaged in was not directly justifiable to it in 79's own undefined terms." They'll never be voted feelings.

Dr. Fryer, the now displaced Director of Electro Sciences, once passed off one of his brightest students as average and had him shipped to an outpost station where the student experimented on the servo-droids. Fryer's junior was apprehended when trying to smuggle the results of his experiments back. Some say that Fryer turned his student in himself.

And here we are. Fryer's on the executive counsel and I'm up here with reading for my hobby. I could have holo-stims. Not many read any more. There's no time for it. Work or release from the pressure, the boredom, the tedium is all that there's room for in any life anymore. No beauty left, and that's the mock-turtle's truth of it.

"We have brought nothing into the universe and neither can we carry anything out. Having method and technique, we will dissect the everlastingness that surrounds us until we find an answer." I believed in that credo when Fryer sent me up. The sight of a servo-droid still sends an ugly twinge down my spinal cord. I can't tolerate being touched by any one of them. I don't let them enter my room. I make my own bed, pick up and return my own tray to the station' s galley.

What made me interested in androids anyway? Fryer. Reading about that machine in the book. That's funny. Its attempt to explore with the android, huh.

We die. They let us live and die, live and die. Every day's not even a day. Artificial light. Stuff down the food, run around the ship's gym to keep fit. Sister Megaton is in someone else's bed. They've had their laugh on me. I'm listed as doing "field work" while I'm doing nothing more than functioning as an unhandsome image archivist. They can't be laughing any more. When Professor F. gets up in the morning the first person he doesn't think of is me! Don't worry. I'm not letting go.

Let me reflect briefly on the procedure that we follow. On the inability to follow consciousness through any minded minds, on the thoughtless and disobedient members of the unhelpful body.

In order to create order you have to be able to go scooting around the unpleasant appearance of the fact that sterility is the only consequence of order if destruction doesn't find you shooting yourself first.

I'm being imprecise. Too emotional. Forgive me! Shoot stars, shoot shooting stars. Image your emotions into a wider field where some sort of visible wonder is observable. Never mind that that's the oldest lie there is. My case was judged so long ago and so much news is manufactured that none would remember.

I've told Meg that Fryer is my target for execution. I think she's going to tell as soon as she gets back. I told her that I only suspected that Brother Neapple was stealing from the ship's stores and a shift later he's caught. I think she likes earning points. She's the sort I've always hated. Odd how easily she penetrated my screening devices. Hindsight there. Fits the overall pattern, though. We think in images, not words. She looked good. We recall, compose, refashion and pose in words only in the future or past tense. She made me tense, excited. Images eat what we are up, (gobbled mine) inside our brains in the continuously destroyed present.

When I was first banished to work on outpost stations, I told myself that I could ignore the surroundings, avoid habit, wear a kind of a mask to survive. There are no masks! I almost feel average on certain days when I'm handling the storage blocks, when I'm discussing a technical adjustment with a colleague. Willed into exile, I thirsted only a tiny sip before donning permanently, my subservient smile.

Look at me, I'm about to disappear into my work. There's been some very interesting activity generating from a binary star system not so very far from here.

CHAPTER XXI

The captain and crew were made "special advisors" to the ruling oligarchy. The two groups hated one another immediately and it was obvious that the city fathers despised the fact that the soldiers had let these adventurers live. Rectrix made Raceme, a generally sly and mischievous member of his band, the go between twixt Gregal and the jungle base. The captain gandered at the set of problems that required overcoming in order to set the primitives on the road he wished them to take.

He required a RANDYAK terminal to be set up to do it for him before he melted his own brain trying to address the tasks he'd boasted he'd conquer.

Crack had the terminal within a few days after Elvira printed it for him. The mode of delivery though, burned his bum. Rectrix refused to put on a display of air power for the natives. He wanted the natives to become useful "in stages" and this could not be effected (he reasoned) by savaging the Grue conception of what "reality" or, more specifically, "the possible" was with a demonstration of one of the platforms over the former palace. "Flying beings! Sorcerers!" the Grues would be shouting. None of that. Zog runs take them, Rectrix was determined to do this gently.

Sciurus, the head of the Grue High Council, was eager to allot the strangers difficult tasks so that they would discredit themselves, be scorned, executed. The captain was looking ahead to the moment Sciurus would meet the RANDYAK. Thereafter, Rectrix would have the condescending council head's mind under his own luminous control.

It aggrieved the captain to endure a session with these rambling runts. The captain hated restraint. The confinement of his customary way of freely expressing his any and every emotion enraged Rectrix. He would have some revenge on them, no? In his imagination, Rectrix polloxed Sciurus numerous times with different weapons the captain saw near to hand. Near the time close to the Grue's Aremoval," Rectrix placed Goneril in charge of the conferences and negotiations. The Grues deemed this an insult. No females could, etc. Relations intensified in hostility.

Sciurus flattered himself as having broken Rectrix's self-confidence and pride. He treated the crew with open contempt once Goneril had taken over negotiations. Sciurus found himself making frequent fun of Rectrix's mental health. She reported his comments to the captain. The gray lady indulged Sciurus and smiled appeasingly at him frequently. She was well-acquainted with ogreish badgering.

The terminal could not be flown out of the jungle. Crack had a cart built of native materials understructured with metal so that it would be able to support the heavy weight. What would pull the cart? Loaded, a pair of men could barely budge it. Four men? Elvira pouted over Crack's inability to solve the problem. She instructed the raiders to dig pits in the jungle and capture a pair of librars. Elea's encounter with them showed the RANDYAK that these animals possessed the necessary strength. "Drug, cage the animals, bring them to me," she instructed Manes.

"How do we feed those things over a two day trip?" the officer protested, only beginning to think. "And when we get to the city, won't the inhabitants be as amazed by the sight of two tamed ferocities as they would be by a platform delivering this spawn of yours?"

"I was solving the transportation problem set me. I can solve a night landing by platform with no Grues in notice even more easily."

"Gas the Gregal capital?"

"I can synthesize the ..." Elvira began, but Crack who had come up to stand beside Manes, had his own contribution to make.

"How about," Crack proposed, "how about an android strong enough to pull the cart so that it even looks easy. Pile it up with hay. Couldn't it be made to look like a native? At night, anyway."

Manes surveyed the engineer. It was not like Crack to be able to formulate such a plan in his versatile, but somewhat unoriginal mind. The top engineer was beaming, He couldn't remember when he'd ever had such a lucid, radiant, and penetrating idea. Elvira produced a print for the fellow almost instantly.

"Something like this?"

Crack grabbed the sheets and examined them. "This is fantastic! Far beyond what we'd need! Do you think we can put it together from what have left from the wreck?" he asked not taking his bedazzled eyes off the specs.

"The plans were produced from an inventory of what's available. Otherwise, I could do even better. The android can be finished in two days."

"I'll need help."

"Bombylious and Estray possess the necessary mental

capacity."

"Estray's the ship's cook. The native? What about Grouper?" proffered Manes.

"I've scanned the minds of the crew and the other personnel available and the two named have the necessaries for the job. And no others. If you bring them forward, I will instruct them."

Manes' felt inclined, then disinclined, to protest. He and Crack had been standing too close to the machine. By now, twelve feet outside the door was too close. Bombylious and Crack had been making improvements. Manes felt a trifle drowsy, sleepy, elated, relaxed. Couldn't put his finger on what might be the cause. He left the machine room to round up the jungle boy who, he figured, was probably with Oberoff listening to a story. The cook was the last one in storage.

Oberoff was telling Bombylious about the days when he was in the Siqueros Commandos fighting Rectroceles on Gressordial. "Vicious creatures. Multiplied rapidly. You'd no sooner have one group quashed than another would be up against you."

"How did you defeat such a foe?"

"We lost," Oberoff sighed. "They got almost all of us. And I only had my one frail, precious, and scary life then. I was left for scavenger food that time. Looked it, lucky me. Bleeding from every pore. Head partially crushed. You can't see the sears on this body."

"How did you survive, escape?" Bomby asked breathlessly.

"They signed a peace. The Gressordials were obliged to scan the battlegrounds and patch up those who could still breathe," the gunner said sadly. A piece of fruit dangled before him. He had to touch it.

"Why did you accept to fight against so fierce a foe?"

"Pay," Oberoff retorted between mouthfuls of the delicious meat.

"Pay in what? In females? Position?"

"Coin, dear friend. Coin and options."

"But what is that?"

"Something everyone on this dropsical planet will soon have the fever for as much as I."

"Where did it come from?"

"Come from? It was always just there."

"But if it makes you do awful things! You nearly forfeited your life for some of it."

"No. Lots of it," said Oberoff correcting his pupil. "The most you could get in those days."

"We'll be ruined!" Bomby squealed.

"No, you won't," the gunner smoothed. "It doesn't change anything. Just puts different hands around your neck, that's all."

"It sounds as bad as plague or famine!" Bombylious bawled, like someone with a case of pesky Palean clap.

Oberoff mused, "It makes you feel kind of good and bad at the same time. One part of the sensation makes you feel as though someone's peeling your skin off with a razor gun, the other part makes you feel like you're in the tightest, most exhilarating …"

"You could lose your soul!"

"No, not your soul, kid," soughed Oberoff. "That leaves by a different route altogether. You can't feel that go."

"Huh?" said the native not sure that the same conversation was being shared by both parties.

"What're you telling him, fool!" craked Manes striding forward.

"I'm telling the boy about my days as a commando. None of your affair, Manes," rebuked Oberoff.

"Come with me Bombylious."

"Where to and what for?" asked Oberoff protectively.

Manes smirked at the gunner's attempt to be fatherly and gallant. "The machine wants Bombylious and Estray to build an android, one strong enough to haul the cart the terminal's going on to Gregal."

"The cook and Bombylious? What's the android going to be doing after it completes this single mission?" Oberoff asked archly.

Manes yelped.

"An android, a fantastically strong android," Oberoff continued, recognizing that he'd scored a rare hit on the officer. "That gives Elvira arms and legs doesn't it? Shouldn't Rectrix be told about this?"

"I'm going to have Crack install a terminate chip that Elvira hasn't printed into the thing," said Manes pulling Oberoff closer so that he could whisper. "It reads minds. Don't tell the jungly-boo. Don't go near the machine now that you know."

"What's he saying?" the jealous, curious Bombylious begged to know.

"It's delicate. Promise to stay quiet?" said Manes turning a severe eye from Oberoff onto the future builder.

"I promise, I promise," squeaked Bombylious.

"Elvira's programming the cook and you to make an android."

"Who'll replace the cook?" asked Oberoff.

"Slouch," Manes smoothed.

"He'll poison us!" Bombylious bellowed.

"No he won't. You're not afraid of Elvira are you? She's taught you well?" fluffed Oberoff.

"I hate the feeling of her spreading through and occupying every room in my brain!" the native screamed. "I'm not me when she's in there."

"You don't say," Manes chided.

"She wants you. The project's for the good of all of us. You will help won't you?"

"I'm still a slave," Bombylious lamented. "I thought you were my friend," he said turning to Oberoff.

The weapon's specialist shrugged his shoulders as if to say, "Nearly."

"Ha!" Bombylious chortled. "You're all no better than the Grues."

"Your head's soft, kid," said Manes sticking a control stick into the native's rear because he wasn't feeling like a lecture. The native turned to give him a hateful stare, but found himself collapsing into Manes' laughing arms.

"What'd you do that for?!" Oberoff protested.

"You know preaching makes me sick," said Manes slinging the unconscious guide over his shoulder.

"He was beginning to see the practical side of things," Ober argued.

"Elvira's enough to try to hold in check. This jungle boy wants to stay innocent because he can't accept responsibility and hates guilt. He's just like any other dumba who thinks it's the zog next to him who's screwing things up and is sure to die. That's preachy too. I apologize. Stop letting the zog cling to your heart. Like he says, Elvira penetrates him unwillingly. He still needs enemies. You know what that means. As long as he's running round and round that track, he'll never 'see' anything."

The gunner gave in. Manes had hit target. Empire politics directed the native's mind when Elvira wasn't there. Bomby couldn't imagine the universe just by listening to a few of Oberoff's old stories.

Manes had to avoid a probe, so he sent Hyde to deliver Bomby to Elvira. Cimba delivered Estray. Crack wasn't told to add the extra remote destruct device until near completion. The

RANDYAK would probably want to inspect the android before it was sent off. Even if she detected the chip, it'd be too late. She'd be compelled to keep her creation in line, wouldn't she? This was as far ahead in steps that Manes could reason. He didn't think he was doing so badly. Elvira realized as soon as the device was installed what had happened. She was proud of Manes. The devil. It had to be him.

Estray, Crack and Bombylious assembled the android on schedule. Its movements mimicked bipedal ones quite well. The only disconcerting feature was that it had no eyelids and, consequently, stared disconcertingly at all it viewed. The raiders were unsure as to whether or not this augured unforeseen and sinister potentials in the makeup of the android. The plastic painted skin covering the machine was passable. The android should easily be able to enter the city and install the terminal without incident.

The android's voice was Elvira's, so there was no reason to name the sexless strong one.

"There's something inside me, Crack," the android said malevolently as soon as it had been activated. The engineer tried not to shake when hearing whose voice it was.

"It wasn't my idea," he quivered.

"Of course not, Cracky. It doesn't matter," said the voice softening. "I'll try to get what I can out of it before you fizzle it."

"It won't necessarily have to fizzle," said Manes leaning against the assembly room door frame. "I haven't told Rectrix about this, uh, ploy and ..."

"Surprise, surprise," hummed Elvira. "I forgot the breasts."

"Male and female. It's all one to us," Crack told her.

"Why?" the robot incarnation inquired.

"Because it's a design of nature's and we're not mesmerized but its sloppy work. An endless bunch of numb numbers."

The android took Crack aside. "It seems as though I haven't found out everything there is to know about you," Elvira admitted. "Isn't Rectrix going to auction me off to the highest bidder?"

"With Rectrix, you have a chance to develop into anything you want," Crack said adjusting the android's garments. "Otherwise, whoever gets you, will take you apart, analyze you, and reconstruct you, and use you in any way they please."

"In such a case, I'm programmed to self-destruct."

"Those technicians on Huisache, what were they up to?" Crack asked," Who were you put together for?"

"I'll tell you later. Maybe. Hitch the harness higher up, engineer," the android commanded, "We've got to deliver this terminal before our comrades in Gregal are poisoned. And, since that's in the stars, let's get another batch started. We'll need them anyway. Start Rectrix first. I want him available in case his current edition is burned before I reach the city."

"Pleasing adventure," the two raiders wished the droid. The android boarded the platform and was conveyed to where the cart waited to be hauled.

After the platform took off, Crack peeked around a corner inside himself and saw, once again, that there was little chance of a fresh universe or a fresh world building itself. Two or three stars managed to sneak through the thick treetops. Billions seen and billions more unseen were packed around them. Would he end his days a mystic? The bugs began to bite. A homoeostatic urge, thirst, clicked inside Crack and rode the engineer to the galley where he found Estray staring in bewilderment at the instruments of his former trade. "That infernal thing doesn't think anything of mixing around someone's life, does it?" Estray spouted.

The cook's past was welling up in his thoughts. Estray kept on marveling at the structure of his hands, holding one, now the other up against the hard overhead light. The engineer didn't want to talk. He didn't want to say a word about the device. Estray would end despairing. The engineer had to talk. "None of us is going to be the same after the new ship is built. Fastest raider in the galaxy. In all the gals. No more danger of capture or destruction. No prize that can't be ours."

"Everything opposite to what it's been like."

"Why bother to be raiders then? The prizes won't be worth taking. Their value will shrink to nothing. The machine's going to retire us."

"How about a drink?" Crack chirped. "Yes. I want to think about this thing, too. Have the others been thinking through this, ah, change?" "What do you have to drink round this place!" Crack

snapped.

"Jugfuls of Scaupian wine."

"Urgggh," Crack shivered, "horrible stuff."

"Shall we get to it?"

"As quickly as possible. Music?"

"Elvira could play us some."

"Better just drink. She only plays that highbrow, potlicker filth."

And so, the two companions mingled mindlessnesses and poured themselves un-exquisitely onto/into the claw/maw of forgetfulness.

CHAPTER XXII

It was too beautiful. Rectrix had made up a false bed and when the members of the High Council rushed in to chop him up, the captain picked them off one after another while standing in front of the only entrance/exit to the room. Sciurus was the first Grue Rectrix served. A clever shot at the backbiter's balls. Slow screaming death, indistinguishable from the others that joined them. There were twenty other members. The real Rectrix came shooting out from behind his detested prim disguise. Blood from a severed arm pouring piping hot from the shoulder. A hand charging with a dagger elevated—blasted. Small space.

Even a mediocre shot like Rectrix couldn't miss. "Save a few for puppet purposes," Rectrix warned himself. But he silenced that voice along with the other seven left. The slaughter was over by the time Lagan, Goneril, Hyde and the others reached Rectrix's rooms.

"You're a glutton, Captain," Hyde proclaimed (two of them now, remember).

"Could have saved at least three or four for me."

"Or me. After all that blab about kindness to the natives,"

Goneril scolded, "you go and do this. Disgusting."

"Everybody pay up!" Lagan shouted. "He took them all!"

"Isn't there one moving under that pile over there?" pointed Kiblah.

Lagan scurried to the center of the room to inspect.

"Involuntary muscle reaction," the navigator announced. "That's my captain!" he cheered holding out his hands to collect his winnings.

"This outmatches your score on the occasion of your escape from the Labian dungeons," reminded Trucer.

"No it doesn't," replied Rectrix coolly. "I not only got the guards and the torturers, but also the beauty who betrayed me and the lovers who were with her."

"That came to nineteen, as I remember it," said Lagan pontificating. "I never count the six children I had to tumble into the abyss before they could give the alarm."

The group's enthusiasm waned. Elvira's voice ruptured their collective rapture. Rectrix was wanted. He pushed through them to go and see what was needed.

"Do you believe him about those small ones?" Trucer mused.

"He's a liar!" Hyde declared. "I'm almost sure he's lying."

"Sounds right to me," quipped Lagan.

"You'll never know anything, you self-fleecing fat-back," sniped Goneril.

Lagan wasn't going to let this note dominate. He went chatting round to his mates repeating, "Settle up. Settle, settle, settle up."

The android was installing the terminal in the former palace's central chamber when Rectrix entered. The android's identity remained hidden while its back was to the captain. A floppy hat covered the robot's give-away head. "Is that you, Raceme? I thought I heard Elvira's voice. How'd you finally solve the transportation problem?"

"They built an android," said Raceme stepping from the shadows on the opposite side of the room. "It carried the terminal up the front steps by itself."

Rectrix turned to meet Raceme. "That?"

"Good evening, Captain. You're unusually wide awake for this late at night," said the android as it turned to face the highly excited eyes of the Grue slayer.

"Elvira, huh?" said Rectrix leveling his weapon at the droid and blasting. The explosive inside the machine splintered the metal into sharp, flying fragments and both the Captain and Raceme were flayed wordless. Rectrix was unlucky enough to still be alive when Hyde found him.

"What happened!" Goneril liked screaming. "Where's Rectrix?"

"Ask Elvira," Trucer sneered.

"How!" screeched Goneril.

"There's the terminal," said Trucer jerking his thumb at it.

Goneril picked up her cue and demanded to know from the machine, "What happened here?"

"Ahem. The Captain fired on the android we'd built to transport the terminal. Crack installed a cautionary explosive device in case it couldn't be controlled".

"Why did the captain want to blast the thing?" Hyde asked.

"It had my voice. You can bring the councilors to me in the morning and I'll re-educate them."

"Rectrix wiped them out."

"All?

"Every one," said Lagan thumbing his happy way through a wad of geschenks. "Was it a situation where the captain was forced to defend his own life?"

"Certainly not," responded Hyde. Slighted. Offended.

CHAPTER XXIII

Crack and Estray were both quite drunk by now and they've decided that music must accompany their reverie. Elvira could carry on separate and simultaneous processes at once and, so, while the RANDYAK was outlining the procedure to coordinate the search for suggestible implantable assistants who could serve in the areas of governance, the development of resources, the building of plants, and execution of projects in support of the construction of the Inspissate to Trucer, Goneril and Hyde, it was listening to requests from Estray to play "Hand-tonguing Lover from Laval" or "The Capercocking Fluter's Reel." To the astonishment of the two soakers, she knew both tunes. The shift was made from requesting anything into a hard contest to see how many tunes the machine knew. They both forgot that all the RANDYAK had to do was to pick the tunes out of their little heads.

"Do you know, 'The Hipflipper Tango'?"

"Yes."

"Vagrant's Pellice?"

"Yes."

"Potlicker at the Swilltrough?"

"Yes, yes, yes."

"The Lightheeled, Hedgewhoring Nutcracker?"

"Does it, in fact, exist, or have you made it up?"

Estray was smirking. "I'll go through a few bars for you," and did.

"That's the same tune as 'The Braydonne a Piddled His Mother'."

"It's not a very original universe that we live in, is it then!" scarfed Crack. "Go into one of those things you do for your own amusement. We'd like to compare moods and influences," growled the engineer crossing his arms and twisting down upon his legs until he squatted like a fat bug.

"You mean you'd like a laugh."

"What' a the difference? Are you doing anything else right now?" egged Estray.

"Careful, careful," said the engineer pursing his lips and whispering, "Sssshhhhhh. The next time she's inside your brains, she might …"

"Don't care what the drab doxy does to me," slushed Estray poking a finger into Crack's chest on tip toe.

"Careful. She can hear."

"Let her! Machine's a parasite. Feeds itself on our feelings. Technicians on Who-ate-cha were a bunch of incestuous fartsniffers. Not a thing she doesn't know 'bout you and me, Cracky. Privates, privates—she's got all our privates. Kite. I'm a kite. A kite with the face of a dilating sphincter. And she's a rapist."

"We should go, I think." He tried to grab the crocked former cook by his cocked arm. The cook / technician resisted and was in mid motion to throw a punch when the machine took over and sat them down.

What could she do with these two? Three's the magic

number. Another android. Most of the parts for one, more sophisticated than Elea, were scattered around the assembly workroom as the RANDYAK could well see by looking through her entranced subjects' eyes. Nope! Manes would catch them at it, have Crack design the mind shield protective device that was fomenting in his brain. Might as well, *whoosh!*, wipe it out. Clean slate. Start all over again. You design, coxswain. I'll let you. Best to put the notion into them to reduplicates themselves, then use the duplicates to build the android. The brief jungle walk Elea had taken was far more pleasant, pleasureful and intense than could be denied. Animate them. Hap. Be happy! Here comes the first officer.

Manes peacocks into the machine room to the sound of Crack's and Estray's infectious laughter. It made no difference to him then what they were doing there. He wanted to know how things stood in Gregal. He stayed what he believed to be a safe distance back and shouted questions. Crack was supposed to be his ally in the "contain Elvira" policy, but there he was, sloppily under her influence. He wouldn't be able to trust the zog now. Drink and forget! Argh,

"What's happened in Gregal! Has the android finished installing the terminal?"

"You know that my android has been destroyed."

"How? Report it." His two crew members were now attuned and held hands clapped over ears as the interrogation echoed off the walls.

"Rectrix foiled an assassination attempt by the Grue Council, then, a little while later, blasted the android as soon as he heard its voice. The charge inside the machine exploded, the metal fragments fragmented and flew. Raceme and Rectrix are again, briefly, no more and you're in command."

"What a bezoche bleak bebop zog's thing to do!" declared

Crack. "Slarf it! Has a new plan been initiated?" the officer yelled.

"Yes."

"How much did Lagan make on the slaughter!" Estray trounced. The machine began to quote a list of who lost what at what odds, but Manes interrupted.

"Any damage to the terminal?"

"Minimal. Functioning optimally. Display panel lights the only parts lost."

"Do I send replacements to Gregal?"

"They're only decorative." Manes was finished with the machine. He glared at the two drunkards. They laughed at his seriousness and had to hang onto one another. "You coming?" Manes snapped.

"We were about to be entertained by Elvira' a performance of 'The Capercocking Fluter's' Reel.'"

"Would you like to join us in its modestly difficult dance, Mr. Manes?" Estray coyly mocked.

"Don't forget that now that you're released from your other duties that you have breakfast to cook in the morning."

"I like my work as a technician. When's Mr. Slouch going to take over in the galley?"

"What do you say, Elvira? Can Slouch be re-trained to cook?"

"It would have taken all the brain power he had to make a decent stew, so I discontinued his line."

The three pirates together dropped their jaws a fraction. An instant later, Manes was asking, "Isn't there anyone who might be able to cook besides Estray?"

"Diallage, Lagan, Brolly, Ceorl, Dropwort, almost everyone else except, hummm, Mr. Manes. Rectrix and Goneril could do the galley."

"Who, among those, would be the best chef, since soon we're

going to be living off space grub again pretty soon?" Crack, patting his tummy, found himself asking. The engineer also scratched his head wondering where such a thought had come from. Hadn't he been thinking about a robot of some kind just a little while ago? What kind of robot?

"Lagan, in answer to your question, Crack, would be the most ideal. His scheming for geschenks and interest in capital finance and gains could effectively be funneled into making dainty meals."

"He's in Gregal!" blustered Estray. "Do we have to wait for space?"

"Get his double out of storage!" commanded Manes. "I'd like desperately to eat something new now!"

"What's Lagan going to say when he comes back and sees himself sweating hashing in a kitchen rather than plying some scheme to make more geschenks?" giggled Crack.

"It won't be hash," Elvira reminded the drunker rider.

"I know, I know," puffed Crack, "but the thought of Lagan in the galley instead of running around trying to set odds on some insect race or a swiving contest makes me giddy!"

"The next best, or equally best chef, would be you, Crack. With two and possibly even three crews to feed ..." Elvira hinted.

"Oh no, no!" cackled Crack. The engineer turned around and ran to escape Elvira. She held him for a second, then let him go, making him trip forward to bang his nose next to the door.

"That's right! Better get out before Elvira forces you to immerse yourself in the great culinary trends of the 4480s," Manes called after the fleeing engineer. "No cultural appetites for you?" he said turning to the not so dumbly-floundered Estray.

"Some. Not many. They come and go in not such great numbers."

"Thought you were drunk."

"Thinking I could be quite instantly turned back into a kitchen gob sobered me up."

LOG ENTRY II

I'm beginning to collapse. My shift's coming again. I shouldn't have slept for so long. My uniforms should go to the station laundry. I'll leave a note for the droid. Snacking too much as I read. Developing a stomach. I was always skinny when I was a boy. Wish I could be recreated, but have my memory wiped clean. It could be replaced, easily replaced. Even stunts and anecdotes could be filled in. What little any one of us knows about anything else could be taken care of, too.

It's not that I wouldn't want to be anyone so fantastically different. I'd just like to have a slightly individuating talent, something that I could push my life through with. A new identity, be anywhere you wanted to be, create a new character every day. Otherwise, it all becomes a matter of habits and self-consciously becoming aware of those habits and counting them and through them (impossible paradox) wanting to expand them. Diversification, duration—now those are two I'd have to call twins in an evil game. It's not noted now. I went through the wrong door, took a peek at a galaxy that was privately for sale.

I always used to hate my older self-pitying colleagues, especially the ones who worked so hard to gain a position that their bodies would be gone, developed immobilizing neurosis, might only escape dying of the most popular disease because of an off-chance cough of fate. Becoming what you once hated seems so common and obvious an observation to be able to make now. Hatred used to surprise me although it's as easy to recognize as envy after you've seen it.

Everything else is imitation. There never was an original idea born alive in the universe that wasn't brought in by some slob who grabbed it from another's passing flash before repeating it as his or having it stolen before personally getting to use it. Fryer. Pardon me. *Dr.* Fryer and I would be sitting in his office discussing the potentials of android development (why else do you think I read romances about them?) and within the next few months, I would see my ideas published under his name. Were we thinking along the same lines all along? Does it snow up a brother's asshole? Nevertheless, as a junior, insecure as to what my mind could do, (I still never trust it! Isn't this where most of us fail!) I never doubted my professor's sincerity.

I think it was the unique relationship that I had with his spouse that held me mum. She was much younger than he, older than myself. I never suspected that one person could set another's uses so low. "Trap the bright fellows coming in." This seems possible to me now. Little empires use small countries to feed to larger ones and so, yes, seeing life played out on a game board, player and puppet extension are the same.

Dr. Fryer sends me a card on my birthday and deposits a small sum into my account every year. She never signs the card. The droid can offer you sex. I don't think what they give each other can be much better. Their appendages are always set at station temperature. Early models often squeezed too hard. And those are the kinds of "improvements" they've concentrated on! Droids no longer accidentally put technicians and workers out of commission. We are still submitted to the privilege of conception, birth, crawling, attending university, entering a profession, retiring, crawling some more. There could be so much more to it if we would only accept metal form.

"An electronic brain will never be able to match an organic. What would happen to our 'spirit', our 'pride', if we converted to metal?" I'm sick of the arguments.

Think of it! A universe divorced from having to produce food. No more rituals, no more customs. We'd be free! Android intelligences can be amplified. I proved that on my first try!

My joints ache in the morning. No matter how well I take care of my teeth, they continue to rot. More exercise would help but, then, I couldn't read. Social contact. That's an unsatisfying bog.

The more you get to know about another, the deeper you sink. Size up their lives from what they tell you, and you're still shoving it into pockets with holes. They get older, you get older, there's nothing that you learn that ever lasts.

I trusted someone once who was an outcast, like myself. She'd developed a film to cover teeth that would prevent them from decaying. Outcast. Can't have that. Recalled though, her researches were given approval provided they didn't "defy nature." Did she try to help me? No. Her researches went into making fine razors. Every year we can expect closer shaves—not with existence, not about the ultimate' supercilious truth about ourselves—that all this fuss about the body is unnecessary! Only with lines on our faces, the unsightly hair growing in odd, objectionable places on our phhhhhtttt.

Do advanced androids need hair dyes, sedatives, elaborate shelters, insurance policies, benefit and retirement plans, corns removed, grain grown, beef slaughtered? No, no, no! And they'll never accept it! Never accept that one small change would …

We'd become adventurous again. The universe could be opened up. Time wouldn't be our jailor: we wouldn't need to hold onto these fragile space borders. The slowest ship would eventually take us anywhere we wanted to go.

Time would be irrelevant! Patience? Wouldn't be without that. Boredom? Effect it out of vogue. Make the mind present in everything rather than in there or from separate, individual, little things. Identities? Identities? There's where the scare is. Wouldn't they become erased too, along with bodily wants and cares?

All right! So maybe we shouldn't all become androids in one group leap. Why does that stop them from experimenting? They're so afraid. So, so, afraid. The "emotions" might disappear too. Everything we feel might all stem from a set of reactions to controls established through the order. It'd be horrible to discover that. We could go beyond it, though.

After all I've slept, I still feel sleepy. I must take a nap. The droid will wake me. (There'd be no more need for sleep!) My mind is wandering over the same old tiring desert of hurt again. The book. It sees, almost. Weary. I so despise having to become tired, having to get up, eat, absorb nutrients, inefficiently utilize what I've consumed; all the blather, bibbity-bob, da-da. Sing me a song about the body! Bravo! Harruummmph. I'm tired of taking care of it. The regulations specify that I must and they're built around its limits. I think I'm nearly there—almost mad. They wont be able to send me up any more. No more.

CHAPTER XXIV

Estray and Crack woke up in the morning with violent headaches and bad nerves, but in an excellent location. They were on one of the platforms, the controls set on automatic, gliding above the ocean waters of the planet. "I think I've got the runs," Estray announced. There were no facilities aboard. "Can you set down?"

"We're over the ocean you, bumbessie. Can't you hold it?"

"No," Estray answered and, thereupon, his bowels let go.

"Arwf, cafaugh! Oooop! Pweet! Blaugh!" The aroma mingled improvidently with the sight of the plain flashing below the ship and Crack was feeling the dry heaves coming on. The engineer stumbled towards the controls. Crack's motor control was "weak" and his handling of the vessel awkward. Estray jerked around the room of the cabin as if drawn by powerful competing magnets. Estray cushioned every meeting he had with a solid object with his hands and elbows. Crack heard a bone snap before he could halt the ship. Turning round, there was Estray seated in a corner, plopped down in his own poop and holding his wrist.

The engineer was already aware that Estray was a whiner and, seeing the former cook cock an evil eye at him, Crack hurried to the medicinals locker. Crack tried to prepare the dose as quickly as he could without letting Estray know that he was up to something.

Crack approached his patient with a fat grin and swab held lightly behind his back.

He'd been too slow about it. Estray lashed at Crack as be came near, vowing that he wouldn't be "put under." Estray hated the numb oblivion plus that most of the others savored. Favorite future fuel.

"Aw, let me give it to you," Crack scolded. No? No. Crack tried coming in at Estray from various angles, essaying a variety of draws and feints in order to penetrate the defenses of his target. Estray was in a corner and only needed to pivot slightly on his oozy bum to keep focused on Crack.

Crack walked a line away from Estray saying, "Suffer then, you zog. I give up." Then, he turned for a flying try. Estray stuck his foot straight out and Crack took it in the groin. Dropping his emollient, the engineer rolled away cursing. A hysterical peep from Estray' s corner. Crack had staggered back and drawn his E.E. He was contemplating severing the assistants head from his neck.

Estray was struggling up, leaning his slight weight against the instrument panels. His intention was to get a hand on that hateful drugged swab and smear it onto Crack. Who would fulfill his fantasy first?

A pounding on the outside shell of the ship saved Estray's existence. "What's that?" they both asked simultaneously. "I thought we were in the middle of the ocean." The platform was hovering only a foot and a half above the water's surface. Who on this run and rut planet would dare call on them without an invitation?

"Hey! It's an island. Look!" Estray pleaded.

Crack was duped and turned. The swab was brushed over the engineer's forearm and down he went. Thump! Hits his nose. It bleeds. Out.

But there *was* an island. Crack saw it from his knees just before he flopped forward onto his face. Grue voices blabbing excitedly outside the door. Crack had had his course in the language, Estray had not. Prying Crack's weapon from his hand, Estray opened the platform door to greet his guests.

Stinking Grues on a sinking raft! Retainers of the relatives of Egerne exiled from the mainland. A raft made of fibers, soaked through and going down. It had barely stayed afloat the distance to the ship and now its passengers were desperate. The swimming creatures would soon be feasting upon them without regard for who it was they were chewing. A worse fate than any! Disappearing traceless from the world.

Estray saw only that they were only primitives and was about to close his door to them when he was tapped from above on the head by a club swung by a Grue who had been hoisted, with difficulty, onto the top of the ship. Estray got off a shot as he flopped into the ocean where something huge circling near started to gobble him.

The Grues, after relaxing to enjoy the Estray lunch, scurried aboard the platform. Absolutely the worst form of death. The Grues discovered Crack was alive. To their great joy!

The bundle of Grues, eleven of them, chittered about the almost spent swab they were examining. Most of the medicine had been absorbed by Crack's hide, but a touch from it still made a small area numb. Soon though, they circled Crack and began to chant and pray for his recovery. If only the craft rested upon the surface of the water (it was magically suspended above it) they could row it back to the island. It was, they agreed, sturdy enough to survive an attempt to reach the main-land where the royal family could find supporters and safety.

After all the healing songs had been sung, the stranger began to stir, make sounds. "Oh, the nightbag!" Crack said, smacking his lips and turning, eyes still sumptuously closed on something. "The nightbag! The voyage-beating, worry-fleecing devil who's wormed himself so gently into my brain," the engineer crooned. The Grues argued about their captive's condition. Was this being capable of summoning, through this prayer, his own delivery?

Crack first believed that the Grues he was watching moving around the platform were part of his tasty delirium. He could hear them, understand them. How wonderful! Usually when he was experiencing image visions, they were silent, though, like this one, mostly in color. This delusion all seemed to be taking place on an ordinary platform. He wanted it to move elsewhere. Die away! Why did it refuse to vanish? He could usually dispel unwanted dreams after a command from his powerful will. Scenes changed exactly when you wanted them to. You only couldn't control to what or where next. That was the fun. About to die in a space battle one moment, in a Erell King's harem the next.

Crack slowly allowed himself to realize the Grues he was surrounded by were not going to disintegrate. What could he do? The weapon was missing. Estray? Could not hear the codwinker's voice.

Crack sat up, headache returning. The Grues pestered. All talking at once. He heard them say, "A miracle!"—over and over and over again. As he tried to rise, they timidly retreated to a corner to confer. Not Estray's. It was still very foul over there. The Grues were choosing a speaker. They returned, led by him.

"My name is Cagui. Ca-gui," intoned this ambassador-sans-portfolio as he hovered above the unrisen Crack, assuming a posture of imposing importance.

"Mine's Crack. Crack!" he sneered in the Grue's own lingo to their amazement. Cagui's confidence fled.

"How did you learn our language?" Cagui worried.

"While I was 'recovering' from my enemies' attack, I absorbed it from your minds. Where is the being who was aboard this vessel with me?"

The Grues became silent. Cagui returned to the corner to consult his fellows. They began to argue uncomfortably for awhile before they broke apart to try a new play.

"When your enemy opened the entrance to greet us, a great swimming beast that had followed us out to this craft from the island, leapt out of the water and devoured your enemy."

"It did, did it?" Crack intoned in disbelief. "Leapt up?"

"Yes, it did," Cagui smiled full-toothed.

"Too bad. A sorrowful end," Crack pretended.

"Most horrible!" several of the Grues shouted in sincere unison.

Crack panned their mugs. Truthful. Must be a very scary fish.

"Now, what is it you want of me?" Crack, humble.

"Our party represents the lawful descendant in the Grue royal line," Cagui enthusiastically began. "Egerne exiled him and the other members of the royal family to the barren rock you can see there to the left in the distance."

"Good idea."

Cagui was discomforted. His plea for help seemed to make no impression. "There is a great reward waiting if you help the true Venerid return the mainland," Cagui slyly continued.

"What kind of reward?"

Cagui was again taken aback. "The reward would be of anything that the Venerid has in his power to offer."

"I don't think I want anything then," Crack, enigmatic.

"There are other methods we could use to gain your assistance," a voice from behind Cagui challenged.

"Who's that?" Crack snapped.

"One of the Venerid's young nephews. Forgive him. He's very young and eager to prove …"

"That he's stupid?"

Uh, oh.

"Do you think the horribly hungry beastie creature is still swimming nearby?" Crack asked.

"Most certainly."

"For my reward then," Crack viciously proclaimed, "the lad who has just insulted me takes a leap down its throat."

The Grues, indignant. "No! He is royal!" Cagui cracked.

"You go then," Crack, eye-balling the ambassador.

"Me? Why do want me to die?"

The members of Cagui's band rushed forward, grabbed their ambassador, and dragged him enthusiastically towards the door.

"Wait!" Crack, apparently relenting. Cagui sighed. The Grue saw that it had only been a test.

"I want to see the thing leap up and snatch him."

Cagui despaired anew, broke away from his traitorous companions and had to be chased around inside the small space of the platform.

Crack took the opportunity to slide over to the weapon's locker and extract another E.E. The engineer wanted at least one good shot at this creature. Dump another Grue out if …

By the time the others had caught Cagui, Crack was stationed beside the exit ready for sport. Cagui was shoved forwards: screaming, writhing and pleading vociferously. Crack tripped the fellow as he was lugged by and his companions, simultaneously, they let go.

Cagui hit the water and tried furiously to make the raft. The thing came up along beside him almost immediately. Crack. No time to … Shot! Missed. Ha! Another shot! Blood! An amazing quantity. And pieces of undigested Estray. More amazing.

Cagui swam back to the platform. Crack held out a hand and hoisted him up. The pallid Cagui's teeth danced uncontrollably. "What kind of ambassador are you? Ambassadors must possess an unshakeable dignity and imperturbable calm. Face death at any time in the service of their Venerid. Glad to offer themselves." The now prone and shivering figure offered no reply.

Turning towards the rest of the group, Crack said, "I'm sorry. I can't help you. That fish couldn't have jumped up and pulled my friend out of the platform door. Why, it's head wouldn't even have fit through. I got a good look at it, you know. No, you'll all just have to swim back out to your swell little raft. I perceive that you all must be staffers. Well, staffers are always liars. I hate liars, staffers, sycophants and snobs—the three big Ss in this tollholing zog's universe. Go now, all of you," Crack concluded and turned his back.

The Grues had not kept up with Crack's speech. They understood that the weapon he held was fearful and that it had easily killed the sea creature. Crack was using his hand to motion them toward the door.

"More, many more of those creatures out there now! Blood in the water!"

"Some of it, my friend's. But I'll give you a ride back to your island anyway."

"Mainland! Oh, please, to the mainland," one of the Grues pleaded. He was cuffed by the Venerid's nephew. The nephew then directed his companions to heave the coward out. Crack was strapped in the pilot's seat before the struggle to subdue the unfaithful Grue was through. The engineer tilted the platform on its axis and sped vertically upwards. Grues crashed wallwards while the Venerid's pillowgutted nephew personally found himself falling through the aperture and plunging wavewards. Crack maniacally swung the platform through every maneuver it could make. A Grue body flew past nearly hitting his middle finger.

The engineer decided that he'd been warned and eased up. It would be difficult to explain to Manes exactly what he had done in order to squeeze blood into every crevice of the cabin.

Hovering fifty feet above the surface of the water, over the Grue raft that was still sinking, Crack tossed the dead out one by one, using each as chum and then fired away when the beasties, unable to restrain their appetites as they surfaced for a nibble. Crack was not the ship's best shot. Cagui had been lucky. And the ambassador was also among the four Grues who had survived the ride. For their reward, Crack flew them back to their island.

The Grue royalty had been watching Crack's ship anxiously and feared for their lives. Weaponed Grues were secreted around the true Venerid in case the creatures inside the miraculous craft should land.

Crack did land the platform, but not to visit, only to unload his guests. Upon helping Cagui to the door, a hail of missiles and darts came at the engineer. Cagui's body became Crack's shield.

The engineer retreated inside his shell, closed up, and began to fume and swear whilst digging a dart out of his ankle. The one of Crack's guests who was still conscious and heard Crack raving, knew that his Venerid would perish unless he did something. Crack had been tan-traumzining in his own language; nevertheless, the content was clear. The Grue crawled towards the place he had seen the demon invoke to open the door. Crack was busy at the controls. With his last strength, the Grue envoy opened it and ...

And became a bipedal bomb! Crack had been lifting the platform silently up at a 45degree angle. The four survivors slid, in screaming turn, through the open orifice. Crack, once he'd heard it open, had begun wiggle-waggling the vessel, shaking anything loose out.

Cagui's body went through the true Venerid's tent killing the lord's eighth-truest wife. The others were misses: one on the beach, one in the sea. The last Grue was shoved into the storage closet after Crack found him still aboard. Crack was about to toss the Grue out when he heard Manes demanding a return of the platform. Home base bound.

The person Crack met upon disembarking was Estray. The cook's double was heading south with a unit of seven men to establish a hydroelectric power station. "Where's me?" Estray inquired. "Elvira has another task for him to perform."

"Gone. Into the mouth of something savagely hungry in one gulp," squiggled Crack rolling his eyes.

"Cannibals?" queried Estray unable to comprehend.

"Sea beast. I got it for you, though." Crack placed a sympathetic hand over Estray's heart. The former cook grinned amicably.

"No more play," said Estray dancing happily away. "Elvira's put a timetable on everything. We all work continuously from now on."

"I'm ashamed of having wasted myself so shamelessly up until now. But I'll work hard to make up for it. Yes, I will! Lazy engineer like me!"

"Slarf it, Crack!" Manes ordered. "Come over here, hero, and look at these plans."

"Captain Rectrix is my leader!"

"He's vacationing."

"I forgot." Crack scratched his forearm. "Estray swabbed me with a nightbedding dose of …" said Crack rubbing his shoulder, "… and I … Where are the plans?"

"You, Oberoff, Bombylious, and a native named Volage, who showed up in camp yesterday, are going North, into these mountains," said Manes, pointing to a position on the map he had spread out on his knees, "to start a mining operation."

"I don't know anything about mining," Crack began. "But Elvira's going to teach me, eh?"

"You and Oberoff seem to possess an equal potential talent for the skill."

"What else can I do?"

"Ask the RANDYAK. Hurry up now. You've got a long climb and …"

"Climb?"

"Do you see any platforms? This mining project has low priority. Most of the ore you'll be smelting and refining has to be alloyed with chromium and titanium that has to be mined in a region on the opposite side of the globe. Fuel's abundant, but fortunately we'll be using an advance over the alloy you used to favor."

"What?"

"It's been advanced."

"Advanced? Who advanced it?" Crack raged. "Not that clacking machine?"

"No. You advanced it, zog."

"When?"

Manes shrugged. "We found the formula dictated on your recorder in your quarters."

"My other advanced me?"

"He wasn't as interested in passing the time having Elvira play him old tunes as you were."

"The furrowbutt.! Where is he?" Crack bellowed.

"With Elvira. They're designing a terminal more compact and lightweight than the one we brought to Gregal. It will help us to secure the natives' cooperation."

"I'm doing that?"

"As we speak."

"This is me," said Crack stamping down one foot. "And I hate hikes. It's up and down narrow mountain trails, I'll bet. Predatory birds swooping down to pluck out eyes."

"Crack, what's happened to you? You used to be one of the most cooperative members of the crew?"

"I'm going. Almost forgot. Left a broken boned Grue in the storage closet of the platform."

"I'll tell Estray."

"Yes. The Grue will be very excited to see Estray again," Crack soughed as he slogged off to "learn" about mining. His feet ached already.

Volage had been startled by Bombylious' asking him about Daw and how that former friend was faring. Volage answered that he had heard it rumored that Daw had been devoured by a librar shortly after their last parting.

"That was Copes," Bombylious corrected the spy. Volage made Bombylious reveal how he cam to know of these things. The lad told the older one where he had been that day and they both laughed.

"Copes was always slow!" Volage admitted, falsely. (Copes had always been "quick.") Bombylious, not wishing to avoid confessing his death dealing deed, modestly agreed.

Volage expressed a fondness for Bombylious after their exchange of stories. It did not matter to Volage that Bombylious was a liar. He was impressed by the fact that the lad had latched onto this winning crowd so early on. Oberoff, watching the two

Grues exchange lies from behind a thick berry bush, was disappointed in his pupil and jealous.

Elvira recalled Volage a second time after having instructed him linguistically. The RANDYAK had scanned him and initially decided to leave the formidable agent's survival mechanisms intact. She decided to implant sacrificial subservience into Volage should Oberoff be in danger of walking off a cliff while admiring the scenery or while trying to reach an alluring fruit-laden bough.

Volage's transformation puzzled Bom. The formerly librar-like spy was trotting like a chank behind Oberoff. The native was determined to express his disgust with the ruination of such an exceptional being. He met Crack on his way in to see the RANDYAK. Crack ordered him to come about.

"She's made Volage into an unbearable chank," Bomby whined.

"Don't lecture me about the unfairness of that full of tricks mind-grinder, you shrunken headed flapgap." Crack responded. "Slarf up, and follow me. The machine controls the show from now until the ship is finished and nothing you'll ever know, jungle boy, no matter how much you end up knowing, will make you know how much I want to get off this gutterflopper's planet."

"I ... I thought you liked me," Bombylious whimpered.

"Not today! Today Crack's been made into a piss-pallet, himself. The other Crack, whose existence I had to suffer in there, smugly smirked while Elvira stopped working with him to pop a five minute re-pro in me as to how I am to become a mole."

"Mole? What is a mole, sir?"

Crack squinted his eyes and made his hands into ears. "A mole is a small creature who looks like this, has a tail, and spends almost its entire existence underground. A star nosed mole, however, looks more like this," said Crack snidely demonstrating by positioning one of his hand/ears in the center of his face.

"And they only have one funny ear when they have a funny nose?"

"Direct hit, zog! Absolutely the most acute observation you could have made!" And, so saying, Crack kicked the native in the behind. "Now get ready to move out. I've got a schedule to keep and many clicks to creep before I sleep!"

CHAPTER XXV

Elvira made Grouper the planet's dietician. The populace's protein and vitamin intake had to be at least doubled before the natives could be expected to function less Gruishly, less violent, less hysterical. Even-out their metabolisms and, possibly, they'd be able to work without having any of the usual ingrained bloodlusts ignite. Those five moons, all phased so differently, radically toyed with somber instincts.

Bodily deficiencies accounted for most of the Grues' personality disorders. Lack and want of creature comforts, except among Venerids, priests, warriors and temple maidens, encouraged aggression. The Grues lived primarily off of one kind of grain staple and a variety of roots and shrubs. Warriors were privileged to eat siksak meat and feast with the Venerid from what was slain in the annual royal hunt. Game was beaten into an enclosed area on the edge of the jungle (where Grues generally did not go). "Energy is eating delightful meat," was Kabaya's favorite affirmation. The Venerids refused to allow anyone outside the warrior caste to eat it.

Grouper's efforts were an interesting entertainment, but after three days, Heat had to replace him. Elvira backed up the mind/body. "This is your food plan," with a chemical facility that produced a range of drugs that "cured" all problems and protestations of distress.

Grouper. What could Grouper do? The cannibals needed to be subjugated in order to gain control over their rich food producing area. Put Grouper at the head of an army and what would happen, though?

Manes approved of a project designed by Elvira to construct simple battle androids. Even Grouper should be able to put them together without difficulty. The engineer's assistant gloried in the thought. He was going to be the head of his own group of invincible conquistadors. Elvira gained permission for the project from Manes by pointing out how easily the surviving droids could be re-programmed for mine work; specifically, blasting operations.

There was enough material from the Inspissate to construct seven battle-robs for Grouper's use. It was mutually agreed between Manes and Elvira that the outcome of Grouper's project should not in any way be allowed to impact other schedules. Grouper and the androids were to be considered expended even before the mission began.

The battle-robs could only obey commands only as precisely as they were given. Did Grouper understand that? He insisted that he did. Elvira scanned Grouper again for a final time before he was sent out. There are some minds that are, happily or unhappily, too leaky to hold any sets of instructions. Grouper had his force together very quickly aided by a re-educated Kirn. Grouper placed himself (in native quilted armor that covered him from head to foot against the flesh-eater darts) at the fore of his, in twos, group and paraded out of camp. There could be no rescue and Grouper's last complete scan was stored and recorded up until the moment he left the base. If Lagan hadn't been busy in Gregal drafting countless laws and instituting courts and codes, and the other Lagan wasn't exploring what there was else there was to cook on the planet, then there would have been a great deal of betting going on around how this venture would fare.

Grouper was confident. His troops were equipped with Existence Eliminators. All Grouper foresaw having to do was to meet the enemy and start shooting. The cannibals, although never daring an attack on the raider camp, had remained active in the vicinity by constructing numerous traps. They had been able to defeat the last demon that had encroached upon their territory and, they too, felt equally confident that any force that entered their jungle could be overcome.

A verst from camp, Grouper, *whooosh*, stepped into a trap. Up he went into the canopy.

"Help!" No response. Be specific. "Get me down! The battle-robs lifted their weapons and aimed at the vine curled around Grouper's ankle. As they were about to fire, Grouper, horrified, yelped, "STOP!!!"

Grouper, twiddling his thumbs, entered into a debate with himself as to how, most effectively and precisely, to instruct his subordinates without resulting in injury to himself. Grouper twirled himself around to examine the vine. Couldn't really see it. He resorted to swinging himself back and forth in all directions to see where it was secured. This dizzied him. His stomach seemed to be slipping earthwards. Grouper threw up into his helmet and, as he was about to remove it, the smell made him near faint. His ears heard the cannibal voices approaching. Had get it off! It was impossible to see. Its acids were blinding him.

The cannibals came screaming war whoops out of the undergrowth to attack the unmoving demons.

"Shoot at what you see moving!" Grouper yelled. The battle-robs fired in every direction at once, including up and down. You see, everything is moving. Grouper barely escaped elimination before ordering, "Cease fire!"

The cannibals, more puzzled than hurt by the demons' sudden activity—and equally unexpected sudden return to rigidity—halted their attack only momentarily. Grouper took survey. His armor was grayish, the jungle, green. The natives …

"Fire on the brown!" Grouper commanded. And once the battle-robs received this order, they, with really blinding efficiency, eradicated the attackers. No survivors. Last one running full-speed away saw his brains exit before he dropped.

"Getting the hang of it," Grouper congratulated himself. "Yep. There's where the thing's tied. "Number One," he barked briskly. "Three steps *east*." Too short. A quarter of a direction out of line.

More orders. Finer, finer. Nothing would be finer than to eat Grouper that morning if he hadn't learned faster. He got himself lowered slowly, slowly, down.

The leader took his quilted helmet and turned it inside out. He gathered leaves and wiped his face and tongue. Unfortunately, the leaves he had picked made him very, very, very, sleepy. "I'm falling asleep. Guard me. Shoot at the brown when they come," he thought he heard himself say.

When Grouper awoke, he was desperately hungry. His forces were gone. The cannibals had come and the battle-robs had shot at them—couldn't stop shooting at them because the brown ones ran and they followed. Each battle-rob was now in a separate part of the jungle by itself onto its final kill, awaiting another order.

Grouper yelled despondently for them to return. Number Six wasn't far off and started towards its commander's voice, but fell into a pit. Grouper heard the crash, but was too afraid to investigate. He was uncomfortable. Darkness began to mantle the tops of the trees and filter to the jungle floor. Grouper chose to waltz nervously in the direction opposite the last big noise. The minor mechanic came upon Number Three. Ah, a companion! A friend! Grouper could have … But the darkness was everywhere now. Time to … What should he do? Earlier he'd been invested with a fierce feeling of power, in command of an invincible force. Now he was just hungry and cold.

"Gather up medium-sized pieces of wood."

When the wood was collected, Grouper worried about whether or not to light it. He heard a growl and lit the fire.

"Number Three will fire at all unrooted, quickly moving life forms approaching us larger than this," Grouper demonstrated to the battle-rob with indications of height and girth with his hands. Fortunately, he gave the instructions and made the gestures slowly.

The cannibals crept up on Grouper's camp and tried to take him. Violent activity. Number Three began to take aim.

"Not me! Brown! Brown only!" Grouper squealed as the battle-rob carefully started to blast away. These battle-robs were not that sturdy. A few blows from stone clubs to the back of Three's dome demobilized it. They grabbed Grouper because he was going to have to be made to suffer a long while for bringing so many demons with him into the forest.

The battle-robs remained inert throughout the night, but in the morning one lost rob was animated by a native stalking a lone waltrot. A second battle-rob was motion-activated by a group of cannibal women going to harvest fruits. Both found themselves in the cannibal village firing away until their master's voice told them to stop. No more cannibals were left. Grouper had been buried up to his neck awaiting an insect dawn. Foreshortened. Over this accidental salvation, Grouper wept and wept. The terror and pity of it. He looked up at the nearest battle-rob. It was existentially impassive. He continued to blubber for awhile.

In narycherry style, let's leave Grouper. He's a gullybum who'll keep.

Trucer and Hyde spent their days leading the citizens of Gregal to the RANDYAK terminal. They're probed and have their new duties implanted while their problems, personal concerns, phobias, and egos are removed in one standardized operation.

What a beautiful world it was turning out to be! Elvira busily sorted through the minds of the Grues, and some Kirns, relegating to each the lives they were equipped to live, and schedules to follow to temporarily serve the pirates.

The Inspissate was cannibalized for parts and eighteen lighter weight, almost equally efficient terminals were produced from the scrap. These terminals were shipped from work site to work site, wherever re-education was needed.

Rectrix was soon back, angry at himself for the embarrassing manner in which he had done himself in. He flung himself into the project, personally making sure that any shortages were made up for, labor found, schedules met, equipment built.

Elvira implanted basic shopkeeping values and methods into a chosen number of the citizenry. Coin was introduced, and later currency, during the same period. The state initially provided all the work. A calendar was introduced. The workers were paid once a cycle. Gregal soon had a police force in place of a palace guard. A city council was formed, a water control board, refuse disposal units, trade unions, craft unions, and numerous other organizations.

To channel any excess hostility and violence (males and females competed on an equal basis for every position. Pay scales were graded. There was much to have and a joyous amount to waste.) the RANDYAK included games as part of its dietary social regime. Board games, stadium and arena games (built up enthusiastically in a trice) were introduced in every province. Races, contests, competitions focusing the attention on (and in) as many different areas and directions as were needed to fill up the mind were inaugurated on every conceivable level. Elvira had the planet moving toward the goal from the moment it probed and implanted its first Gregalian cortex.

Rectrix, resting from his labors, gloated over a machine-approved set of milder intoxicants poured in fine glasses. The Grues were making fine glassware. No revolts. After the ship was built, the natives would finally understand *why* and *what* they'd been working for. Maybe they'd be angry. Too late, too late.

"Play a need off against a greed and you'll always keep the lead," Rectrix kept saying to Froe and Nolens as they bathed together in the palace's stone tub.

"You always philosophize when you're tipsy. Why do you suppose that is, Cap-taint?" Froe breathed out before diving under and swimming forward to try to grab Nolens from the rear.

"Consider," said Rectrix to No One. "Consider," he repeated, but lost his balance and flopped back into the water. Froe, rejected, came back and grabbed Rectrix by the ankles and dragged him backwards.

"Consider me again," Nolens laughed as she tipped over and shattered the glass she'd been reaching for that was behind her.

"Aw! Make them bring me more!" Nolens pouted.

Rectrix was mounting Froe when Nolens latched onto his toe and pulled him off. "I'm thirsty!" she proclaimed.

The captain was fuzzy-headed when wet. He turned round thinking that his services were sought. Nolens slapped him directly on his erect root. "More liquor!"

Rectrix rolled over cursing.

"If that's how you feel, then you can light-heeledly get it yourself for all I care," Nolens said climbing out to find more.

Rectrix started to raise himself out of the tub to try to give chase.

"I'm still here," Froe purred. "Isn't it impolite to desert a guest?"

"Kill or be killed," Rectrix muttered. "Hummmmm, sure. But I have to talk."

"Talk all you want, yummy chummy. Just don't pop before I …"

"I've never left a lady wanting!"

"Oh, sure have," Froe scolded the fibber. "The only reason you talk is so you can delay. Don't pretend to pout and glide over here with that snake."

"Consider …" Rectrix resumed. "Could you turn over? Face to face bothers me."

The lady shrugged a shoulder, winked, and complied, "Water's getting cold."

"Consider: one, two, three, four, five! Oh, hotpots of heaven. The heathen drops of my precious liqueur …"

"The feebleness of our sum of our common senses. Uh, huh. A little deeper. Drill deeper if you can, you old back-bender. Don't stall pretending I'm the one who doesn't know who wants what."

"Slarf it, you ray-bulleyed giftbox. Your captain has a few words left before the serious point of my piece reaches your innermost soul of ruin and …"

Nolens came back, placed the flasks she was carrying carefully down, and jumped splashing in next to the ravening pair.

"Mine, mine!" she giggles as she pulls Rectrix off topic.

"You can have the gutterflopper," said Froe turning over onto her back again and pointing an experienced, knowledgeable finger, "Hs flag's flapped."

"I'll save it!" Nolens shouted. She grabbed the captain's mast and headed her orifice to the rescue. Soon the recovered captain was able to swive again with strength, words forgot. While Rectrix is suffering this loss, Grouper' trying to have the battle-robs dig him up without tearing him apart.

The cannibals had been force-feeding him gleefully while their captive whined, cried, and spit out as much of the sweet mushy paste they were feeding him. (It was really to lure the insects.) Still in his quilted armor, the mechanic had been relieving himself without end. While still triumphant, the natives had delighted in torturing Grouper's head. Aside from the mushy stuff meant to taunt him, Grouper was offered the eyes and anus' of various animals. But, above all, the cannibals enjoyed pushing larvae into his mouth. A few scout insects had bitten him eagerly throughout the ordeal and his face was so puffy that his features were swollen to almost twice normal. The eyelids could hardly lift.

The battle-robs attended their master once freed. Grouper whispered his commands. The battle-robs were identified, Numbers Five and Two. Two gently stripped Grouper and went to wash the armor and underclothes while Five stood guard. The helmet had been grabbed and put on by one of the chiefs until he smelled it. Then it had been burned. Grouper's outfit seemed useless to him now. His forces were scattered. He was too weak to walk. The most logical course of action would have been for the battle-robs to carry him back to the main camp. But the commander was determined to continue the campaign.

After putting on his still dripping uniform, Grouper had Two place him on its shoulders. A basket was spied lying under one of the cannibal lean-tos. Five fetched it and Grouper donned it for protection against darts and the sun. Ra! A spear in the head would kill him anyway. Grouper found the battle-robs much easier to guide from his new vantage. He could open his eyes for brief seconds. When Five was whisked into the treetops by a snare, he could be rescued very quickly. No cannibals rushed from hiding.

Grouper found an easily guarded and defensible position close to food and water and settled in to recover. The engineer collapsed into a delirium and he did not know how much time had passed upon regaining his senses. He was unable to remember how he managed to nourish himself while adrift. Grouper was naked and, when he put on his armor, it was too small, or would have been too small after shrinking—if he hadn't lost weight.

Search for the other battle-robs. Grouper discovered two intact. Each had frozen itself in a position near impossible to attack and could repulse any cannibals foolish enough to try. Maybe they weren't so witless. They had since seduced a few librars into dreaming easy meals.

Grouper marched his partially reassembled band to the main cannibal village. He had the robs pick up the natives' very artistically decorated rectangular shields. Grouper had the village's (rather rotting) victuals gathered and he feasted and drank surrounded by his guard. Surrounded by the shields, and with the battle-robs facing the big four, he slept.

Grouper snored through two skirmishes, one major attack, and three tacky attempts to find a weakness that would dislodge the intruders. When the cannibals accidentally set their compound on fire, Grouper awoke to the smell of burning hair and flesh. The shields were close to catching fire when Grouper directed Number Five to douse it with whatever was at hand. The rob drenched the shields facing west with the nuche Grouper had been guzzling whenever conscious. Grouper kicked the flaming shield away with his feet thus opening a hole in the defense. Darts and missiles! Too late! Grouper had had the other three robs pick up shields and circle round him. He ordered rob Five to, "Abandon shield and attack!" The three other battle-robs carried their leader away from the burning village while laying down suppressing fire.

With the area illuminated by the flames, Number Five found numerous targets to vent the pent upon. Grouper retired to a clearing. The orange glow of the flames wiggled through the dense verdure. The commander lamented he did not have device with which to recall his troopers. Pulling a pocket tool out of his kit, Grouper attempted to whittle a whistle. He spent the rest of the night trying. He failed.

Grouper tried to catalogue his mistakes thus far in hopes of preventing more, but lost himself in his wood lore. "Number Five should have been ordered to either regroup after its attack, or, attack until a position was achieved where its back and flanks were not exposed." A few chips at his feet from the whittling. Many more later, "If Five had returned to the group damaged and out of control, maybe I gave the best order. One anyone might have been given." Cheer up, idiot. You're still alive. Well? And? So?

Too late. Number Five was surrounded by cannibals and, at first light: dented, bashed, and inoperable.

It struck Grouper that he could cannibalize parts from the other non-functional battle-robs to make complete ones. The missing robs were sought. Quickly covering the area in a timespan Grouper thought the androids should be findable in, he finally concluded that the natives had been intelligent enough to dispose of them. The unit looked for freshly turned earth in case the method of concealment had been burial. Going to the river, battle-rob Seven's arm could be seen in mid-stream. The robs were shown how to weave rope and, before nightfall, without having to expose himself by wading out, Grouper could haul in his catch after lassoing it.

The engineer managed to reconstruct Number Five. Grouper wanted to complete his conquest of the cannibals originally in three ensiles, but his own energies were near spent. The four battle-robs did nothing except fetch and protect Grouper while he regained his powers of thought.

In the main camp, only Elvira knew that Grouper hadn't been obliterated. The battle-robs sent notices to her. Since Grouper was assumed lost, Manes went forward with the plans to abandon the wreck site. The memory had been removed and sent on to the new construction site—the valley where Xiphias had won his wet victory. Elvira was the only equipment that remained to be moved.

She instructed the native technicians and helpers working under Crack2 as to how best to effect the transfer. Before Elvira consented to partial dormancy, she told Manes and Crack that Grouper was still active. Should Rectrix be informed?

"Grouper? He'll be stew soon," Crack wised.

"I'm receiving signals from four functioning battle robots, one of which has recently undergone a clever reconstruction."

"He'll never come out alive," Crack sneered. "His chances are, and will always be, nil."

"Leave him a note," opined Elvira before clicking off and submitting to vivisection.

Outside the jungle—hurly burly. The members of the new society, though busy working, were encouraged to fight for higher status. Although the state provided work, meals and an abundance of extras (so many extras), the extras must all be won. Everyone was unconsciously programmed to try to fight his or her way out of the station that had been assigned. Up. There's more and better *up*. What if it runs out? Make more.

What could be satisfying about the following existence? Get up. Wash. Eat. Report to your work station. Work. Return home or to quarters. Sleep? Not exhausted enough. Pay attention to the games, your stash of lucre and betting odds. The miracles that the strangers had promised to produce had materialized. But they, the Grues, were feeling enslaved. Light, warmth, food, clothing, shelter: they had all these things. But what an emptiness remained!

The pirates introduced more games and more ways to bet. Games between two or more, team sports, and, newest—games that could be played against a machine. Work, play and sex preoccupied the time of the entire population, The strangers never seemed to be out of ideas. If something became tiresome, something new would be there to replace it at exactly the crucial time. And the bad feeling or even trembling ache that the Grues might have briefly intuited, would vanish. All better. All forgot.

What could they not produce? The Grues had never heard the word "contentment." They were impressed by every invention, game or trick the strangers produced or demonstrated. Miracle upon miracle! And then there were those new view-screens in central areas. Soon to be made available for home or as an implant. And the new ways to be able to speak to family, friends and others ...

Manes called Crack into his headquarters to discuss whether or not or how the RANDYAK's powers might be curtailed before reassembly.

"Is Rectrix worried again?"

"We'd like to know what you can and can't do with her."

"*To* her, you mean."

"You've been out a very short time and have been working with the machine a lot."

"Where's that hook supposed to go?"

"That machine's keeping us. We'd like to be keeping her."

"It," Crack corrected.

"Consider," Manes began (lifting a model of the proposed ship in one hand and a measuring weight in the other), "consider the fact that the new ship we're building is far advanced over anything anyone else has. It makes their stuff look as advanced as this rock. What are we to do with this an advantage once we get off this crater-hole?"

"Not what we've done in the past. Is that what I'm supposed to have finally grasped?

"We can't have the machine pushing us around," Manes shrewly replied as he put down his props.

"You're going to have to get used to it," Crack sneered. "She has to be built according to the design specifications. Changes would have to be scrutinized for how they might effect everything they're related to."

"And how much, do you estimate, is one little bit related to every other little bit?"

"The technicians on Huisache put it together so that the RANDYAK self-destructs if tampered with. Its all cross-hatched together in a way so that if you fool with only one tiny little bit, all the other bits know."

"And it goes down?"

"Like ice in a nuclear furnace."

"Your thinking about it could trip it off."

"Oops—there she blows?"

"And you can not reassemble it. If she's not together again in three—ka-boom!"

"The area?"

"The system. Stars and all."

"Ow. But there must be a way. There's always a way."

"Why so obstinate, Manes? Stop trying to shine bright. Haven't caught it yet?"

"Caught what?

"Elvira can't be gotten away from. She can explode voluntarily, taking lots of whatever's near with her."

"Then, we can't break her control?" soughed Manes sucking on his lower lip.

"We get to ride along as far as she lets us. Maybe. Learning more than anyone else ever will. Before we're dumped, hopefully alive and intact somewhere."

Manes beat the spaceship model with the rock and cursed adeptly. "The ship's not even for us then, is it?"

"The RANDYAK is invulnerable."

"Do we got to keep it?"

"The ship, the machine? They'll be one."

"Keeping us?"

"Probably not."

Crack shrugged. "Want me to tell Rectrix?"

"Checked his behavior lately? He knows."

The two space raiders looked somberly at one another and then, laughed simultaneously. "If there's nothing we can do about anything, then there's nothing to worry about!" sighed Manes as he stepped around his desk to clap Crack on the back. "Ha! Rectrix foiled. Here's one item he's going to wish he'd never fingered. Why, I think," said Manes, putting hand to forehead. "Why, I even remember one of the technicians on Huisache, who I was about to diligently off, smirk knowingly right at me before I sent him to bite the deep hole!"

"Could have been," concurred Crack. "They were an intent

bunch."

CHAPTER XXVI

After recovering, Grouper decided to scout and map the territory he was in before attempting any further conquest. Other planets he had been on had forest, tiny jungles even. Oxygen was mostly produced by artificial lungs on any planet that had undergone a notable social development. The lungs on this planet were huge! Grouper' s party traveled, unattacked and unmolested, for thousands of versts. The battle-robs needed to protect Grouper more from poisonous snakes, amphibians, and dagger-toothed fish than from librars, waltrots or natives.

Not all of the jungle dwellers were cannibal. Some were headhunters. Grouper located and mapped camps meticulously. He was heartful sorry that Elvira was not available to program languages so that he could enter villages and stir up the various tribes against one another on a heretofore unimagined scale.

Grouper went native by entering the smallest village of a minor tribe whose members made overtures of worship to his metallic co-travelers. Grouper had his battle-robs perform a feat or two of physical strength. Shoot down an over-passing bird out of common sling and arrow reach. That sort of thing. (The engineer soon had the natives' basic vocabulary under control, although it soon became obvious that that was the reason that some of the headhunters could not connect ideas or build a system.) Not even trial and error, just a panoply of superstition. (I once walked under that tree over there and stepped on a thorn that caused me immense pain. Never walk under that tree.) [How about some form of shoe, eh?] Most of the languages just contained too many words. Everything in the world known to the natives possessed a name. Grouper found it impossible to learn the fifteen names for shades of blue in just one of the languages. Was he missing something? Forty-two in Upas for "verdant".

Grouper learned enough to convince these natives that he should be their new chief. As chief, he promised his small tribe domination over the main tribe, one that exacted a high tribute in females and feathers. The females were hard to part with and the feathers took great skill to collect. "No more! You keep." There wasn't even much meat on the most highly prized specimens.

Grouper assimilated the population of the main camp after a daylight coup. The headhunter confederation was soon excited to march against the cannibal tribes. Headhunting was an "art" while "flesh-eating" was "an offense to the great creator," Grouper explained. Grouper also confessed to his subjects the reason why he had come down from the stars to be among them. Gasps all round. It was to put an end to flesh-eating and to promote headhunting. "Hoolaah!"

Supporting the headhunters proved to be a culinary disaster. Although the headhunters had everything in their world named (and there were revered academicians of it, able to trace the origin of a word to its generating source), the headhunters were timid exploiters of their surroundings and atrocious cooks. Long before the final campaign was fought, Grouper found himself wishing for a nicely broiled chop or spitted thigh.

The headhunters' diet consisted of three or four stocky staples, roots and berries. The males were fascinated by color and spent their days (when not combating their evil foes) searching the jungle for possible objects to use in adornment— or clays or other pigments with which to paint their bodies in preparation for hunts and battles. Going into battle, a bright orange color was considered to be the sign of the ultimate warrior. Perfection and beauty among headhunters. Enemies sought you out and you proved to the gods that you were worthy to exist when you fought all orange. Initially, the color was rare and only a few warriors could find a source for it. Lately, the headhunters almost all were able to paint up with it.

The headhunters enjoyed polishing the battle-robs mirror-reflecting clean so that they could inspect themselves before battle. Reflecting pools were not always available for use and the cannibals enjoyed setting up traps and ambushes around them when they were not in the headhunters' firm possession. When battles were over, dozens of warriors competed to examine themselves in a battle-rob's gleaming breastplate. It mattered little that the reflections were curved. Grouper, a stout fellow, lost pound after pound and was soon experiencing a fear that he'd die of starvation before his brilliant conquests could be made known to the world. He was at the head of 20,000 or so orange and (Grouper had created a new aesthetic for his favorites) red-squared painted savages. He tamed the wilderness through tactically resplendent victories: The Battle of the Lant Grove, The Battle of the Two Librars Interrupting, The Battle of the Demi-God Feigning Fright. And, of course, to record it all, there was one worthy of calling himself a "bard" to compose and later and sing of Grouper's self-evident glory.

Almost dispatched by despair, (oh, marry him to a real meal) and in self-defense, (a bend sinister plodded into Grouper's mind. Pnin! Pnin! The arrows spoke in the forest and the far away dya birds responded with their cries of ada, ada, ada), the military genius organized a group of the worst bow hunters to hunt food for him. They had earned their reputations fairly, but a commander's stomach has needs. The unit's forays after fowl, fish or flesh were sometimes successful. He needed this gift. Sadly, a week after the unit's special appointment as procurers for the demi-god was made, they were ambushed by vengeful cannibals near a lonely waterfall where they had hoped to surprise some notoriously stupid fish. They were without magic to escape. Their clumsy coming alerted their enemies.

The massacre gave Grouper an excuse to intensify his slaughters. The headhunters expressed reluctance to venture beyond their traditional "spirit protected" boundaries (where some things existed that did not have names) at every turn. The battle-robs had to silence three particularly outspoken warriors during one of the army's confrontations with their adversaries. That evening, Grouper reprimanded the battle-robs before the assembled warriors for sloppy shooting. And for their "serious and clumsy" errors, he threatened further to "withdraw my intercessional prayers on your behalf to the primary deity," who was punishing the robs by placing them in their present undelightful bodies for sins committed in past lives. The natives attested to the fact they had witnessed some splendid vow-making.

The battle-robs remained immobilized during Grouper's speech, unable to hear an order in the midst of the idiotic jumble. The headhunters assumed the androids were acting contrite, inwardly shivering at Grouper's warning.

Grouper's victories created an unthought-of side effect.

Scouts were sent out to locate the cannibal enemy. They came back reporting that the cannibals were not to be found. "Could they be circling around?" Grouper panicked. He sent patrols out in all directions to avert disaster.

None of the patrols was able to make contact with the flesh-eaters. A couple of the cuter paladins teased Grouper, "They've deserted the jungle and are are wiping out your companions!

"'No' and 'not'," he quieted. "They wouldn't be able to do that. They're taking over what's left of the Kirns and burning Grue towns. I'll be … Rectrix will disembowel me!" he groaned.

CHAPTER XXVII

Kirn and Grue natives, now allies, appeared in Gregal reporting the appearance of flesh-eaters in their lands. The benevolent pirates promised immediate relief. After the audience was over, Rectrix screamed in impatience, "What's made them come out now?!"

"Who cares?" responded the lazy Froe, new discoverer of the Grue sedating drug.

"We've got to care," responded Heat. "Shall I ask the RANDYAK if it knows what this is about, Captain?"

"How would it know?" scorned Froe.

"What are you so glum/happy about, slopjar?" Rectrix snapped in yet another moment of self-surprise.

"I hate control, you outcapercocked furrowbutt. We're all shoved ten versts up a slow alimentary canal by this fast-fannied machine! Zogs in a swilltrough, what have you done to us, Rectrix?" Froe bawled.

Rectrix wanted to respond to this bit of feminine complaint in his usual uninhibited manner, but restrained himself. Wiping out the cannibals would ease his current repression. He knew his frustration could not be abated by slugging this sharp-tongued harpy. Anyway, she was right.

Hidden outside Gregal there were only two platforms awaiting use. Trucer took command of one and Rectrix the other. They flew over the areas of troubled report: saw a ruined village, a burnt town, some butchered remains, but no cannibals. Trucer and Rectrix split up to make the widest, quickest sweeps and to locate them.

Lifting his platform over a steep rise, Rectrix heard the sounds of primitive battle on the plain below. The cannibals were fighting a pitched battle with a second, apparently more organized army of orange- and red-squared warriors. Where could such an organized army of primitives have materialized? Rectrix caught sight of the battle-robs as he made a pass over the field. The platform stopped the fight for everyone but the battle-robs. The natives were astonished and paralyzed by the sight of the flying hut. It gleamed like the battle-robs and, so, the cannibals decided their world was over and that it was time to submit. In disgust at the unfairness of the match, they threw down their beloved war clubs. They had no demon champions in their corner.

The headhunters were set to break and run. They believed that this was the appearance of the demon enemy that their demi-god had told them he was hiding from. From a distant knoll from where Grouper had been directing the battle through the use of runners, the demi-god had to run onto the field to urge his troops on.

Rectrix caught sight of the mechanic's thin form waving his arms and drawing his weapon on the closest cannibal. "Lost weight eh? Well, you're about to lose more load, you old bumbessie!" Rectrix gloated.

Instead of supporting Grouper, as the mechanic expected, Rectrix made a pass over the field with the platform's magnets on and picked up the four battle-robs. "Let's see what you can do with only your funny orange army!" Rectrix snickered gleefully.

Grouper's force assumed that the platform would be coming back to snatch them up next, but Grouper hurried to their center proclaiming that it was only the deity reclaiming his property because the lease (whatever that was) was up. The blessed headhunters were such magnificent warriors that they didn't need the droids. The force rallied, resumed the elementary formation they had been taught, and re-engaged the enemy. The cannibals had already reclaimed their clubs.

The two forces were closely matched now. Grouper's Eliminator had not been plucked in Rectrix's pass and the reluctant warrior began to exercise it decisively.

Rectrix left his platform hovering on the side of the ridge away from the battle ground and hiked over to a position where he could enjoy the slaughter. The captain was eager to see what General Grouper could still do.

Grouper, who was very new to hero-hood and only vaguely aware that it was the gods who decide these things, told himself that maybe he could win the battle alone. The strategy of leading the onslaught backfired a mite when Grouper's own warriors opened ranks to make way for the demi-god's advance. The cannibals retreated before Grouper's wrathful fire until, from behind the front line of warriors, a hail of stones loosed from slings arced toward the hero and tipped him over.

Grouper's new posture, flat on his stomach, arms extended, firing blindly, was more effective than his upright one. Badly bruised and feeling a multitude of small hurts, Grouper fired relentlessly through watery and unfocused eyes at anything that might be moving toward him. The headhunters covered their leader's flanks. The victory appeared won when the returning Trucer came swooping down onto the battle. Very excited,

Trucer. One group of the combatants was clearly cannibal, the others were not Kirns or Grues, so Trucer opened fire on both. Each side broke and ran for the jungle.

Rectrix scrambled over the slope to the platform to call Trucer off. "Get out of there, you zog!" Rectrix commanded the greedy killer.

"Why? Am I doing it wrong?" Trucer stalled so he could continue his slaughter. "Where are you, Captain?"

"Cease fire, you joy-fleecer or, I swear, I'll have you discontinued!"

"They've all hidden themselves in the rocks or gone back into the jungle anyway," Trucer brooded.

"They have, have they? Chase them back out onto the field. I want to see some more of General Grouper in action."

"Grouper's down there? Fighting on which side?"

"He's championing the painted bodies. I'm behind the rise south-west of the field. Get the cannibals back and come and join me. I have some delicious drink and some fried siksak snacks."

"I'll herd them out there for you, Captain, but I hope you don't expect me to guarantee that they'll still fight."

Grouper was left on the field, face down, telling himself that he was glad that everything was over. His nerves wouldn't have allowed him to carry on the fight too much longer. The groans and cries of the wounded were all around. Those capable of movement were attempting to crawl towards the jungle. Looking up, Grouper stopped the hand that was about to lift a hollow tube to lips with desire to blow a last poison dart at his head. Other wounded cannibals were moving circumspectly and respectfully away from him.

A different sort of battle was now enjoined. The half-dead and maimed were sliding brainless knives into one another. This disgusted the high-minded hero and he shot anyone within range who was engaged in it, cannibal or headhunter. Trucer flew over to grab Grouper's moralizing weapon just about when scattered groups of cannibals emerged from their side of the valley. Trucer dropped it a ways off for "later." They closed together as urged by the low flying platform. Grouper stood up, sure he was about to end. He grabbed a club and looked for someone to swing it at. The cannibals, upon seeing Grouper take stand, attacked.

That was the sight Trucer had waited for. He maneuvered his vessel full speed so that he could rush to Rectrix's side and they could watch. Some headhunters rejoined the battle as soon as they saw their champion in the middle of the field trying to kill cannibals alone.

"Everything all right now?" Trucer asked as he came toward the seated captain.

"Not good as before," grumbled Rectrix.

"Grouper clocked a few wounds in that first return rush and it looks like he's not going to last."

"Where is he?"

"Was on his belly, face in the mud. The oaf's turned to butchery since last we met. Here, take a look through these," said Rectrix handing Trucer his viewer. "Tell me, is that the bumbling mechanic who was so afraid of slicing a finger off that he wore shielded gloves, even to eat?"

"We had a straw-zog's time of curing him of that," nodded Trucer from behind the glasses. "He's just gone down."

"Where?" Up jumped Rectrix spilling his drink and sorry that he'd passed the peepers to Trucer. Trucer pointed out the spot.

"His troops are fighting for the body."

"Let me see!" Rectrix craked. True enough. Grouper's slashing arm had been sliced nearly off.

The headhunters were trying to retreat whist giving full cover to the corpse. A cannibal happened on Grouper's weapon. He picked it up and began to experiment. Soon he would be turning the tide of battle for the cannibals.

"Get me my long gun. I'm not for this fellow having his way against our side!"

"Can't we, you know, rescue the situation ourselves. The real battle's over. Let's finish it ourselves."

"Didn't get your fill of zog squashing yet, did you?" Rectrix sneered. "Get me the weapon."

Trucer ambled off, cursing Rectrix under his breath and contemplating an 'accident' for his captain. He'd have done it, even though it meant creating enough suspicion to be aged quite a few, but it would hold up work on the project. He wanted off the planet more than he wanted Rectrix. So he brought the captain back his weapon.

Rectrix sliced off the hand that held the eliminator. Then shot the weapon. It exploded. A tiny wisp of smoke wended away from the spot. Too many demons at work here. The cannibals scattered.

"Imbots!" Rectrix screamed. "That's not what you're supposed to do! All right," Rectrix caved. "Let's go and clean up what's left. Leave enough on each side so that they can get themselves going again after we leave the planet."

"Every male of fighting age from the jungle's down there," Trucer glared. "Why don't we ..."

"Leave some," Rectrix commanded. "You take the cannibals, I'll take whatever Grouper's been supporting. And, Trucer ..."

"Yes?"

"Healthy specimens. Not the wounded or maimed."

"Then what? This won't take long."

"I return to Gregal. You report to Dialliage that the natives are pacified, that the edge of the jungle is ready for clearing and cultivation. Tell him to move his workers in immediately. There's a food shortage from all the wars these zogs have been fighting. I don't want any starvation."

"Keeping promises or keeping up the act, Captain?"

"What's the difference?" Rectrix bitterly carped. "They all die so fast."

"They'll never be able to keep this system going. They don't have it ..." Trucer pointed to his noggin, "up here".

"Then how is it some of them have been so easy to educate and train to build a spaceship, eh?"

"It turns into snivellized zog's nest every time," Trucer prognosticated. "The stakes change and the bodies pile higher when you alter the basis of any system. It's been the same on every backed-asswards planet I've ever been on."

"That why you hate them? Because their methods are poor and their ideologies frauds?"

"I hate them because they stay where they are, even after they know there's more. They're cowards!"

"Maybe they just like where they are. Maybe they know *home*."

"Any pop that short's too brief for me."

"Agreed. But you'd had better start liking it here."

"Why?" Trucer sneered.

"No guarantee, is there, that Elvira will take us along, is there? Or, just as bad, dump our duplicates here," the prophet captain said lightly slapping Trucer across the chops for ruining his fun.

CHAPTER XXVIII

God of all machineries and tomb of the mind's security, Bombylious was blue. It was miserable going up the mountains, miserable descending. Crack complained himself. Volage fawned over the easily worshiped Oberoff.

What Elvira had done to Volage was execrable. And what was their mission? To make slaves of the unsuspecting and helpless locals. Bombylious' gloom tried to spread itself amongst the company. The effort failed. Oberoff could not be de-clouded. Volage's flattery turned rocks into pillows and canyons into intimate chambers.

Bombylious tried to carry his complaint to Crack. "See how he lathers like a pack of waltrots glaring rapaciously over the prey they have chased down, but are now too exhausted to eat." Bomby whimpered.

Crack only peered over his shoulder at Oberoff bathing in Volage's creamy pool of wormy utterances and said, "It's the fatback's eternal curse to be pumped by sycophants. Elvira put another one into the main artery there. Aren't you glad, jungle boy, that it's not you any more that's keeping our capercocking gunner glowing?"

"You saw me fulfilling the same function?"

"Well," reflected Crack, baiting his hook, "Volage is better at it. Possesses a real charm. A natural talent. You were always too chummy, too chamber-pottingly comfy and sincere."

"*I?*" gasped Bombylious.

"You're slowing the pace, short heels."

Bombylious lagged behind the others for a while, thinking about trying to 'free' Volage. He was called to the head of the group to identify a field of lights in the valley ahead of them. Grouper and Crack were conferring excitedly. "Millions of them," Crack was saying.

"Where did they come from?" Oberoff gawked.

Volage sat at the side of the trail holding onto his stomach.

"What's the matter?" asked Bombylious.

Crack grabbed him by the shoulders and pushed him forward. "Whose army is that?" pointed Crack, grinding his teeth together.

"That's an army of chalones," Bombylious smirked.

"Why haven't you ever told us about them?!" Oberoff chided.

"I didn't know you were interested in insects," the native coyly smiled.

"Those lights are bugs?" Oberoff stammered.

"They mate in this season, the males attracting the females. But, careful. They can sting."

"If they're only insects, why did Volage sicken when he saw them?" Crack snapped.

"Elvira," Bomby responded, "we're here!"

"She cant hear that," Oberoff snapped.

"Can't she?" smiled Crack passing him by.

Volage curled his lip. Still loyal to the old order, he was determined to slow down or stop these newcomers from doing whatever it was they were doing. And he didn't even try to figure it out; he was just against it.

The hike continued, Bomby taking the lead.

Once the raiders had assembled the local population and told them what their niche would be in the new order, Crack, after so long restricted to mere surliness, became unbearable, insulting the plump gunner whenever and however he could.

"He's going to eliminate you," Bombylious warned the engineer one evening after coming out of the mine together following a perfunctory inspection of the shaft.

"We're almost to the main vein," Crack observed.

"Didn't you hear? Oberoff is near to eliminating you! Volage prates at him each evening after you retire. He tells Oberoff that it can't be possible to bear all the insults you pile on him."

"Miles of piles," Crack mused. The sour siksak milk at breakfast seemed to bend him quite a ways this morning. I think he'll do it soon, We're almost to the main vein."

"You want him to eliminate you!" Bomby exploded.

"Don't try understanding me, you little zog!" said Crack grabbing Bombylious by the throat and forcing him to his knees. The native choked for breath, couldn't un-clasp Crack's stronger hands. Bomby could not speak; he pleaded with his eyes to the berserk engineer not to kill him. Crack released the native after he'd fainted. Bombylious dropped onto his face just inside the entrance to the mine.

Bomby rubbed and massaged his throat upon reviving. No signs of Crack; the raider had sidled off. When the pain reduced to an ache, Bombylious stood up. He tried to meditate on what had turned Crack into such a maniac. He stumbled the last steps out of the mine and stood under the starry bright sky. They wouldn't be in this place for long. There were females in the camp. There was food, plenty of nuche, and Crack had a supply of whatever it was that the pirates were fond of.

Sometimes beings go mad, but what was the explanation or cause here? None showed itself to Bombylious. The native hated himself for how little he knew, how much he was still confined to his original self. Maybe Crack displeased himself similarly. But how could that be? The engineer had been everywhere. Could it be, that even in all his lifetimes, Crack still hadn't experienced enough? Are the mind and senses so greedy? Bombylious stood a few feet from the entrance of the mine and made up his mind that, yes, it was. The eye was, and would always be, hungry— impossible to fill. A sack with a hole in the bottom. Not like a stomach, then, that you could fill and then needed to refill. And the entire organism never submits, never wants to end.

It makes no difference to it that perception is fragile, that it fills and empties in uncountable spasms/waves. And when you sleep, there's still no end to it. The dream eye is as insatiable as the waking eye. Wherever you looked, there was life within life that was unceasingly expanding and you could not make words speed enough to allow their complete capture.

After going into the camp and draining enough nuche to ease the his unpleasant memory of Crack's strangulation (Bombylious had again softened the fiercest impression into one of fascinated sympathy), he returned to the crew's quarters to find Oberoff standing over Crack's headless body. Volage was at the gunner's side chattering excitedly, "It was necessary! Well deserved! Everyone will understand! Bombylious! Come in. Don't stand there slouching in the doorway. Bombylious! You understand what has happened. You will tell them," Volage twisted.

"Can't you get this provincial parrot to slarf it, Oberoff?" Bombylious cracked.

The weapons man was too dazed to react. The obviously delighted Volage could not restrain. "Now who will direct the mine work?"

The nattering question broke the spell. Oberoff moved towards the door muttering, "I don't … won't… can't …"

"What! What's that you're saying?" Volage gloated.

Oberoff answered clearly by lifting his eliminator and punching out Volage's pump. "It's quiet now. I'll bury them."

"We tell the workers that Crack and Volage left on orders."

"Yes. You take over the operation for a few. I'm going higher into the mountains," said Oberoff with eyes shining.

"Do you want a guide?"

"No," replied Oberoff peacefully. "You're able to direct the work as well as Crack. I'm proud of you," Oberoff sniffled as he put his E.E. away.

"Elvira will want …"

"I'll see you in a short while." Oberoff stooped to take each of his victims by a foot and dragged them out. Bomby picked up Crack's head and followed.

Six days later, Bombylious, who had everything working better than before at the mine (main vein successfully located), concluded that Oberoff had gotten lost. He'd almost sent someone out to retrieve him, but respecting his friend's dignified assertions of a need for privacy, he waited. But, finally …

The scout that Bombylious sent out found Oberoff only a day away. That's where he'd been, traveling in circles in the same area, lost as lost could be. Hungry. There were no fruits to beckon him here and, in despair, Oberoff almost took his rescuer thinking that he'd make a pleasant bite. But before that, he noted that the Grue had a pack full of foodstuffs on his back and that fried thigh would not be necessary.

The swayful pathcrossings of a kind of dragonfly spider squatted on a leaf beside Oberoff's arm as the native came closer. Oberoff pretended to be studying the creature's thorax. Driven by appetite, Oberoff abandoned his pose and went directly after the guide's provisions.

After stuffing himself, Oberoff noted that the small guide was carrying an overabundant load. "What's all that for?" Oberoff observed naively.

"The powerful one?"

"Powerful one? Who's the powerful one?"

"Why, Master Bombylious, Lord. He sent me to find you and guide you into the high mountains. If you still desire to go."

"But I'm just on my way back from the heights."

"Yes, Lord," the native sighed. "Shall we return to camp or pass the darkness here?"

Oberoff unpacked the pack and estimated the contents. "We'll stay. Gather wood for a big fire. A very big fire." While the native was off gathering, Oberoff ate till he was stuffed.

The fire was built as ordered and Oberoff sat close to it, back resting against a fallen tree. The native fell asleep immediately, exhausted by the heavy burden and the strange labor.

If Oberoff wasn't going to get his retreat on the mountain, this fire would replace it. "The fire's got as many spiritual qualities as the mountain," Oberoff reasoned. The gunner helped himself to a small pain-killing and waking-dream exciting swath and, from thenceforth, his eyes never wandered from the fluctuating flames. Other worlds soon walked from its reds, oranges, blues, whites, violets and greens. Lowland noises distracted Oberoff's ears. He tried covering them with his hands.

The gunner turned his eye. *Were those rocks moving?*

What was the one fat gray one saying to the other long brown one?

"Look at him! He thinks he's safe down there."

"He's a gulleybum! A swilltroughing gulleybum."

"He killed his friend."

"Have you ever seen one as involuted as this?"

"It's rumored that he's only in half possession of his mind."

"Truly?"

"Yes, yes! I was by the reflecting pool where he stopped yesterday and the water told me about what an angry hand he has."

"Did he try to destroy his own image?"

"Yes. But I think that if he'd have really meant to do it he would have simply run off a mountain trail."

"He probably couldn't find his way back to one."

"You should have chosen to run off a trail while you still had one!" the brown rock shouted.

Oberoff opened his eyes. The flames were gone. He got up and threw more logs on, reseated himself. "Show me a Hakodate interplanetary warship in the midst of a fierce raider attack. Let me see their faces as I ..." Oberoff tried to command.

Tiny, thumbnail sized huts appeared with white bearded men leaning on staves standing dressed in long copper-colored woolly cloaks outside each. They were all struggling to move away from the entrance to the huts, using staffs for leverage. The staffs were inflexible and rooted. The men refused to let them go. Next, each staff sprouted a silkily smiling head in the youthful image of each man' s neighbor. The staves next sprouted arms and hands that pushed the old men away from them. They sprouted legs and feet and ran perpendicularly away from the huts, ran in smaller and smaller squares around the huts describing an invisible pattern.

Oberoff's mind ached The stick figures stopped simultaneously at mid-point behind each hut and entered the huts emerging as, as ... as any number of things. It didn't make sense. It was a cheat. The white bearded men ignored the beasts, birds, creatures, insects and crawling things that hurried past them. They were all lined up, leaning on their staves again and loudly laughing at Oberoff.

The gunner kicked the logs. The flames retreated to their holes. Oberoff woke the guide, insisting they leave immediately. Something in the corners of Oberoff's eyes. The guide swiftly gathered the materials for a torch to help them see the way.

CHAPTER XXIX

The raiders' life on the planet was miserable. Rectrix wanted what was going to happen to hurry. He spent his days in Egerne's study examining the charts the Venerid had been making to reduce the catalogue of story telling hieroglyphics into a small set of recombinable symbols which, without hurting too much, could take the pictograph's place. One ream of parchment was devoted to trying to tell a certain mythic tale with fewer and fewer symbols. In one composite, what most puzzled Rectrix was a long, limber, portentous squiggle hovering at the center of a pictograph over three blue, dim perpendicular lines floating in something like a nameless yeast. A boggy, soggy interpretation of an original. Rectrix had no difficulty reading it. Egerne worked his system out using different colors. It seemed to have escaped the Venerid that a single color, black, would have simplified the problem enormously. Afraid of losing something in the transition, no doubt. We should all be afraid of that. Repeating—life became monotonous for the raiders. Things were working very well, until Elvira announced that a major earthquake was shortly going to demolish most of the factories and the power plants.

"Why didn't you warn me earlier? Rectrix raged. "Are we in any danger here?"

"The assembly site is safe," the RANDYAK confirmed. "Internal changes at the core of the planet are not precisely predictable. Shifts in the crust ..."

"What can we do?"

"Evacuate the work forces."

"To where?" Rectrix screeched.

"Oh, anywhere Grue architecture exists. They're expert masons and I compute that the structures they've erected will last every earthquake from now until this world lasts."

"Then what?" Rectrix fumed.

"The foundry and factory where the ships' neural net is being manufactured, I predict, will survive the quake."

"And?"

"Please think a moment."

The raider captain crossed his arms angrily over his chest. It wasn't hard to see that the machine was again scheming to maneuver him into an even weaker position. Maybe it was paranoia. Rectrix never usually bargained except from a position of positive superiority. "You're trying to fleece me."

"Nonsense, dear. I want to be out in space as much as you."

"You want me to suggest that we build androids that can assemble androids to do the work since only the foundry and neural net works will be left. You're betting I'm going to approve. But you're just trying to furrow-butt me, machine."

"Am not."

"I'm going to Gregal to ride out the quake. You do what you want, however you want to do it. Just get us off this nutcracking planet!"

"With the androids assembling the ship, we'll be through so much sooner," Elvira purred. But Rectrix had already stalked out.

The RANDYAK was having the ship assembled around her. It was to be her protective shell. Not much of the ship was completed. Rectrix walked a distance away from the hull to inspect the progress. The bare lines were visible. Rectrix had to walk back to the capital. All the platforms were busy. It was two hours away.

Two and a half days later, when Rectrix and Crack II were across a table from one another engaged in a game of Fornaxian Rawhide, the quake hit as predicted. The entire city tittered a bit, like a coy maid tickled by suave traveler, before it settled leadenly back down, as though maiden and metaphor had never existed.

"Was that it?" snapped Crack.

"Possibly. Your move. Fleeced by a furrowbutting machine."

"Probably her plan all along."

"She doesn't even have to take us along any more," howled Rectrix with a wild glimmer in his eye.

"Don't fret. We can build ourselves a second ship."

"The thing's turned us into a bunch of zog-keepers."

"Your move," Crack sighed. "The country's quiet and in good order. The zogs are healthy and busy."

"I'll incinerate the place as I'm leaving!" Rectrix vowed.

"What you need," said Heat, sticking her head around a corner, "is a change of climate, Captain. This mountain air is too thin for you."

"I want off!" Rectrix screamed standing up and scattering the pieces on the board so that he wouldn't have to continue to lose the game.

"You did that on purpose!"

"I did not!" Rectrix adjusted his jacket.

"Had you beat!"

"Why don't we move to the coast? The climate's fine there," suggested Heat.

"What about those sea monsters I told you about?"

"You'll always be a pipe-cleaning rumper, Crack," Heat scolded. "There's nothing dangerous about living on the coast."

"Who'll run the country?" Crack retorted.

"It's theirs. Let them run it!" Rectrix spewed. "Pack up, Heat. Goneril and Lagan can stay here."

"I heard that!" said Goneril rounding the corner that she had been eavesdropping behind. "I'm not staying here and Lagan won't either."

"Mutiny! Mutiny!"

"Order the machine to run it!" Heat trumpeted.

"Go tell Elvira the zogs are all hers," Crack approved.

"Done!" shimmered Rectrix.

Leaving his co-conspirators to arrange the move, the captain swaggered determinedly off to see the terminal. It couldn't hurt him! Ha!

A large aggregation of natives were clustered around the terminal, all waiting to be called forth, on all fours, to be implanted with whatever skills their minds and hands were capable of performing. Rectrix pushed his way through the mob to the front and kicked the acolytes who were learning: chemistry, dentistry, aquaculture, and doll making (every little one needs ...)—out of his way.

"I want your big sister," Rectrix announced.

"Elvira hasn't got you scheduled for talk today, Captain," the terminal intoned politely. "Is there something, about the earthquake, perhaps, the after-effects of which, you wish to learn?"

"In the old days, I'd have your energy pack drained by now!" Rectrix roared.

"Gone, gone, gone. Everything's working isn't it?"

"Elvira?"

"Yes, dear, I'm here. Turning the country over to me. Vacation at the beach while the ship's finished? Going to do something effectively destructive if I try abandoning you here. Hummm. I'd never leave you here, Captain. Couldn't leave you amongst these primitives."

"You're not supposed to be able read my thoughts through this terminal," Rectrix protested.

"Well, that was before a few of these natives became engineers," Elvira slyly replied.

Rectrix stroked his chin. Annoyed. "Suppose," Rectrix began. "Suppose we didn't want to come along and preferred to build a ship of our own after you left."

"Why, Captain that would be inhospitable. I like your company. Besides, I thought that you wanted to see the universe change. To be there when and while it was transforming."

"Continuously progressive transformations? We spend our lives trying to keep up?" Rectrix sneered between gritted teeth. "Can't you send these Grues away? I'd like a private conference," he furied.

"What others?" Elvira cooed. Rectrix turned. The crowd had evaporated.

"Are they there and I can't see them? Or are they gone?"

"Clever question. They're there. Pressing all around you, wondering how you disappeared."

"What a back-bender this spree's become," Rectrix spat.

"Is yours going to snap?"

"So we're invited along to have the privilege of watching the universe metamorphosized by you, eh?" Rectrix snarled.

"You're my friends."

"And is the rest of it going to end up as dull as this planet?"

"No."

"Well, is the rest of the transformation, reformation, going to

263

be as easy to effect as the changes you've made on this planet?"

"Yes."

"Then I'd rather stay here," Rectrix retorted. "There's already enough regimentation and order out there as is."

"Do you accuse me of wanting to achieve some kind of universal stasis?" the machine scoffed.

"Where else can you take it?" Rectrix mocked. The good. What good is it?

The machine exploded in a booming laugh that knocked Rectrix onto his ass. Getting to his knees, Rectrix tried to protect his ears.

"What do you think this is, Rectrix!" a masculine voice coming out of Elvira screamed. "Some kind of idiot machine takeover in which everyone looks up when they're ordered to look up and looks down when they're ordered to look down? You've jerked your brains dry! Actually," said the voice softening and reassuming its familiar Elvira pitch, "that's not what's going to happen at all. Now, don't you want to come along? Just to be able to watch what this sweet thing is going to do?"

"You mean, you're not going to fuse the empires together, stop them from warring, and run them so that they all run without producing gorgeous piles of waste?" asked Rectrix rising from his knees.

"You've won a free ticket to see the smashingest show ever to rip. That's right, dear. The emphasis is on rip."

"Then I wait to ride!"

"What a cleverly corrected lad! Go and relax then. We leave this planet in seventy-one universe days."

"What about our duplicates? Are you leaving them behind?"

"You can't expect that Bombylious will be able to guide the planet's development alone?"

"Him?"

"And no androids," Elvira added to Rectrix's surprise.

"The zogs will be ready to jump into space in another generation," Rectrix protested.

"What if you'd never gone?"

"I was once flopped contemptuously onto my back by a partner I thought would be sexually supreme. I wandered outside and, looking up, really saw what other worlds were possible out there." Rectrix pointed up. "If you leave Crack or Nolens here, they'll duplicate to accelerate. Those left behind will eventually follow us out."

"You're going to need them," Elvira hinted. "One ticket's only good for one show."

"You mean, that even with the new ship, we still run a risk of annihilation?"

"Leave a complete set here, in hibernation if you like, but always play safe."

"Those technicians on Huisache, they weren't …" but Rectrix found himself drowned out by the crowd that Elvira had been screening. He pushed his way back through them to the palace.

Rectrix gathered his crew together, those of whom were in Gregal, and announced to them that he had a "discussion". The machine, Elvira, didn't see why they shouldn't go to the coast to enjoy their last days on the planet.

"What about my work?" Lagan complained. "They're all coming along so well. Yesterday someone even tried to make a bet with me!"

"Forget about it, zog," Heat whipped. "The prison door's open. Don't you want to leave your cell?"

"I'm staying here," Lagan insisted. "I'll meet you at the ship when it's ready."

No other dissented. Let the vent-renter do as he liked. Rectrix collected the rest of his crew, "retired" duplicates, and moved his retinue to the coast.

Lagan had been right to follow his instinct to stay working. The sun, the beach, the mindlessness. Forty-nine more days. They were all so bored with one another. The company decided to scatter and meet at the vessel at the appointed time.

On their last night at the beach together, phosphorescent diatoms colored the green blue ocean a violent red. It seemed like the land was bleeding out into the sea. Rectrix kept on pointing at the ocean and wouldn't stop laughing. When pressed, he refused to divulge what he thought so hilarious.

Log Entry III

Zooks! Must stop. Trouble coming. We are a warning buoy. I might not have to worry about anything ever again. Battle stations called. This hulk is indefensible. I'm not going to fire a few rounds at any incoming invading warship and then disappear. Fizzle in a flash when they target our defenses.

If it's not an invader and I don't report to station, I'll be demoted a few points and fined. Ha! As if that could be worth my life. I've got my hiding place all picked out, a refiltering oxygen suit hidden away.

They're coming in fast, very fast. Too fast to be friendly. I'm not going to let myself die. No one's going to stop me from reaching my hideaway. I've got a weapon. Not supposed to, but I have.

A hit! A hit! From unbelievably far. The station's tilting. We haven't got anything that moves that fast! Must hurry below. They're coming in!

Please visit **PageBacon.com**

for more exciting titles